DATE DUE

MAY 12 '77				
FEB 26 '79				
SEP 1 '05				

Chariot In the Sky

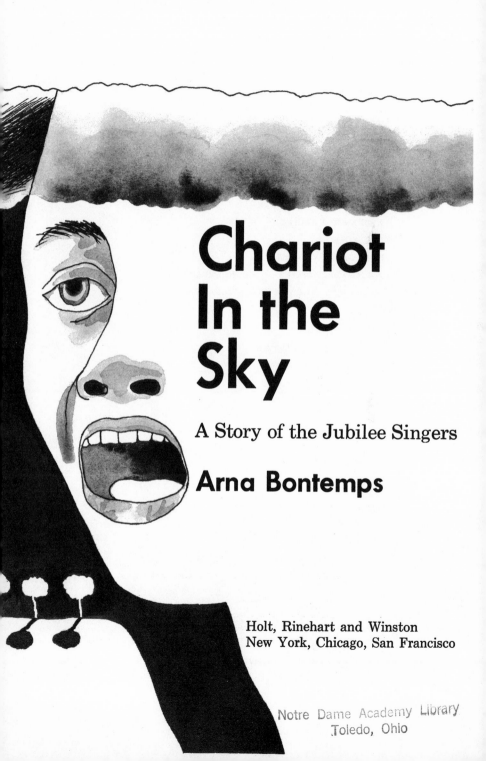

Chariot In the Sky

A Story of the Jubilee Singers

Arna Bontemps

Holt, Rinehart and Winston
New York, Chicago, San Francisco

OTHER BOOKS BY ARNA BONTEMPS

Written by Arna Bontemps

SAD-FACED BOY

WE HAVE TOMORROW

STORY OF THE NEGRO

BLACK THUNDER

FAMOUS NEGRO ATHLETES

FREDERICK DOUGLASS

LONESOME BOY

MISTER KELSO'S LION

ONE HUNDRED YEARS OF NEGRO FREEDOM

STORY OF GEORGE WASHINGTON CARVER

Edited by Arna Bontemps

GOLDEN SLIPPERS

GREAT SLAVE NARRATIVES

HOLD FAST TO DREAMS

AMERICAN NEGRO POETRY

Published simultaneously in Canada by
Holt, Rinehart and Winston of Canada, Limited

ISBN: 0-03-080216-4 (Trade)
ISBN: 0-03-080217-2 (HLE)
Library of Congress Catalog Card Number: 73-160162

Printed in the United States of America
First Published October 1951
Tenth Printing, October 1967
New Edition, October 1971

FOR POPPY AND CAMILLE

Foreword

The year is 1873. The place is London. In the spacious studio of Edmund Havell a group of the artist's friends are standing before his latest painting. It is an impressive canvas that almost reaches the ceiling and covers most of one wall of the room. But there is more to this painting than its size. Havell's visitors are fascinated by the figures in the group portrait.

Havell's eyes are on his friends, and he smiles to note the changing expressions on their faces. Not all of them recognize the four erect young men and the seven beautiful girls in the painting, but they soon guess their identity, for by now nearly everyone in London has heard about the Jubilee Singers. Not all have been fortunate enough to get tickets for their concerts, and seeing them for the first time in the artist's life-size painting—well, they are unable to believe their eyes.

Who were these American singers that London was talking about in 1873? What was it about them that caused Prime Minister Gladstone to invite them to sing for his guests, including the Prince of Wales and other members of the royal family? What was behind their invitation to sing before Queen Victoria at Argyle Lodge? And what was this gossip about invitations from Germany, The Netherlands and other European countries?

Certainly Havell's painting tells an important part of

the story: the lovely complexions of the girls, ranging in color from cream to chocolate, the unruffled dignity of the young men, their calm patience and endurance. But there is another part that does not show, and it is this as much as their personalities that has astonished the musical world.

Just eight years before, most of the eleven young people in that picture were slave children on Southern plantations. Two years before, when the little band, accompanied by two white teachers, left their struggling school in Nashville, Tennessee, the marks of slavery were still on them. They were wearing clothes borrowed from their missionary teachers at the Fisk school. It was hard to believe that this was the same group, these girls in silk dresses and velvet capes, these boys in well-tailored broadcloth. Only their voices remained unchanged—their voices and the songs they had brought with them out of bondage. Now the whole story was being told for the first time.

In 1871 it seemed that the Fisk school would have to close for lack of money. But George L. White, a veteran of the Grand Army of the Republic, who served the small school as treasurer as well as singing teacher, had one more plan he wanted to try. Something seemed to tell him that the people of the North, once they saw the kind of students who came to Fisk, once they heard the sorrow songs of slavery as these gifted and attractive young people could sing them, would surely be moved to help. He proposed a singing campaign.

It took much time and effort to get the approval of Fisk's board, its faculty and the parents of the students involved. Frankly, Mr. White's plan seemed risky, and perhaps the fact that he was one of the younger teachers did not help. But in time consent was given and the preparations began. Fisk's new principal emptied the school's lean treasury to help buy railroad tickets for the group to Cincinnati, but this was not enough. Other gifts were solicited. Finally George L. White sold or pawned everything he owned to make up the balance, and the tour started with fear and trembling. Within a fortnight the little band was down and out in Springfield, Ohio, not knowing where to turn for their next meal.

How they survived and how they came finally to have their picture done in oils by Queen Victoria's own portrait painter in London is part of the story of CHARIOT IN THE SKY. The point here is that their school was saved. When the singers returned the following spring, they not only brought with them enough money to pay the school's debts but also enough more to buy the hill beyond Nashville where once Fort Gillem had stood. This, they hoped, would some day be the site of a larger and finer school, perhaps a university, for free young people who like themselves would be eager to learn.

A second tour a year later was even more successful. The group sang before European audiences of kings and queens and nobility as well as enormous throngs of common people, and with the funds they brought home, a new building was erected on the hill their first tour had purchased. By now the little group of students from Fisk was known throughout the musical world as the Jubilee Singers, and the building they erected was called Jubilee Hall. At the time of its dedication that building was described by many as the finest educational edifice in the whole South. It has remained a symbol of liberal education, without limitation as to race or color or previous condition.

Another result of these tours by the Jubilee Singers showed itself in the way they began to think of themselves. As children of slavery, attending school in the South during the reconstruction disorders, they caught a glimpse of the wider world, and they expressed the attitude which this view awakened by an act that has even sharper meaning today. They collected bits of wood from the trees in the countries they visited and from those in other countries with which they made contact, including Africa. All these pieces were appropriately worked into the banisters and floors of Jubilee Hall.

The Negro spirituals which this group introduced soon came to be regarded as the only native American music. From the Negro himself had come the sorrowful, the hauntingly beautiful melodies. And the world listened. When Johann Strauss, composer of wonderful waltzes, heard the group in Boston, he waved his arms and tossed his hat into the air. The approbation of later musicians has scarcely been less enthusiastic, and the influence of the spirituals on American musical composition since then, both popular and serious, is certainly beyond measure. These songs of slavery, so jealously guarded before the Jubilees' tour, have ironically enough become the folk songs of the American land that had held the Negro slave in bondage.

Though they had been slaves, the Jubilee Singers could never again feel that they were alone on the earth.

Contents

Chariot In the Sky

A Runaway Slave

Caleb saw nothing distinctly in the dark palmetto grove, but he knew he was being followed. Somewhere in the deep shadows footsteps fell.

He paused, leaning against a tree. He had been running a long while, and he was beginning to feel tired. But now he would have to run again. The footsteps kept coming.

They did not seem in a hurry. Caleb could easily out-run them. At times he was so far ahead that he lost the sound altogether. But when he stopped to catch his breath, pretty soon there the footsteps were again, trudging ahead tirelessly, following, following.

This was a race he just couldn't afford to lose, he muttered to himself. It meant—he was about to say it meant life or death. Caleb was running toward freedom.

Many times in his young life he had heard stories about slaves who fled. Somewhere—somewhere up North these unhappy bondsmen found the freedom for which their hearts yearned, the stories said. But the journey was hard and long.

Caleb was not sure he knew the way. He had never been more than a few miles from the plantation on which he was born, and the only helpful direction he had been given was that a certain star guided runaways. If they would keep their eyes on this star as they journeyed, it would lead them at last to free ground where they could walk like men and not be afraid. They called this star the North Star.

This meant they must always travel by night when the stars were in the sky. During the day hours they could rest and sleep if they were able to find hiding places. Along the way they would have to beg their food, depending on the kindness and good will of other folk who also longed for freedom and who would therefore be ready to help a fugitive.

Right now, however, Caleb's mind was not on food or sleep. When would those footsteps cease to follow? At that moment his own bare foot landed on hard, smooth ground. He took another step or two before he realized that he had run out of the woods and onto the big road. Which way now?

Caleb gave a quick glance in each direction. Somehow he failed to recognize this road. Had he run so hard he had become confused? Where was he?

Well, never mind. Perhaps one way was as good as the other. He turned to his right and began running again. A few moments later he thought about the footprints his feet were making in the dirt road. These would certainly be easy to follow by daylight. Maybe he should keep to the woods.

Again Caleb stopped to listen. His heart pounded noisily, and the woods were as full of sounds as ever. He waited. A moment passed. Another moment. Could they have lost him?

When he was sure they were no longer on his trail, Caleb sighed with relief. Still he did not feel safe enough to stop running. He swung around again and plunged into the dark grove.

It seemed hours later that he came to a hut. By this time Caleb was so exhausted he could scarcely drag his feet. It made no difference who lived in this tiny cabin, he had to rest now. He couldn't run another step. He put his hands against the side of the hut and began feeling his way around to the front.

"Anybody here?" he called breathlessly through the opening that served as a door. There was no answer. "Yoo-hoo! Anybody live here?" he repeated. After another pause he added, "Can I come in, please?"

By now Caleb was inside, his eyes adjusting slowly to the deeper dark. The cabin seemed empty. He dropped to his knees and began patting the dirt floor. Yes, it was empty all right, except for something dry and flaky in a corner. Corn shucks, Caleb thought. Maybe the hut had been used as a crib. Anyhow, it would do well enough for his purpose.

Caleb stretched out on the shucks and closed his eyes.

Presently he heard music. He opened his eyes and saw silver in the cracks of the wall. A jasmine fragrance filled the air. Where was he? What had happened?

He sat up, rubbed his eyes and shook his head. The tunes came from a mocking bird. That shiny stuff in the chinks was daylight. The perfume was blown from big clusters of blue flowers that hung on a vine over the doorway. There was no miracle.

Why had he awakened so strangely? Suddenly Caleb remembered his dash for freedom and how he had stumbled into the log hut and fallen asleep on the corn shucks. He also recalled wearily some of the events that led to his running away.

Two nights ago he had stood under a pride-of-China tree listening to an old gray-haired slave. With him in the circle were a dozen other shadowy figures. Not all of them were boys like Caleb. Grown folk bent their ears and listened too. The stoop-shouldered old man spoke in a sort of chant. "Freedom's in the air, sweet people."

3

"Yes, yes, I know. We heard about it," the others chimed back.

"Well, what you aim to do?"

Caleb waited. When nobody else answered, he spoke up, "I don't know what to do, Uncle Mingo. Folks run away and get free sometimes. I've seen them scampering off like rabbits or squirrels. I've heard tell about the Underground Railroad too."

The old man lowered his voice to a whisper. "I'm thinking about flying, me."

Nobody laughed out loud, but Caleb smiled indulgently. "Like a bird? Is that how you mean?"

"Don't you know about flying Africans?"

Some said they had heard rumors. Others knew nothing of the legend.

"It sounds downright funny to me," Caleb said.

Uncle Mingo's forehead wrinkled like a mask in the moonlight. "Don't make light of what old folks tell you, son," he warned. "If the old folks say they seen slaves pick up and fly back to Africa, like birds, just don't you dispute them. If they tell you about a slave preacher what led his whole flock to the beach and sat down on the sand with them, looking across the ocean toward home, don't ask no questions. Next morning nobody could find trace of that preacher or his people. And no boat had been there neither. One day when I was chopping cotton in the field, I looked up and the old fellow working in the row next to mine was gone. He was too feeble to run away, and I couldn't see no place for him to hide. None of the others in the field saw him leave either, but later on an old woman drinking water at a well, told us she noticed something pass in front of the sun about that time, like a hawk or a buzzard maybe, but she didn't pay it much mind."

Uncle Mingo paused, looking up at the moon. Presently

4

he added, "Freedom is a powerful word, children. Make you fly like a bird sometimes."

So Caleb had made up his mind to run toward freedom too. While he didn't believe Uncle Mingo's yarns about the flying slaves, he was sure he understood how the old man and the other slave folk felt in their hearts. He wanted to be free as much as any of them. That was why he had left them working in the cotton field yesterday and started running toward the palmetto grove.

Now it was morning again. Caleb rolled out of the corn shucks and cautiously poked his head through the door. The sun was higher than he expected. He must have slept a long time. Maybe that was why he felt hungry and thirsty. He would have to find food and water.

Caleb understood why the journey to freedom had to be made at night, but the day hours seemed important too, now that his stomach had begun to feel empty. He would have to search around among the palmettos and see what he could find.

He crept out of the hut and began walking cautiously.

It was late afternoon when Caleb put his feet on another big road. He had found creeks from which to drink, but he was still hungry. Now he would have to look for a friendly house or cabin. If he could see someone working in a field, perhaps he could ask help. In any case, he would have to follow the road for a while. Caleb hoped it was taking him northward.

When a cloud of dust arose a few moments later, he hoped that that might be a cotton wagon on the way to the gin. As it drew nearer, however, he discovered that the two horses were not pulling a wagon. They had saddles on their backs and men were riding them. He hoped —but there was no need to hope for help from these horsemen, for Caleb could see that they were strangers, and they looked terribly unpleasant.

All he could wish now was that they would pay no attention to a lonesome-looking colored boy minding his own business and walking the big road. Yes, those were guns in their hands, and those badges pinned to their shirts seemed to mean something or other. Caleb decided to look at the ground as they passed. Presently they were right in front of him, and a harsh voice shouted angrily, "Where you going there, boy?"

"N-nowheres, sir, n-nowheres," Caleb stuttered, without looking up.

"Stand still when I talk to you, and stop that confounded stuttering. Whose boy are you?"

"I b'long to—I ain't nobody's—I mean I was just—"

"Come along," the second horseman ordered.

"Please, sir," Caleb pleaded. "I don't aim to do no devilment."

"Start walking," the first deputy barked. After a pause he added, "A young slave scamp ran away from Colonel Willows' plantation yesterday. Did you see any such boy that looked like he might be running away?"

Caleb tried to swallow the lump in his throat. "I ain't seen nobody, sir."

The deputies laughed strangely.

"I think we've caught the bird," one of them smirked. "Keep walking up ahead there. We'll turn you over to Colonel Willows' overseer."

"You can tell him who you are," the other commented.

Strangers

The penalty for trying to escape from slavery was always severe. Sometimes it meant being sold to another master in another state or on a plantation covered with swamps in which rice was cultivated and the chances for running away were fewer. Sometimes it meant being assigned to harder and dirtier work with longer hours and less food. Always it meant a whipping with a rawhide lash.

Caleb couldn't tell how long or hard he was whipped because he fainted after a few lashes, and when he regained consciousness he was back in his own sleeping place on the floor of the slave cabin. Nor was he able to tell what other punishment his master's overseer had in mind for him. Two days passed in which he worked in the cotton field as usual, with nothing more said about his attempted flight, and he began to wonder what the overseer had said to Colonel Willows about him and what Colonel Willows had said to the overseer.

Then one morning very early, when he was on his way to the cotton field, the overseer met him on the path. "Come with me," the tall white man said, his cheek bulging with chewing tobacco, his mouth twisted and stained. "You're not chopping no cotton today."

Caleb became uneasy. Was this more punishment for the unsuccessful attempt to run away? "Yes, sir," he murmured.

The overseer led him past the slave quarters and toward the stables and carriage sheds. A sleek chestnut colt with white tail and mane was hitched to a democrat wagon in the driveway. Old Mingo waited under a tree, corncob pipe in his mouth, a buggy whip in one hand. The overseer pointed. "You're going with him in the wagon," he said.

Caleb did not answer, but a moment later he climbed slowly over the wheel. Mingo took the driver's place, gave the lines a sharp jerk and clucked to the horse. The little buckboard began to roll briskly; presently it turned into a big road.

After a long silence Mingo said, "How come your face is long as a mule's this morning, son? If I was in your fix, I'd be kicking up my heels. I'd have a smile on my face like a wave on the ocean."

"Stop joking, Uncle Mingo. You joke all the time," Caleb scolded. "I don't know what you're talking about."

"Can't you see which way we're headed? We're going to Charleston, boy. Looks to me like you won't have to chop no more cotton in the hot sun or help the stable boys clean up after the horses. Looks to me like you'll be working in town from now on."

Caleb was tempted to tell Uncle Mingo that if he had not talked so much about flying Africans, about mysterious wings passing in front of the sun, and other such nonsense, a boy might be able to put more trust in what he said. But Uncle Mingo was an old man and had to be treated with respect. "I'll wait till I get where I'm going," Caleb told him thoughtfully. "If I like it there, I can get happy then."

Mingo took the pipe out of his mouth and began to laugh, his old face splitting up like a smashed pie. "Now you talking sense, son. It do me good to hear you talk like that. Old fellow like me—all beat up and full of fool-

ishment—don't amount to nothing nohow. But you—
you is young, Caleb. You got to talk sense."

The sun was pushing up. Spots of perspiration began
to show on the colt's back where the harness rubbed, and
a thin cloud of dust trailed off behind the wagon. For a
while Caleb said nothing, and Uncle Mingo commenced
to nod in his seat. Then, quite abruptly, the boy turned
to the old man again. "Where you taking me in Charleston?" he demanded.

Mingo scarcely opened his eyes. "You'll find out," he
muttered.

"Is it a secret?"

Mingo's watery old eyes fluttered. "Kind of," he said.
"Kind of a secret."

"It's not like you to keep secrets, Uncle Mingo." Caleb
spoke impatiently.

"This is different, boy. But don't you mind. You'll see
the place directly."

Caleb pondered these words. Presently suspicion began
to grow in his mind. Was Uncle Mingo joking as usual or
was this indeed a serious matter—so serious that the old
man hesitated to name the place? No one was ever sure
how much Mingo knew or what he was thinking. At
night, in the moonlight and under the China trees, he
chattered a lot about freedom, but during the daytime
Caleb had often seen him talking to the overseer. What
he said to the overseer at these times, and what the overseer said to him, only Uncle Mingo and the overseer
knew. But it was a fact that old Mingo was trusted beyond most slaves. It was because of this that he was permitted to drive to Charleston in the buckboard behind a
tall, high-stepping young colt. The master trusted Mingo;
Caleb began to wonder if *he* could trust him as much.

A moment later a shocking thing popped into Caleb's
mind, and he reached over and snatched the reins from

9

the hands of the drowsy old man. "Hold on a minute, Uncle Mingo," he shouted. "Let's stop here."

"What's the matter with you, Caleb? Turn loose them lines. You going crazy?" The boy and the old man tugged at the reins. Their pulling back and forth confused the horse, who first began to slow down, but later picked up speed and went into a gallop.

"Stop the horse," cried Caleb. "He's running away."

"Turn loose them lines, I say."

Caleb released the driving lines reluctantly, and the horse began to respond to the steady hand of the driver he knew. Presently he was back to his usual gait. A moment later Mingo brought him to a full stop.

"I want to know something," Caleb began. Now that the wagon was still, he discovered that his hands were shaking; there was sweat on his face, and his voice trembled. "I want to know where you're taking me, Uncle Mingo. I want to know now."

"Did you have to snatch the reins out of my hands and make the horse run away?"

"Never mind about that. Where in Charleston are you taking me?"

Mingo rubbed the frizzled whiskers on his chin. "You going to a new job today. I told you that."

"Is Colonel Willows fixing to sell me, Uncle Mingo?" Caleb's voice dropped low. "Don't look at me funny like that. Tell me, is the old master sending me to Charleston to be sold."

"Lord a' mercy, why'd the Colonel want to sell a young boy like you, just sixteen years old?"

"You ain't forgot I tried to run away, have you? You know as well as me what happens to slaves that run away."

"The ones that don't behave get sold to the plantations on the rice swamps. But one thing you forget, Caleb.

The rice swamps don't pay so much for the ones that run away. Colonel Willows ain't fixing to lose no money on you. He got something else in his head."

"Then you're not taking me to the auction block?"

" 'Course not. Didn't I tell you this was your lucky day?"

"I'll believe that when I see it, Uncle Mingo."

"Well, keep your hands off these reins and let me drive this horse where I'm going."

Once more the little wagon began to roll on the big road. Neither Caleb nor Mingo spoke again until the wheels hit the cobblestones of Charleston.

Mingo tied the horse to a hitching post on a narrow side street shaded by flowering locust trees, while Caleb waited. Then the two entered a small shop together. A bell tinkled faintly in a back room as the door opened and closed.

It was a clothing establishment, but the front room was deserted at this moment. A tall mirror stood against one wall, reaching from the floor almost to the ceiling. Caleb stepped in front of it, his hat in his hand. Almost immediately an expression of disappointment came over his face.

Was this how he looked to other people? Before him in the glass stood a scrawny brown boy, the figure as tall as a man, but the hair wild and neglected, and the clothes in rags, the feet bare. Caleb shook his head sadly.

"What's the matter?" old Mingo grinned. "Don't you like yourself?"

"Why didn't you tell me I looked like this, Uncle Mingo? If anybody'd told me I looked this bad, I'd run away again."

Mingo laughed softly. "What good would that do? You can't run away from yourself. Besides, you ain't all that monstrous. You dirty and ragged all right, and your head

11

look like a cuckoo's nest, but you'll learn how to fix up a little if you stay in town."

"I hear somebody coming," Caleb whispered, stepping back quickly and facing the door that led into the back rooms. Mingo moved nearer the entrance and waited. A small man in a tailor's apron entered, his eyeshade pushed up from his forehead.

"Good morning, Mingo," the tailor said pleasantly. "Is this the boy?"

The old slave bowed stiffly. "Yes, sir, Mr. Harvey," he answered. "This here's Caleb. This the one our master's been talking to you about."

"Colonel Willows is my friend. I'm sure he wouldn't send me a worthless boy to learn tailoring."

"No, sir," Mingo assured him. "Caleb ain't worthless." This must have sounded silly to him because he grinned as he turned to the boy. "Tell him 'bout yourself, Caleb."

Caleb was so confused by the unfamiliar surroundings that he let the first thing that came into his mind pop out. "I tried to run away," he said.

The tailor nodded; he had heard about that. "But I don't aim to do it again," Caleb added quickly.

Mr. Harvey paused, as if to weigh the boy's words. Then he turned to the older slave. "Well, Mingo, I reckon you can go now and leave him with me."

"Yes, sir, Mr. Harvey." Mingo bowed and moved toward the door. "Good-by, Caleb."

Caleb's answer was so soft it couldn't be heard. A moment later he looked out the window and saw old Mingo climbing over the wheel of the buckboard wagon, the driving whip still in his hand.

"When's the last time you saw your master?" Mr. Harvey asked as the wagon disappeared.

Caleb shook his head. "Can't remember the last time, sir. He don't spend much time at home."

12

"You're lucky to belong to Colonel Willows," the little tailor said. "He's a fine man. Most any other owner would have sold you to one of those rice planters to work in the swamps, after you tried to run away. But not Colonel Willows. He turns you over to me to help in my shop and learn tailoring."

"I'm much obliged to him," Caleb murmured.

"But that's not all. When's the last time you saw your ma and pa?"

"Don't know, sir. It's been too long."

"Colonel Willows was thinking about that, too, when he decided to let me have you. Your ma and pa live here in Charleston. He's going to let you live with them."

Caleb felt completely bewildered. He twisted the old hat that he held in his hand. He was glad, he was terribly pleased by Mr. Harvey's words, but he wasn't sure it was safe to smile. In slavery a boy learned to keep his feelings to himself. If people found out what made him happy, they might make him pay for it; they might deny it to him and make him work doubly hard to get it. Everything that happened in slavery, Caleb had learned, was a trick to get more work out of a fellow.

"Doesn't that sound good to you?" asked Mr. Harvey.

Caleb answered cautiously, "I look a sight in these rags, I ain't fit to be in here walking on your clean floor and touching your clean things. My ma and pa won't hardly know me when they see me." He kept his eyes on the floor.

Mr. Harvey laughed. "We'll clean you up a little," he said. "At least enough so your ma and pa will know you. There's a pump in the yard behind the shop; you can go out there and scrub yourself. While you're at it, I'll look around in here and see if I can find something you can put on to be decent in the streets."

Caleb followed him through the door and into the large

cluttered room in which Mr. Harvey worked. A long cutting table stood in front of the windows, facing the light; shelves stacked with countless bolts of cloth covered two of the other walls, and there were sewing machines, wooden mannequins for fitting clothes, an ironing board, a stove, a small desk covered with papers, records and accounts, and shaded lamps suspended from the ceiling. Caleb's eyes darted from one object to another as he passed through. He reached the back door, and Mr. Harvey pointed to the yard beyond.

"I'm much obliged," Caleb murmured. Mr. Harvey closed the door behind him.

Around this end of the premises stood a high wooden fence, the heavy green of two magnolia trees made a canopy overhead. Near the pump there was an outdoor fireplace and a huge iron kettle in which clothes had been boiled upon occasion. A wooden tub half full of water sat in front of the pump to catch the drip. Near by, Caleb found a drinking gourd and a broken pitcher containing homemade soap.

It took him only a moment to throw off his rags, lather himself from head to foot, and start splashing in the wooden tub. When he rinsed away the soap, the water in which he had sat became so dirty he decided to empty it along the fence and draw more. He repeated this three times before he felt that he could safely put on clean clothes. Later Mr. Harvey came outside.

"Put these on," he said, hanging pants, shirt and underclothes on a clothesline. "I guess these shoes will fit your feet," he added, dropping them on the ground. "The socks are balled up in them."

Caleb opened one eye. "Thank you, sir." A moment later he began wondering how he would get himself dry enough to put on the fresh clothes. If he waited for the sun to dry him, Mr. Harvey might think he was worthless and lazy; if he dressed while his body was wet, that would be bad too. But when he stood up and looked around, he saw an old cloth he could use, probably the one Mr. Harvey used to dry his hands when he washed them at the pump. Caleb decided to use it without permission; afterwards he washed it out with soap and hung it on the line to dry.

The clean clothes felt wonderful; Caleb didn't give much thought to the fit. Even with the shoes, the first he had ever put on his feet, he was not critical; he was dressed and he was clean, and this was a new experience. It was almost like a new life. He examined the yard to make sure no puddles remained in the places where he had emptied the water. But what could he do with the filthy rags he had worn to town from the plantation? Best leave them on the fireplace; next time Mr. Harvey had need for a fire in the yard, he would see them—and perhaps understand.

"I could let you go down the alley and see your ma and pa for a few minutes now, but it wouldn't do any good," Mr. Harvey said when Caleb returned to the big workroom. "They aren't there at this time of day. Your ma cooks in a boarding-house and your pa works on the dock. Your master hires them out by the day; Colonel Willows has more people than he can use."

"I feel like doing some work now, Mr. Harvey," Caleb said, smiling gratefully. "Can I start tailoring?"

The little round-shouldered man was bending over the cutting table, his mouth bristling with pins. He burst into laughter, scattering a few of them across the pattern he had just laid out. "You're too anxious," he chuckled. "People don't just sit down and start making suits and capes and jackets, Caleb. There's more to it than that. But don't worry; I've got work planned for you."

"Yes, sir," Caleb muttered, ashamed of himself for speaking up so bold, "I didn't mean—"

"You'll get around to tailoring soon enough. Right now

I have something for you to deliver." Mr. Harvey pointed to a large parcel wrapped in heavy paper. It was on a shelf beside the bolts of broadcloth and other suit materials. "Evening clothes for Mr. Cardoza," he explained. "Walk down this street three blocks—or is it four?—till you come to a house with two poplars by the gate. Turn and go four more blocks; you'll see a big white house setting back from the street. Go to the back door. Understand?"

Caleb took the parcel off the shelf. "I hear what you say, Mr. Harvey," he said, but his face looked blank. "I reckon I understand."

"If you don't find it right away, just ask somebody to show you. The name and address are written on the bundle."

Caleb looked at the marks on the wrapping paper. They meant nothing to him. And Mr. Harvey's directions stuck in his mind rather awkwardly. Three blocks—or was it four? Two poplars. A gate; four more blocks. A big white house; the back door. The tailor walked through the little reception room with him and stood in the entrance of the shop while Caleb hesitated.

"This way?" the boy asked, pointing.

Mr. Harvey shook his head and jerked his thumb in the opposite direction. "No, no," he said. "The other way. Watch for two poplars by a gate."

Caleb nodded and began walking. Half an hour later he paused to take his bearings. He had seen so many gates with poplars, so many big white houses, and counted blocks to four so many times his head spun. He was hopelessly lost. He wasn't even sure now he knew how to get back to Mr. Harvey's tailor shop; he would have to ask help.

A large dark woman, with a basket of laundry on her head, approached on the opposite side of the street. Caleb crossed over to meet her. "Please, ma'am," he said. "Will you tell me where Mr. Cardoza lives at?"

"I would if I knowed," she smiled.

"It's wrote on here—if you can read writing."

"Read writing!" Her laughter was loud and musical. "Son, I can't even read reading."

Caleb sauntered along a few more blocks and came to a livery stable with an entrance wide enough to admit carriages and coaches, and with a watering trough and a hitching bar outside under a tree. A smell of hay and horses and leather saddles came out of the place. Caleb stuck his head inside and heard stableboys and coachmen chatting somewhere back in the shadows. A clatter of well-shod feet on the wooden floors could also be heard. Caleb ventured a few steps farther and discovered a man with rings in his ears repairing a broken harness inside a dim room.

"I'm looking for somebody," he said carefully.

The harness-maker growled. His shirt was open, his chest matted with black hair. "A likely story," he sneered. "What's in that bundle?"

"It's from the tailor. Something for Mr. Cardoza," Caleb answered.

"From the tailor, huh?" the man mimicked savagely. "For Mr. Cardoza."

"Yes, sir."

"How do I know you're not trying to make off with something you stole?" He took two steps forward and caught Caleb firmly by the arm. "How do I know you're not a runaway looking for a place to hide? I've got a good mind to report you."

Caleb managed to point a shaking finger at the writing on the package. "Read that, please," he begged.

The harness maker snatched the parcel from under the boy's arm and carried it to the light of the entrance way, where he could see the writing better. After a considerable pause he muttered, "Well, I don't know. But just to be sure, I'll take you to Mr. Cardoza's myself. Come along," he snorted. "And no monkey business either."

In the sunlight the stoop-shouldered harness-maker looked almost as fierce and dangerous as a Barbary pirate.

A half hour more of walking and they reached a waterfront street; Caleb became aware of fishermen's wharves, taverns crowded with merchant seamen, warehouses, docks piled with bales and barrels, hurrying rousters, lumbering drays and moored trading vessels. It struck him as a strange neighborhood in which to seek a fine white house with a sweeping driveway, but he was afraid to question the harness-maker. A few moments later they turned into a narrow passage between two buildings, and Caleb's companion stopped suddenly and caught the boy's arm in a harsh grip.

"We can stop this make-believe now," he muttered between his teeth. "Just behave yourself and you'll get along all right. Give me that bundle."

"It belongs to Mr. Cardoza," Caleb whispered, trembling. "I got to take it to him."

"I said give it to me."

"But Mr. Harvey said—" Caleb saw the fellow's closed fist rise to strike. At the same time he felt the parcel slipping from under his arm. Then heard it drop on the ground.

"I haven't got time to argue with you," the man threatened. "And the sooner you forget about Mr. Cardoza and Mr. Harvey, the better. You're doing what I tell you from now on. Come along."

When they turned from the alley into the street again, Caleb caught a last glimpse of the package with which he had been intrusted. It had fallen against a wall near a pile of trash. He turned quickly and began walking fast to keep up with the long strides of the hairy-chested man with earrings in his ears.

His heart pounded and his breath came short. "Colonel Willows won't let me go with you, sir," he cried. "I belong to him."

His captor frowned angrily. "Do I have to *knock* sense into your head?"

"No, sir."

"I've heard all I want to hear from you. Do what you're told from now on and keep your mouth shut—if you know what's good for you."

A few moments later they stopped in front of a noisy tavern, and the harness-maker seemed to be looking around for somebody he knew. Spotting a pale, hatchet-faced man in dark clothes, he beckoned furtively. With this stranger he and Caleb crossed the street and walked a few paces to get safely beyond earshot of the patrons of the tavern. For some reason Caleb seemed to lose a little of his fear, but when the men began to talk he turned his eyes away.

"You selling anything today?" the harness-maker asked.

"Couple of rice planters are here," the stranger confided. "I promised to see what I could line up for them."

The fellow from the livery stable lowered his voice. "What do you think of this boy?"

"I don't know. Where'd you find him?"

"He strayed into town. I don't think we'll have any trouble if we get rid of him in a hurry. He won't be missed for a day or two."

"What are you asking?"

"Twelve hundred. He'll bring two thousand at auction; that ought to leave you a profit."

The stranger shook his head. "I'll be mighty lucky to

get twelve hundred for him myself. This infernal anti-slavery agitation in Congress has knocked the bottom out of slave prices. I'll give you eight hundred for him."

"You're robbing me, as usual," the harness-maker complained, "but I haven't got time to haggle. Take him."

"Stay here," the man in dark clothes said. "I'll settle with you after the auction." He turned to Caleb. "Come along, boy."

Caleb followed the man, walking behind him. When they reached the corner, he saw the harness-maker crossing over to the tavern. The sharp-faced stranger led him toward a dilapidated building in front of which a crowd was gathered. A string of carriages were tied to hitching bars across the street, and a dozen miserable-looking Negroes were herded together around the entrance. Caleb slowed his steps and dropped a little farther behind the man he was following. When he realized this was not noticed, he hesitated even more and let a still longer distance develop between himself and the man. A moment later he made a lightning-swift decision.

He spun suddenly and darted across the street. When the dark-clad stranger realized what was happening, Caleb was dashing into an alley. With the speed of a frightened cat he bounded and swerved in the cluttered passage, slipping around carts and drays, till he emerged on another street. He turned without considering the direction and began to watch for another alley. When he found one, he scampered into it blindly and soon found himself blocked by a high wooden fence. Hesitating only a second, he decided to climb it and take his chances in the yard beyond.

When he landed on the other side, a dog began to bark. Caleb restrained his urge to run long enough to walk around the house and go out the front gate, the dog still at his heels. No sooner had the gate clicked behind him, however, than he began running again. The street was quieter, and he followed it for several blocks before it occurred to him to look for another alley. When he did discover one, he was calm enough to look ahead and make sure of an opening at the other end.

As he turned into this alley, he glanced backward to see whether or not he was being followed. No pursuit was apparent. If an alarm had been sounded, if the dark-clad stranger or the earringed harness-maker were after him or had found others to join them in the chase, they must have been coming another way. Either that, or they had lost him. Caleb slowed down and tried to catch his breath; his legs felt tired and heavy.

When he came again to a street with trees, he decided to sit on a step and rest. Several minutes later he raised his eyes and saw Mr. Harvey's tailor shop across the street and not very far down the block. Caleb got up and walked slowly toward it.

Friends

Caleb's father and mother lived on an alley, in a loft above a carriage shed. They reached their rooms by a rickety stair on the outside. Pigeons had once inhabited these quarters, but since Moses and Sarah came there to live, the place had become as tidy a home as slaves could hope to occupy. They kept it swept and mopped, and they pasted old newspapers on the wall. They planted honeysuckle and columbine outside and carefully guided the young vines upward toward their door and window. Now the openings into their rooms were surrounded by flowers and fragrance.

Sarah was a tall slender woman with deep eyes and a low-pitched voice. Her husband was short, barrel-chested and powerful. Both were quiet people, and both had been hurt in many ways by slavery, but they remained gentle in manner and in speech; nor did they appear to be unhappy.

Neither did they appear to be expecting a visitor that evening as they sat together on the steps that led to their door. Moses was whittling on a fishing pole, Sarah's arms were quietly folded. Twilight was falling. Two shadows moving in the alley did not disturb them; they were accustomed to shadows; the alley was always full of shadows. Sarah continued to dream, Moses to whittle.

But when the two figures stopped directly in front of them, they couldn't help notice.

"Do you folks know this fellow?" Mr. Harvey asked.

Neither of them seemed pleased or surprised. "He do look kind of familiar," said Moses.

"I'd know my boy with my eyes shut," Sarah admitted.

"I'm bringing him to you to keep," the tailor added. "He's working for me now."

"Yes, sir," Sarah whispered.

"Do you reckon you can make a pallet for him and give him something to eat?"

"We'll try," Moses said.

Mr. Harvey turned to leave. "Have him in my shop bright and early," he ordered.

Sarah muttered something inaudible, but she didn't move from her seat on the step. When the tailor was safely out of earshot, however, she sprang up quickly and threw her arms around Caleb's neck. "I'm glad enough to holler," she cried, making the words hum like music. "My, my—how long has it been?"

"I'm glad too," Caleb whispered.

Moses dropped his fishing pole and put an arm around the boy's shoulder. "Come upstairs," he said, still afraid to show all his joy.

"We got something up there in a basket," Sarah revealed. "Your pa would of et it all if I'd let him, hungry as he was, but I held a little back. Something must of told me company was coming."

She led the others up the narrow, creaking steps. The room they entered was already dark, but Caleb could make out the shapes of a bed, a table and two boxes. Also visible was an opening into darkness beyond, but his eyes were heavy, and he didn't look closely. Instead, he reached for the bed and sat down on the side of it.

Moses stood his fishing pole in the corner, found a

match and lighted a wick in a bowl of tallow. Sarah's basket was on the table, covered with a large napkin; she began rummaging in it for fragments of food. There was a ham bone that wasn't quite clean, two broken biscuits, a baked sweet potato, some crumbs of cake. Caleb watched her weakly.

"Somehow or another I don't feel much like eating," he said.

"You don't?" A strange look came over his mother's face. "Tell me what's the trouble now, son." She sat down beside him on the bed. "I knowed something was wrong time I set eyes on you." She put her hand on his. "Tell your ma what's happened, Caleb."

"I'm going to be all right, Ma," he said softly. "Don't mind me."

Moses became attentive. "When a growing boy like you don't feel like eating, something must be the matter."

Caleb was sorry he had made his parents unhappy; he hadn't aimed to do this. "I'll eat a little bit maybe," he said, trying to cover over his first remark.

Sarah patted his hand again. "Never mind," she said. "Rest yourself first. We got plenty time, and you don't have to eat if you don't feel like it."

"Stretch out on the bed if you're tired," suggested his father.

Caleb leaned back and closed his eyes. When he opened them about an hour later, a big moon was shining through the door, and he could see a peculiar object like a carved stump of a tree in the corner of the room. The tallow flame was no longer burning, and his parents were out on the steps again enjoying the night air and the honeysuckle. Caleb got up, went across the room, and touched the strange object. It still seemed like the stump of a tree, but it was hollow and one end was covered by a tight skin. Caleb thumped against this tight covering. The thing resounded oddly.

"Somebody's meddling," his mother called from outside. "Must feel better." She came in and re-lighted the wick in the tallow.

"I believe I could eat something now," Caleb told her.

"Sit down on this box and help yourself. We fixed you a pallet in the other room whilst you was asleep."

He pulled up a box and began to eat. Moses came in and sat across from him. "I'd like to know what that thing in the corner is," Caleb said.

"Your pa can tell you about that contraption later on," Sarah said impatiently. "Right now I want to hear what *you* got to say."

Caleb's face fell. He hesitated again. "Well, first thing, I tried to run away," he confessed. "The patrollers stopped me."

His mother's eyes became stern. "You know what happens to slaves that run away?"

"I found out," Caleb said calmly.

"I hope you learned your lesson," Sarah snapped.

"Mind how you talk, Sarah," Moses spoke up. "Anything that's equal to a ground squirrel wants to be free. No need to fault the boy on account of that."

Caleb said softly, "Colonel Willows is going to let me stay here with you all and learn to tailor in Mr. Harvey's shop."

Moses beamed. "It do us proud to have you here, son. But how come you look so tuckered out and can't keep your eyes open?"

Caleb told them about the parcel he had tried to deliver to Mr. Cardoza for Mr. Harvey and the trouble it had led him into. "After I got back to the shop," he concluded, "Mr. Harvey went with me and we found the bundle again. By then it was too late to take it to Mr. Cardoza's house, so we left it at the shop and he brought me here."

"If you stay in Charleston, you got to learn who to talk

25

to and who not to talk to," Moses told him. "Plenty no-good men around here is just waiting to pick up a lost colored boy and sell him off. You got to know where you going and you got to be ready to tell them who you belong to. Big city like this, full of strange folks, with ships coming in all the time and stagecoaches going out every day, is more like a jungle than anything else. You got to learn how to come and go."

"If you learn how to read numbers, that'll help," Sarah said, lowering her voice. "You'll know which way to go, and you won't have to ask questions."

"Read numbers? How can I learn that, Ma?"

Sarah put her finger over her lips. "S-h-h. . . . You don't talk out loud about reading. It ain't allowed—for slaves. It's against the law for anybody to teach slaves. But there ain't no law to say you can't teach *yourself*."

"You have to be powerful smart to learn how to read all by yourself," Moses said hopelessly. "Not many can do it."

Caleb lowered his own voice. "Maybe I can do it though."

His mother's stern face and deep eyes did not change expression, but her voice was not the same when she spoke again. "I got me a piece of gold money—five dollars," she said. "Sometimes I cook for people at night and on days when the boardinghouse is closed, and Colonel Willows lets me keep what I make. When I saved enough to make five dollars, I changed it to gold and sewed it up in the mattress of the bed. It's right there now. But I'll take it out for you, Caleb, if you learn how to read. It'll be yours." Her voice faded. A moment later she added, "Maybe you better lay down on your pallet now and get some sleep."

He went through the opening into the tiny adjoining room. The sleeping place was on the floor at his feet.

The next morning Mr. Harvey sent him out with the same bundle again, and Caleb had no trouble finding the place. This caused him to wonder how he had become so mixed up the day before. Not only did he find the Cardoza house, but he hurried back to the shop and promptly delivered two other packages containing completed work for customers of the tailor. With neither of these did Caleb have any difficulty following directions, and it was still early morning when Mr. Harvey gave him a few simple instructions and put him to work on the ironing board.

Soon afterwards a customer entered the shop. Caleb listened as the tailor took his measurements, announcing each distinctly as he set it down on a slip of paper. Waist, 32, he heard. Chest, 36. Hips, 36. Arms, 35. Mr. Harvey wrote the words and numbers as he called them, and it occurred to Caleb as he bent over his iron that if he could see that writing, he would then know how words like *waist*, *chest*, *hips* and *arms* look when written. He would learn to recognize by sight the marks for *32*, *36*, and the other numbers. But he would have to listen carefully and remember everything in order to get the right meaning. When Mr. Harvey finished writing, Caleb checked back in his mind to make sure he hadn't forgotten. And when the tailor went into the reception room with his customer, Caleb set his iron aside and examined the handwriting on the measurement slip.

So that was the way those words looked. Those marks beside them were the numbers as Mr. Harvey had called them off. He would have to look at all these markings many times before he could be sure of recognizing them any time he saw them, but somehow this did not seem impossible to Caleb. The words *hips* and *arms* were especially encouraging. Why, they were as good as learned already. A few minutes later he heard the customer go out the front door, and he put the slip where he found it and returned to his ironing board.

That night after supper, as he sat with his mother and father on the narrow steps on the side of the carriage shed, he couldn't keep the good news to himself. "I've started," he whispered. "I'm learning to read a few words and some figures."

"Don't crow too soon," Sarah cautioned. "Books and newspapers and things don't let just anybody read them. You got to stay by it a long time to learn how to read."

"How'd you start out today?" Moses asked.

Caleb explained to them about the tailor's measurement notations while the older people listened intently. Finally Sarah turned around, her forehead wrinkled, and said, "Know something?"

"How's that, Sarah?" Moses asked.

"I b'lieve that might work. He can learn reading that way."

"You can't never tell what a growing boy'll pick up," Moses chuckled. "He's apt to learn anything. Anything."

Both of them became silent again, pondering Caleb's first steps toward literacy. To the boy this was wonderful encouragement. He began to feel confidence. Before he knew it, he was humming a tune he had learned from the other slaves on the plantation. Presently he recalled the words and sang softly:

"Peeking around the chinquapin bush,
Peeking around the chinquapin bush."

"Looka here, hush!" Moses laughed. "Where'd you get that bass voice?"

Caleb smiled. "Is this what you call a bass voice?"

"Let me hear some more," Sarah said. "That sounded like right good singing."

Caleb was grinning big now, his teeth pearly in the darkness. "I'm just carrying on foolishment," he chuckled. "I don't know nothing about no singing."

As soon as he straightened out his face, however, he added two more lines!

"Billy goat came and gave him a push,
In Aunt Sally's garden."

"What'll you try next?" Sarah smiled. "First it's reading, and now it's singing. What'll it be next? Don't you think you better slow down?"

"You can't never tell about these young ones nowadays," Moses repeated. "I don't know what's going to come of them—learning so much."

For a moment this united slave family, sitting one behind the other on the steps leading up to their loft, moonlight splashing on them, was a picture of happiness. Life seemed so wonderful there with his parents that Caleb suddenly wiped the smile off his face. There was a danger in feeling too much happiness. Evenings like this, hours on the steps with your parents, could be snatched away without a moment's notice. A master or an overseer or a patroller—almost anybody could walk up the alley, beckon with his finger and say, "Come here, boy," and Caleb would have to go. This was a pleasant night, a happy hour, but he had better not laugh so much. If he felt like singing, he decided, he'd better think up a song that wasn't so playful. A moment later one came to mind.

"O wasn't that a wide river,
River of Jordan, Lord,
Wasn't that a wide river,
There's one more river to cross."

"True, true," Sarah mourned. "One more river."

Caleb stopped singing and turned to Moses. "You ain't told me yet about that thing in the corner of the room that makes noise, Pa."

Moses looked sheepish. "That's not to talk about," he said.

"But Ma said you'd tell me."

"Well, I'll tell you," his father compromised, "but don't you tell nobody else. Understand?"

"I understand, Pa."

"He'll have to know anyway if he's going to stay here with us," Sarah said.

Moses agreed. "I work on the docks," he began a moment later. "I help unload ships that come in and some that go out. Sometime I come across curious things. Heap of times I hear curious kinds of talk."

"Well, I reckon you do—on the docks," Caleb said, remembering his own brief impressions of the waterfront.

"Ships come in from the Sugar Islands sometimes. Sometimes they come from Philadelphia and Boston and New York. Now and then they come from Europe or Africa."

Caleb's eyes rounded. "Sugar Islands?"

"Them's the West Indies," Moses explained. "Ships from Africa stop there. Ever hear any talk about Africa?"

"Uncle Mingo tells about flying Africans," Caleb smiled.

"Mingo ought to stop that," Sarah said impatiently. "That's just his lonesomeness talking."

"Africa is where we come from—our people, way back yonder, maybe a hundred years ago," Moses explained. "Most everybody's people came here from somewhere across the water. They all talk about the old country; it do them proud to say they come from England, France, Spain, Italy, Germany and all such places. It do me proud to say we come from Africa."

"You was fixing to tell me about that thing in the corner of the room," Caleb reminded him.

"Tell him about the drum, for goodness' sake," Sarah prodded. "Everybody knows about Africa."

"You call it a drum?" Caleb asked.

"That's what it is—a drum. A tom-tom. A sailor on a ship let me have it." Moses paused a moment. "Africans are crazy about drums. They make a drum like that talk," he said proudly.

"What do *you* do with it?" Caleb insisted.

"You beat a drum," Moses said. "It makes a nice sound. Just beat on it with your hands. Beat it one way and all the people that's walking slow will commence to walk fast. Beat it another way and all the people that's sitting in the house will come outdoors and kick up their heels. Beat it one way and people will laugh. Beat it another way and they'll cry." Moses stood up and stretched his legs. "I always wanted something from Africa I could keep in the house, and I fell in love with that drum first time I set eyes on it. That's a powerful drum, son."

"Let's beat it now," Caleb suggested.

"Oh, no, not now," Sarah cautioned. "You can't just beat it for nothing, like that."

"Like I started to tell you," Moses went on in a lowered tone, "you mustn't talk about this. That's the only African drum in Charleston now. All the slaves know there's a drum somewhere, but they don't know who got it. If ever any trouble breaks out, I'll beat on that drum, and that'll be the sign. You can hear it two or three miles on a quiet night."

"I'd like to look at the drum some more," Caleb said.

"Look at it all you please," Sarah said. "Just don't go to beating it."

"And put it under our bed when you get through,"

Moses added. "I don't reckon we better leave it in that corner no more."

Next morning as dawn was breaking, the three of them walked down the alley together. Just before they parted to go their separate ways to work, Sarah told Caleb to ask the tailor if they might borrow one of his old pairs of scissors overnight.

Caleb made the request at the first opportunity, and Mr. Harvey granted it without hesitation.

That evening, sitting above him on the steps, Sarah trimmed Caleb's neglected hair.

"Uncle Mingo said it looks like a cuckoo's nest," he commented as she clipped.

"I'll help him to say that," Sarah agreed. "But it won't look so bad when I get through with it."

Even Mr. Harvey noticed the improvement the next day, and it prompted him to search in a barrel of old and discarded garments for more clothes that Caleb could wear. The pieces he found were not clean, and they needed sewing and patching in a few places. "Take these home with you tonight," he said. "Have your ma wash them out. Early tomorrow morning before I get to the shop, you can sew the torn places and press the things on the ironing board. There's no better way to start tailoring than by fixing your own clothes."

With a change of garments to wear, Caleb was able to turn the others over to his mother for washing and then to repair and press them in the shop for wear on the street. Before long he was looking exceptionally clean and tidy for a slave boy.

But this did not take his mind away from the reading he was trying to learn. Every day people came into the shop to be measured, and Mr. Harvey called out each measurement distinctly for the benefit of his customer before jotting it down. Caleb always tried to hold these in his memory till he could get his hands on the slip and examine the markings. Later, when Mr. Harvey disposed of some of these by tossing them in a trash basket, he watched his chance to fish them out unnoticed and put them in his pocket. This gave him more time to study them at night and when he was walking on the street.

At the same time Caleb's work in the shop took on more interest. He was not yet expected to work at the cutting table, but Mr. Harvey began asking him to baste cuts together with a needle and thread. He gave him garments to take apart for renovation by opening old seams and picking out the threads; all the ironing and pressing became Caleb's responsibility. The sweeping of the floor and the picking up of scraps, the cleaning of the lamp chimneys and the trimming of the wicks, the drawing of water at the pump and the occasional boiling of water in the kettle in the yard had been his tasks from the start.

All in all, he was very busy and much interested in his work. When Sarah reminded him one evening that a whole month had passed since the morning Mingo drove him to town, he was surprised. Never in the past had time seemed to slip by so quickly.

One afternoon a few days later he was working so well and humming so cheerfully as he worked that Mr. Harvey couldn't help noticing it. "You sound like you're happy," the tailor said, pushing his eyeshade up on his forehead.

"I forgot myself," Caleb apologized. "I must have been singing."

"You can sing all you please, far as I'm concerned. It don't bother me," Mr. Harvey told him.

"Thank you, sir."

Mr. Harvey rubbed his chin. "Maybe you'd like to get outdoors and walk under the trees on a pretty street."

"That would be nice."

"I got a suit to be carried a good way out." Mr. Harvey

opened his big gold watch. "It's a little early," he went on, "but by the time you deliver it, it will be late enough for you to quit for the day. You can take your time and stroll by the river if you feel like it."

"I'm much obliged, sir."

Caleb waited while Mr. Harvey took the suit from a hanger, folded it and made it ready for delivery. Instead of wrapping the garments in a parcel, Mr. Harvey laid them neatly across Caleb's left arm. Then he handed him a slip on which was written the name and address.

"You've been on that street before," he explained. "Maybe this number is a little farther out than you've been, but you'll find it without any trouble. The name is Claude Sazon." When he saw that the name meant nothing to Caleb, Mr. Harvey added, "Mr. Sazon is a carriage-maker—a very successful man. He has a fine family, too."

Caleb was aware of a change in the tone of Mr. Harvey's voice during those last remarks, but he failed to catch the significance of it. To Caleb's way of thinking, all Mr. Harvey's customers were successful men. Many of them had proud families and stylish homes; all those elegant people looked alike to him. He nodded respectfully as Mr. Harvey complimented the Sazons, but he wasn't really interested.

About twenty minutes later, however, when a handsome and well-dressed young woman answered the back door in response to his knock, Mr. Harvey's words came back to him with unusual force. Caleb had seen many ladies in attractive clothes since he came to Charleston; even on the plantation he had occasionally seen them on the veranda of the big house as they laughed and talked with the master's family. But never before had one of them been an individual with a brown skin, recognizable as colored.

"Yes?" the young woman smiled.

34

Caleb's amazement left him speechless. Instead, he handed her the slip on which the directions were written. "Oh, Papa's new suit," the young woman said. "I'll take it." Caleb started to hand her the garments. "Just step inside," she told him. He was in the kitchen when the door closed and Miss Sazon relieved him of the clothes. "May I offer you a glass of water?" she asked. She pointed to a pitcher on a table. "Or some lemonade?"

Caleb took a step backward. "I'd be much obliged," he managed to say, his eyes fixed on the lemonade pitcher.

"Not at all." Miss Sazon took a glass from the cupboard and filled it to the brim with lemonade. "It must be very hot in the sun."

As he drank, two more Sazons entered the kitchen from the other part of the house. One was obviously the mother, a middle-aged woman with a little gray in her hair, and one a boy who appeared to be no older than Caleb. Both of these, like the young woman who had received the suit, showed more resemblance to people like Mr. Harvey and Colonel Willows and their families than to slave folk like Caleb and his parents and Uncle Mingo and the rest. Yet they were colored. Caleb had heard about free Negroes; Charleston was said to have a good many of them, but he had seen none before—none that he could recognize as free colored people, at any rate. And here he was in this well-kept kitchen with his eyes popping out of his head, trying to take everything in as he drank the lemonade.

The mother looked at Caleb. "This is a new boy, isn't it?"

"Yes'm," Caleb nodded, scarcely taking the glass from his lips.

"Who's boy are you?"

"I belong to Colonel Willows," Caleb said.

Mrs. Sazon looked surprised. "I almost took you to be free," she said.

That sounded like a compliment, but Caleb wasn't sure he knew what to make of it. "I'm trying to learn some reading," he confided. "But I ain't free. Once I tried—" He broke off abruptly and placed the glass on the table. "Thank you, ma'am," he said, turning to the door at which he had entered. "I'll be going," he added nervously.

The Sazon boy followed him outside. "What did you say your name was—Willows?"

"I'm named Caleb."

Mrs. Sazon stood at the door while the two crossed the back yard. "Tell Mr. Harvey," she called, "that either my husband or my daughter Mathilde will see him about the bill."

"Yes, ma'am," Caleb answered.

They were around the corner of the house when the Sazon boy said, "Don't you know it's against the law for anybody to teach slaves to read?"

"Nobody's teaching me," Caleb explained quickly. "I didn't say that."

"Somebody must be helping you. Where'd you get your book?"

Caleb didn't know whether to be angry or disappointed. "I ain't got no book," he said. "You talk like *you* don't want me to learn neither."

The Sazon boy looked at him sternly. "You tried to run away too, didn't you?"

"What if I do want to be free?" Caleb suddenly lost his shyness. "Would *you* like to be a slave?"

"That's not the question. You said you were learning to read. Somebody must be—"

"Somebody, nothing!" Caleb snapped. "There ain't no law to say I mustn't learn by myself, if I can."

"Listen," the other boy said, his manner friendly again. "I'm not trying to change your mind about learning. If I was sure you wouldn't tell anybody where you got it, I might even lend you one of my books."

"I wouldn't tell," Caleb promised.

"Wait here then." The Sazon boy hurried back through the front door into the house. He returned a few minutes later around the house. "Put this inside your shirt. I want it back some day, but if anybody catches you with it, say you found it. Don't mention me. Lot of people in this city would be happy if they could accuse our family of teaching slaves or helping them to escape or something like that."

"I'll bring the book back," Caleb assured him.

"But not till you can read it," young Sazon smiled.

Caleb started home, walking rapidly, the small book held firmly against his body by his left elbow. He had never seen the inside of a book, and he wasn't sure he could resist the temptation to take this one out and look at it before he got home, but at least he would try.

The African Drum

A few nights later Caleb was tossing on his pallet when the shingles on the roof of the carriage shed commenced to rattle. He sat up suddenly, put his hand on the book under his head to make sure it was safe, and tried to determine the cause of the noise. Wind was blowing on Charleston; it was blowing on all the cities of the Carolinas and throughout the southern part of the United States. Caleb didn't need to be told what it meant. Summer was past, the autumn had come.

What he didn't know, of course, was that another wind was also blowing in the nation. It was the wind of strife. Election time was near, and Abraham Lincoln was a candidate for President. One of his opponents was Stephen A. Douglas, and the issue of slavery that came between these and other candidates for high office meant so much in dollars and cents to people who owned and depended on slaves that no one who lived in a slave state could take it lightly. People in states that had taken a stand against slavery were just as disturbed. Banners and flags were waving in hundreds of towns and cities, and large audiences stood on their chairs in many auditoriums, cheering their favorite candidates. Trains decorated with streamers and placards crossed the country as crowds milled about little flag stations to shake the hands of the men who greeted them from the rear of platforms, or lined themselves along fences by the tracks to catch a glimpse of the homespun "rail splitter" or the eloquent "little giant." The wind of strife was rising to a hurricane.

Neither did Caleb know about the small wind, no louder than a whisper, that was blowing in the hearts of many Americans. It was the wind called conscience, the wind that wanted to know whether or not it was right for men who were made in God's image to hold in bondage—slavery—other men who were also made in God's image. It was the wind that said, "Are not all men equal before God?"

Not knowing about any wind but the one that rattled the shingles above the carriage-shed loft, Caleb put his hand on the book and sank back into sleep. The next day he noticed that the leaves were turning red, yellow and gold. Yes, summer was gone. And the world seemed to change as time passed. Caleb had changed a good bit himself since summer began. He wore shoes, his clothes were clean, his hair trimmed, and he was walking about Charleston as if he belonged there. He was a tailor's apprentice, learning the craft of making clothes. More important still, there was a small book hidden safely under the eaves of the loft, a book that had turned out to be a combination reader and speller, a book in which the alphabet was shown and easy words and syllables constructed.

When he first came to Charleston, life had seemed to center around Mr. Harvey's tailor shop and the new tasks it offered. Now the center of Caleb's world was the book. From it he tore himself in the morning when it was time to go to the shop; to it he hastened when the day's work ended. There was no more time to sit on the steps with Moses and Sarah in the twilight; there wasn't even time to sit at the table and ask questions after the three of them had eaten the food Sarah brought home in her basket.

A few weeks passed like this before Caleb looked up suddenly from his book one evening and saw Moses squatting in a peculiar position in the corner, the African drum in front of him. A flicker from the tallow flame fell across his face and his glossy, rousterbout's shoulders. With his finger tips he tapped on the savage drumhead so lightly that the sound could scarcely be heard across the room.

Caleb gave a jump. "You fixing to beat it, Pa?" he cried out in astonishment.

"Set yourself back down, son," Moses smiled calmly. "I'm not ready to start folks to running out in the alleys and asking one another what's the trouble. If I beat it for nothing, they wouldn't know what to do when I beat it for something."

Sarah was leaning out the door, shaking crumbs out of her basket. "Might as well keep your hands off it then," she scolded. "It ain't to play with."

"Now that's where you wrong, Sarah." Moses was still hunched over the tom-tom, still tapping it silently with his finger tips. "The drum is for good times too."

Caleb sat down on his box again, but he couldn't get his mind back on the reading. Moses had made it so plain that the drum would be used only to announce possible trouble of concern to the black folks of Charleston. The sight of his father with the drum in his hands had startled him.

Sarah muttered. "Back in Africa, maybe. They don't beat drums for no good times here."

"I talked with some sailors from New Orleans today," Moses said. "They told me that the white folks let the slaves beat the drums one day every month. They let them have the day off. So they come from all out in the country—every which way—and beat the drums and dance in a place they call Congo Square. They beat the African drums and they do the African dances."

Caleb could see that his mother was still unimpressed. "New Orleans," she scoffed. "Maybe the white folks ain't so mean down there. I never heard tell of no slaves dancing in the square in Charleston."

"Maybe they'd let us, if we asked them," Moses argued.

"You'd have to catch them when they was feeling mighty good."

"That's just what I'm thinking about," Moses chuckled. He got up and placed the drum back under the bed. "Everybody's talking about election day. White folks around here going to be happy as jay birds after they win this election."

Sarah nodded. "You right about that. I hear them talking in the boardinghouse every day. Abraham Lincoln is the one they want to beat."

"All right then!" Moses rubbed his hands together. "That's when we beat the drum in the square and all the slaves come out and dance."

"Election's next week," Sarah said.

Moses couldn't hide his excitement. "I'll be ready. I'm practicing on the drum now."

"Do that mean freedom?" Caleb asked suddenly. "Do it mean they'll let the slaves come and go like free folks after that 'lection?"

For some reason both his parents behaved as if they had not thought of this before. When they looked at Caleb, it was almost as if they wanted to reprove him for saying something out of place. Presently Moses bowed his head and explained, "Wouldn't be no drum-beating and no dancing if it was like that, son."

"I don't think I'm going to feel like dancing," Caleb said.

"Me neither," Sarah murmured.

"Wait till you hear me beat the African drum. You'll dance, both of you," Moses promised. "That's a powerful drum we got."

"But we got nothing to beat it for now," Sarah insisted, "nothing but trouble."

"Never mind that, Sarah," her husband reasoned. "We're obliged to beat the drum when we can—when folks will let us. When they hear how the election come out, that'll be our time."

"How will all the slave people know to come?" Caleb asked.

Again Moses began to show enthusiasm. "That's what we got to think about now. We'll tell the ones we see in town to pass the word out in the country. We'll whisper to everybody we see. We'll talk to the coachmen down by the dock and the boys driving the cotton wagons. Sarah can talk to the cooks and the women hanging out clothes when she walks down the alley. You can say something to the ones digging among the flower beds when you go to take the clothes Mr. Harvey sends. My hands are just itching to get at that drum."

"Will their masters let them come?" Caleb asked, still perplexed.

"Don't need to say nothing to their masters. Just come on and dance. After that election their masters'll be feeling so good they won't make no trouble on account of something like this."

Sarah's stern face looked pessimistic, but she said no more. It still seemed somewhat confused to Caleb, but he was willing to do his part, if his father advised it.

In the days before the election, the city of Charleston saw several big celebrations. A candidate for a local office gave the voters a big barbecue, Southern style. His opponent tried to outdo him the following night by inviting prospective voters to an ample banquet under the pal-

metto palms of a summer hotel on Sullivan Island, in
Charleston Bay. To entertain the guests he invited the
band from the United States Army post at Fort Sumter
on another near-by island in the bay. Elsewhere there
were balls and parties and merriment that reached even
to the street corners and the waterfront taverns.

But none of these was like the festivity to which
Moses' African drum called the slave people after the
ballots were cast and the voting citizens were grimly
awaiting the outcome. Charleston became deadly serious.
It also became strangely quiet. Caleb and his mother
were so disturbed by the stillness they decided to hold
back awhile. But Moses could not be detained. He picked
up his drum from under the bed and hurried down the
alley toward an open field. No moon was shining.

A few minutes later Caleb heard the drum begin to
beat. Deep throbs that at first seemed like the beating
of his own heart. Slow, slow, then faster and faster. Soft,
then loud. Weird, wild, frightening—the ancient drum of
Africa.

Sarah's eyes moved in the darkness. "You're trembling, son."

"I don't know why," Caleb said. "I don't know what
makes me shake."

"Come on. Let's go where you pa is." Sarah took his
arm.

In the dark alley Caleb became aware of dim figures
hurrying past him and his mother. Before he knew it, he
and Sarah were walking much faster; presently they were
fairly running toward the tom-tom.

In the open field to which they came, Moses was
crouched over the drum like a man of the jungle. His
pounding hands fluttered like shadows in the darkness.

Most of the slave folk were bewildered. They had been
born in the New World, and their parents and grand-

parents had been here so long that the link with Africa had been broken. Slavery had separated them from the power of the drum. They had never learned the dances that went with it—rhythms that had already had a tremendous influence on European people such as the Spaniards. The slaves moved about nervously, wanting to respond to the drum but not knowing why.

Suddenly a group of West Indian seamen pushed through the crowd and began to sway and move in beautiful harmony with the beating throbs. When Moses pounded faster and changed the rhythm, the island seamen leaped and whirled. Then they settled back into the steady motion. One by one, two by two, the slave folk joined them and fell into the same patterns of motions. Caleb could stand still no longer. He drew away from Sarah and began leaping and turning with the dancers.

It was past midnight when the authorities broke up the dance. Caleb heard mule whips cracking in the dark and harsh voices bellowing curses and oaths.

"I'll take the living hide off you," one of them roared. "Slaves cavorting like this—what in God's name are we come to?"

"You can't hide nothing from them," another shouted. "They heard how the 'lection come out. They're beside themselves on account of Abe Lincoln. That's what he's done for us already—him and his abolitionists."

"Back where you belong now—every last one of you." This voice sounded like the voice of the harness-maker who had tried to snatch Caleb from his present owner and sell him to the rice planters. Caleb thought of the men he had known who were capable of such tones: the overseer on the plantation, the patrollers who had picked him up when he attempted to run away, perhaps even the auctioneer in dark clothes who had come out of the tavern when the harness-maker beckoned.

It made no difference now, the slave people were dispersing so swiftly they couldn't be followed. The dancing and the drum-beating were over; even Moses had disappeared. Caleb looked for Sarah. When he did not see her, he struck out alone, came to a wall and began creeping alongside it in the shadows.

"Some of these Charleston people is mad as wet hens," Moses whispered to his wife and son as he shoved the African drum back out of reach, under the bed. "This 'lection's got them stirred up like I-don't-know-what. The drum-beating and the dancing last night just made it worse. They don't want to think about nothing like that now."

Sarah tied a clean apron around her waist, hooked her arm through the basket-handle and prepared to leave. "Keep your eyes straight in front of you when you're going around town for Mr. Harvey," she told Caleb. "Don't see nothing and don't hear nothing—if you know what I mean. If anybody say something to you, don't know *nothing*. Understand?"

"Yes'm," Caleb assured her. He was in the other room straightening out his sleeping place on the floor.

They left the loft together and separated as usual at the head of the alley. An hour or two later, when he had finished cleaning the shop, and started a fire under the pressing irons, and was looking around for something else to do while waiting for Mr. Harvey to arrive, Caleb opened the tailor's large measurement book and began turning pages. He discovered that the notations there were the same as those on the slips Mr. Harvey wrote when measuring a customer. Obviously he had copied them here before throwing the slips away. Like a flash an idea popped into Caleb's head. Certainly Mr. Harvey couldn't object too strongly; he might even approve. In any case, Caleb knew that he would have to mention it

45

to the tailor. He couldn't possibly resist the temptation.

Meanwhile it was important to make double sure the shop was completely in order and that everything Mr. Harvey expected of him had been done. Caleb went from the front door to the back, swept the floor again, straightened the bolts of cloth, put in place the scissors and pincushions and tape measures and spools, rubbed the mirrors again with a cloth and went outside to examine the little yard space.

By the time Mr. Harvey reached the shop, however, Caleb had decided that this thing which meant so much to him should not be the first thing he said to the tailor that morning. It would be better to wait till it could be said in an offhand way, as something that had just slipped into the mind. The chance he wanted came a few hours later while he was pressing the shoulders of a new coat on the rounded end of an ironing board shaped for that purpose.

"Would it help you any, Mr. Harvey," he said slowly, as if musing, "if I could mark them figures in the measurement book for you?"

The tailor was basting a collar onto a jacket. There were pins in his mouth. His eyeshade was low, and his needle was almost flying. A moment or two later he paused to remove the pins. "I reckon it would," he said. He hesitated. Then he added, "You think you could copy figures, Caleb?"

Caleb moistened his finger and tried his iron. It had cooled off. He took time to put it back on the fire and get the one that was heating.

"I believe I could learn how to do that, sir—if it would be any help to you."

"Suppose," again a pause, "suppose you take one of those old slips home and copy the figures for me. I'll give you a piece of paper and a lead pencil. If you do it pretty well, then we can talk about copying in the measurement book."

"All right, sir," Caleb said, choking back his excitement.

They became silent, each doing his work, and for Caleb the rest of the day passed slowly.

That night by the light of the tallow wick his mother and father saw him take up a new occupation: learning to write. He struggled with the marks till he could no longer hold his eyes open. Then he set aside the best specimen he had been able to make and went to bed. But in bright daylight this did not look good to him, and he decided not to show it to Mr. Harvey. Indeed, several weeks passed before he brought the original slip back to the tailor with a copy that seemed respectable.

When he examined it, Mr. Harvey's eyes and mouth popped open. "You did this, Caleb?"

"Maybe I could make it better if I practiced some more, sir."

"You can write in the measurement book if you like," the tailor said, recovering from his first surprise. "I'll be able to read your marks all right."

Thereafter Caleb copied measurements in the book. Evenings, by the tallow light, he copied words and sentences from the book he had borrowed from the Sazon boy. And he began to think it was time he saw that boy again and reported to him on his use of the reader. But Sarah and Moses kept talking about how the white people were upset over the selection of Abraham Lincoln as President of the United States, and how slave folk would have to walk easy till the city got over its touchiness, and he knew without being told that this was no time for a slave boy to be going to the home of a free colored family unless he had business there that all the neighbors could know about. He had no choice but to wait.

CHARIOT IN THE SKY

While he waited, the fears of the people of the South, and those of Charleston people in particular, grew worse. Sarah told Caleb and Moses at night that the men in the boardinghouse now talked of nothing but fighting the Yankees. Lots of them had already joined the state guards. To her it looked as if trouble was commencing for sure.

To Moses it looked the same way. The dock workers could see that something unusual was happening out on the islands in Charleston Bay. There was a small Union garrison in Fort Moultrie; work was going on in the new Fort Sumter too, and there was talk of Union reenforcements coming down from the North.

In the tailor shop there was even more unmistakable evidence of what was coming. Caleb noticed that all Mr. Harvey's customers were being measured for officer's uniforms, military capes and dress suits. No new orders were being placed for civilian clothes; in fact, those already placed were canceled. The men for whom Mr. Harvey made suits were all getting ready to wear gray Confederate uniforms.

Then one day in April, when the azaleas were beginning to bloom and spring was in the air again, it happened. Caleb was sewing a long seam, and Mr. Harvey was at the cutting table, his scissors working double-quick, when a tall man entered the shop, a man who was almost a stranger. He was dressed in an officer's uniform.

"Don't you know me, Caleb?" he said.

"Yes, sir, Master Willows," the boy said, stopping the machine. "I'm proud to see you, sir."

"Well, don't stop sewing. You're going to have to make a lot more uniforms like this one—and in a hurry." He turned to the tailor. "How's the boy doing?"

"He's learning," Mr. Harvey said. "I like him."

"If he's worth anything to you, he can stay right here

while I'm away. They could use him on the plantation, but somebody's got to make uniforms for the Confederate Army. Somebody's got to load the ships and cook the food. So I'm leaving his ma and pa in town too."

"That suits me," the tailor said. "Caleb's a good boy."

"Send that other uniform as soon as you can. I'm in a hurry." Colonel Willows waved his hand as he went out the door.

A strange sensation passed over Caleb when the room became quiet again. He had not seen his owner since before his attempt to run away. That was months—it was actually more than a year—ago. And he had never before seen Colonel Willows in uniform. Never before had he heard him talk in this casual way about the disposition he would make of people who belonged to him. The moment filled Caleb with awe.

Now that the Colonel was gone, Caleb felt less hatred for the man who controlled his fate than he had when he was on the plantation and being driven by the overseer. The tailor shop was a great improvement over that. And being with his mother and father was a privilege seldom enjoyed by young slaves. Colonel Willows had practically promised these advantages would continue.

Caleb turned to Mr. Harvey. "Is there any trouble?" he asked.

"Mm," the tailor mumbled. "I think there is."

Later that afternoon Caleb ran into the reception room and looked out the front window when he heard commotion on the cobblestones. A galloping horse flashed by, with a boy standing in the stirrups and leaning forward eagerly. Children ran out of doors. Windows were thrown open, and women leaned over the sills to look out. A horse-drawn coach swerved around a corner. It was filled with men leaning over the wheels and waving to the people on the street.

"It's started," someone shouted. "We'll show Abe Lincoln something now."

Caleb remained at the window. Even when Mr. Harvey opened the front door and went outside, he did not dare follow. He was sure the excitement was connected in some way with slavery, and he knew that the best thing for him was to act as if it didn't concern him. But that didn't close his eyes or his ears, and he did not turn away when Mr. Harvey spoke to the cross-eyed jeweler who had stepped out of the shop next door.

"Where did it happen?" the tailor asked.

"Fort Sumter," the jeweler explained. "Looks like war."

"I'm not surprised," Mr. Harvey said.

"Me neither." The jeweler chuckled. "If the South is fixed with everything else like it is with buckles and sword handles and ornamented sheaths," he said, "it won't take us long to finish this fight. They been rushing me with so much work I haven't had time to sleep for a month."

"I know what you mean," the tailor smiled. "It's the same in my shop. We're trying to see to it that most of the high officers from around Charleston look presentable in their uniforms."

The men were not boastful, but Caleb understood that each one was well pleased with the small part he had been given to play in the drama that was now beginning.

More people came into the narrow street. More horse-drawn carriages and hacks clattered on the cobblestones. A clamor of voices rose under the young leaves of the shade trees; the words Caleb kept hearing were "Fort Sumter, Fort Sumter." Something significant and decisive had happened on an island in Charleston Bay; soldiers of the South had attacked and captured a Union outpost. War had begun between the States.

Mr. Harvey worked late in his shop that night, and much of the noise had ended by the time he sent Caleb down the dark, deserted alley toward home.

Slave
On the
Block

After the capture of Fort Sumter by the Confederacy, the war began to seem remote to Caleb. He saw soldiers, of course, and frequently men in sailor's uniforms; flags were unfurled on many buildings and sometimes in the windows of houses. But all this dealt with something a long way off. Caleb went to the tailor shop as usual, his mother continued to cook in the boardinghouse, his father never stopped working with the other rousterbouts on the docks. And on warm evenings the three of them still sat together, one above the other, on the narrow steps on the side of the carriage shed.

Time passed swiftly out there in the moonlight. Almost before they were comfortably seated, it seemed to Caleb that his eyelids would begin to feel heavy, and he would have to leave the other two and go to bed. Soon Sarah and Moses would follow, and in his dream he would hear dimly the shuffling of their bare feet on the wooden floor. These evenings were very short.

The moon changed rapidly too. Caleb watched it from night to night and saw it grow from nothing to fullness and then go back to nothing again. Almost before he realized what was happening, the season changed, and he and his parents began spending their evenings inside and trying to keep a fire in a little pot-bellied stove that often smoked and never seemed to draw very well.

They were just getting it to act right one night when they heard footsteps outside on the creaky stair leading to the loft. All three drew away from the door and stood huddled together beyond the table. They were not accustomed to callers, especially after dark, and they had no reason to expect that this one would be friendly. The tallow flame fluttered in the saucer on the table as the door opened. A slender young man appeared in the shadows.

"I'm Phillip Sazon," he said softly.

Caleb recognized the voice of the Sazon boy who had lent him the reader months ago. But the boy seemed taller now. He had also grown more serious; his eyes showed that he was troubled.

"Come in," Sarah murmured as politely as she could.

"You want your book," Caleb apologized. Even though he had had no good chance to return it, he felt guilty. He knew in his heart that he had been reluctant to part with the little borrowed book. "I aimed to bring it back," he added.

Phillip Sazon shook his head. He was a handsome boy, but he was out of breath and visibly upset. "Never mind the book," he said. "I've not come about that."

Moses shoved one of the wooden boxes toward the boy. "Have some sit-down," he offered.

"Thank you. I've been running," Phillip confessed, accepting the box. He unbuttoned his overcoat. Under it he had on sailor pants and a sailor's striped slipover. "I'll catch my breath a minute, if you don't mind."

Caleb reached for one of the other boxes; his mother sat on the edge of the bed, his father stood in front of the stove. "Was somebody running after you?" Caleb asked.

"My family would be better off if we were slaves," Phillip answered bitterly. "Since the war broke out, the white folk don't seem to know how to treat free colored people. They never stop pestering us. I'm sick and tired of it. Sick and tired." His voice trembled, and he slapped the table as he added, "I'm not going to put up with it any more. Not another day."

"How come they bother you all?" Sarah asked.

"They want to make slaves out of us. I can't go on the street without running into trouble."

"You got free papers to show, ain't you?" Moses asked.

Phillip ran his hand inside his slipover. "They're right here, but that doesn't stop some of the bullies. They pretend there's something wrong with the papers, arrest me, take me to jail, hold me for several days and then discover that it was all a mistake. The papers are all right. Sometimes they do it just for fun; sometimes for meanness. I was born free right here in Charleston; my father and mother were both born free. I've had all I'm going to take."

"What can you do?" asked Caleb.

Phillip turned toward Moses, whose back was still to the stove. "That's just it." He hesitated a moment. "I thought maybe your father wouldn't mind helping me, since he works on the docks and knows all the ships."

"Where you like to go?" Moses asked.

"I'm not particular," Phillip said. "All I want to do is to get on a ship that's ready to sail. It can be going any place it wants to, for all I care—any place but here."

Moses looked at his wife and then at his son, as if to get their approval. Then he turned to Phillip and nodded. "It's all right with me," he said. "Looks like all of us is mixed up here together. I'll put you on board."

Phillip rose eagerly. "Right now?"

"Right now is best," Moses agreed. "Might be somebody snooping around in the morning."

A smile appeared on Phillip's light-brown face; it turned the corners of his lips and disclosed a row of even teeth. "I've got some money," he said, "and with my free papers there won't be any trouble on the boat. Those devils on the dock are the ones I don't trust. They wouldn't let me get by to save their lives if they had a way to stop me."

"Are you going away without saying good-by to your ma and pa?" Sarah asked, rising from the side of the bed.

"I said good-by to my mother an hour ago," Phillip told her. "My father—we all said good-by to him. More than a month ago. He couldn't stand the pestering either. He died."

Caleb felt uncomfortable. He could see the pained expression on his mother's face. "I'll get the book for you," he said suddenly, trying to express sympathy for Phillip.

"No," Phillip told him. "Leave it where it is. When you finish with that one, you'll be able to read this." He took another book from his overcoat pocket. "This one's harder. There's more in it. Speeches and poems and stories—all kinds of things. It's called *The Columbian Orator*."

Caleb didn't know how to express his thanks. He clasped the book Phillip handed him. "Thank you a heap," he said, "a real heap." Then after a pause, "But you better take the other one with you. I can read it through, frontward and backward almost. This one's all I need. Maybe you could give the beginning book to somebody else—somebody that's just starting to learn. I don't believe I could keep up with more than one book."

"All right, let me have it then," Phillip agreed. He seemed almost cheerful for a moment, but after Caleb returned from the adjoining room with the first thin volume he became serious again. "Well," he turned to Moses, "I hope this won't take long. You'll need to get back home to sleep."

"We're much obliged to you for helping Caleb with his reading," Sarah said.

"I'm the one that's much obliged." Phillip buttoned

55

his overcoat and followed Moses down the outside steps. A moment later Caleb saw the two in the alley, hurrying along as silently as shadows.

Now that he had *The Columbian Orator* to occupy his time, the winter nights passed even more swiftly for Caleb. But his eagerness to get back to the book, from evening to evening, made the days in the shop seem longer. Yet there, too, new things had been found for him to do. He was now able to write the measurements of customers directly in the book as Mr. Harvey called them off. He was asked to do practically any kind of assignment that came to hand.

As a result, the tailor himself spent more and more time out of the shop. He began taking longer lunch periods, and Caleb noticed that Mr. Harvey spent more time in hotel lobbies and in taverns with other businessmen of the city. When he returned from these sessions, he was usually in a serious mood. Sometimes there was a smell of alcohol on his breath. At other times he did an unusual thing for him, dropping his work to read a newspaper. And once he put the paper down with a sigh and turned to Caleb.

"I don't know how much longer I can go on like this. The South needs all the men it can get. Sooner or later I'll have to join up." He became silent, but Caleb said nothing. Eventually Mr. Harvey spoke again. "When that time comes, I'll have to do one of two things about my business. Either I'll have to close it down and let you go back to the plantation, or I'll keep it open and let you run it for me while I'm away."

Caleb thought about these possibilities for several moments. "I'll be proud to do anything you want me to, Mr. Harvey," he answered tactfully.

"Yes, I know you will, Caleb. And, by George, I be-

lieve you'd do a good job for me here in the shop. You've
picked up tailoring in a hurry, and by teaching yourself
to read and write, you've helped a lot. But you don't belong to me, and I don't know what Colonel Willows will
say to my leaving you here. Don't worry though. We can
cross that bridge when we come to it."

"Yes, sir."

The knowledge that he was being trusted and depended on gave Caleb a warm inward feeling. He found
himself singing more while he worked, and in return Mr.
Harvey showed him more kindness than before. One day,
after he had left most of the work with the boy for nearly
a week, the tailor came in just before noon with an old
mandolin.

"You're smart, Caleb," he said. "You like music and
you sing a lot. Maybe you could pick out something on
this while you're resting after lunch. I tried to learn it
myself, but I never seemed to make much headway. If
you like it, I'll leave it here in the shop. It's just picking
up dust at home."

"It's mighty pretty," Caleb beamed, turning it over in
his hands. "Looks like it ought to be good for something."

"See what you can do with it."

The tailor went out again, and Caleb returned to his
work. Later on he took the pick from under the mandolin
strings and began to try the instrument for sound. He
quickly discovered that playing a mandolin is more than
a notion and that he would probably have to work as
long and hard to learn it as he had to pick up reading
and writing. But it would be a pleasant task, and it would
be a way to fill the time when he was restless to get back
to *The Columbian Orator*.

After a few months he began to find the instrument
almost as interesting as the book, and on several eve-

nings he asked Mr. Harvey to let him take it home to play for his mother and father. The tailor did not object, and during all the following summer there was string music and singing on the steps to the loft above the carriage shed. Frequently there were other slaves in the alley, listening and smiling and joining in when the song was familiar.

One warm evening, as twilight fell, a man who looked like a preacher was drawn to the music. He wore a derby and carried a cane, and he spoke with a deep, vibrant voice. "Want to hear my song?" he interrupted.

"Don't care if I do," Moses smiled.

"Well, here it goes," the man said, taking off his derby and tapping with his cane:

> "There ain't no liars up there
> In my father's house,
> In my father's house,
> There is peace, sweet peace."

Moses nodded approval. "Sing some more, if you please."

The man fanned himself with his derby. "Help me out, son," he said to Caleb, and both of them took it up with "There ain't no gamblers there" while Caleb picked an accompaniment on the instrument.

More and more of the folk chimed in, and presently the whole alley rang with melody.

On another such day, as twilight fell, a fellow who looked like an outcast staggered along the back fences and paused, his eyes rolling wildly, when he came in earshot of the tunes.

"Do you want to hear my song?" he asked when there was a pause.

"Sure," Caleb encouraged. "I want to hear everybody's song. I want to play it and sing it too."

"Then let me have that box a minute." He reached for the mandolin and Caleb let him have it. The ragged fellow who looked half-starved and almost crazy with suffering leaned against the fence and began to play. He played a long time without singing, and Caleb and his parents and the other curious folk in the alley became fascinated. The stranger had a musical gift so wonderful it seemed unreal. All kinds of beautiful tunes came from the mandolin as he picked the strings. Later on he opened his mouth to sing and suddenly a light from the sky fell on his dark, wasted figure. The moon had just risen.

"Shepherd, Shepherd, where'd you lose your sheep?
 Shepherd, O Shepherd, where'd you lose this poor
      sheep?
 Shepherd, Shepherd, where'd you lose your sheep?
 O the sheep all gone astray,
 The sheep all gone astray.

"Shepherd, Shepherd, where'd you leave your lambs?
 Shepherd, O Shepherd, where 'bouts did you leave your
      little lambs?
 O the sheep all gone astray,
 The sheep all gone astray.

"When I was a little boy, played at my mother's knee.
 When I was a little boy, I used to play at my mother's
      knee.
 Lordy, just a little boy, playing at my mother's knee,
 O the sheep all gone astray,
 The sheep all gone astray."

Caleb played and sang the unhappy man's song after him, Moses clapped his hands in rhythm. Presently the father rose impulsively.

"Lord, I feel like beating the African drum," he announced.

"Don't you do it," Sarah cautioned. "You want to stir all these people up and start trouble? Can't you just listen to the singing and the music and be satisfied?"

Moses restrained himself and sat down quietly.

Then the days began to grow shorter again.

Caleb was working alone in the shop on a cold winter morning when the door opened suddenly. Colonel Willows rushed in, his military spurs clicking. His eyes searched the room. "Where's Mr. Harvey?"

Caleb stammered nervously, "I—I don't know, sir. I expect he'll be back directly."

The Colonel shook his head. "No time to wait," he snapped. "I have to get back to my regiment." He scarcely paused. "I'm real sorry to miss Mr. Harvey, but you'll have to lock up, Caleb. Leave the key with the jeweler next door. You're coming with me. We haven't got much time."

"Yes, sir. Yes, sir." Caleb dropped the garment on which he was working, hooked the back door, and followed his master through the front. When he had deposited the key as he had been directed, he hurried back and climbed into a seat that the Colonel indicated in a waiting carriage. The driver knew where to go and started the horses without waiting for instructions.

"Is it some trouble, sir?" Caleb ventured.

His master didn't want to talk, but after a while he answered curtly, "It's trouble all right. The South may not be able to hold Charleston. You wouldn't like to fall into the hands of the Yankees, would you?"

"I reckon not, sir."

"Don't believe what you hear about the Yankees, Caleb. They don't mean you no good."

"Yes, sir."

Colonel Willows became absorbed in his own thoughts. As the carriage rolled along, turning first one corner and then another, Caleb tried to understand what was happening. He didn't feel nervous or afraid, but the more he thought about his master's words and this unexplained drive, the more worried he became. If Colonel Willows intended to move his slave people out of Charleston, where would he take them? And what would this mean to Caleb? What would it mean to Sarah and Moses, his parents?

Then he remembered the mandolin in Mr. Harvey's shop. He thought of the African drum. What would happen to these? What would he do about *The Columbian Orator?* He thought about all the things and the people who had made life different for him since he was brought to Charleston to live with his parents and work in the tailor shop of Mr. Harvey. Was all this about to be changed?

The carriage came to a stop in front of the city slave exchange.

"I wouldn't sell you, Caleb, if I could be sure we were going to hold Charleston, but the way things look now, I just can't be sure. Most of my money is tied up in slaves. I can't wait to find out. If the Union forces decide to attack from the sea, I'm not sure we could keep them from getting a foothold and occupying Charleston," Colonel Willows explained while stepping out of the carriage. On the ground he added, "I'd be ruined if all my slave people were stolen from me by the Yankees. I've got to sell out while I can."

Caleb followed him into the building. The interior was more like a stable than a public building. In one corner of a large, unswept room a sorrowful band of black folks was huddled together. Nearby stood a small platform, an auction block, and across the room a group of white men chatted casually. Among them, Caleb noticed, was the man in dark clothes from whom he had escaped his first day in the city. A cloud of tobacco smoke arose above this group.

The Colonel went over and said something to the dark-clad man. A moment later the two returned to the block. Caleb kept his face turned away in fear of being recognized by the gaunt, hatchet-faced individual. But if the man remembered him, he gave no indication.

"So this is the one you want me to sell now?" the man asked Colonel Willows.

"He's a smart boy, trained as a tailor's apprentice," the Colonel boasted. "Don't let him go too cheaply. I wouldn't sell him for anything if I could take him to the interior myself."

"I'll get you all he'll bring," the man snorted. He turned to Caleb. "Get up there, boy." Caleb stepped on the auction block. "Take off your shirt." The boy obeyed mechanically. "Roll up your pants."

"You're not selling him for a field hand," the Colonel protested. "He's a skilled worker. He can tailor."

"He can leave his shoes on," the auctioneer compromised. "All right, men," he turned to the crowd across the room, "here's a boy I'd like to have you look at. I understand he's been trained by a tailor. Don't think you'll find a thing wrong with him. Any of you like to make me an offer? This boy's one of Colonel Willows' stock." Caleb stiffened. Humiliation turned to anger. Pride forced his head back. He looked slender without his shirt, and on the block he seemed taller than usual. Was there something a boy could do at a time like this? Something he could say? Caleb could think of nothing. Instead, he clenched his fists at his sides, pushed his shoulders back, and looked at the ceiling.

The murmur of voices quieted across the room.

"He's got a proud air about him there," one of them commented.

"Looks first-rate to me," another said. "How old is he?"

The auctioneer turned to Colonel Willows and the Colonel scratched his head. "I calculate he's about seventeen," he said. "You'll never run across a smarter boy," he added quickly. "He'll make a butler, a coachman—anything. He picked up tailoring just like that—" The Colonel snapped his fingers to explain.

The auctioneer showed impatience. "You want to sell him, Colonel, or do you want me to do it?"

Colonel Willows apologized and stepped back. "You're selling him, sir."

"Very well, gentlemen," the dark-clad man said, "I'm still selling this boy. Who wants him? What am I offered for this seventeen-year-old? Speak up, gentlemen."

"One thousand dollars." Caleb heard the bid, but he didn't see the face.

"I'm bid a thousand dollars," the auctioneer sang. "A thousand dollars I'm bid. Who'll make it two? Who'll make it two?"

"Fifteen hundred."

"I got fifteen, who'll give me eighteen?"

"Eighteen."

"Eighteen hundred. Nineteen, do you want him? Nineteen, do you want him?"

"Nineteen!" came from the group of men.

"Two thousand," another called before the auctioneer could cut in.

"I got two thousand, gentlemen. Anybody want him for twenty-two hundred?"

A man with sideburns stepped out of the group with a handful of paper money. "I'll take him for twenty-two hundred," he said calmly.

"Sold to the gentleman in the red vest for twenty-two

hundred dollars," the auctioneer announced. Take your property, sir."

Caleb slept that night on the floor of a building that was being used as a "slave prison." This was a painful experience. His two years in Charleston, living with his parents and working in the tailor shop, had accustomed him to cleanliness. Being thrown into a room with un-washed field hands was a shock to his nose, as well as his other senses. And it added to the deep feeling of loss and disappointment the past day had brought.

The slaves with whom he spent the night in this old wooden building were not being punished; all of them, like Caleb, were being turned over to new owners. They were here awaiting the departure of their masters. But this did not make the crude quarters in which they had been herded any less miserable or offensive to Caleb. He opened his eyes at daylight and went to a window to get a breath of fresh air.

He was stretching his arms and legs to remove the kinks from his bones when he noticed one of his com-panions on the floor looking up at him out of one eye. The peeping slave was middle-aged; his face was covered with frizzly whiskers. It annoyed Caleb to discover that he was being watched by a stranger in such an odd way, but he spoke to the man in a polite voice just the same.

"Good morning."

"Hush," the man whispered, putting a finger to his lips. "Don't wake nobody up." The strange slave rolled over and stood up quickly as if he had been awake a long time playing possum. "Can you read, boy?" he asked excitedly, clasping Caleb's arm like a drowning man catching at a straw. "Can you read reading?"

Caleb hesitated cautiously. Perhaps it would do no harm to let the quaint man know he could read. After all, it was no longer a secret. "I can read reading," he nodded. After a pause he added, "I can read writing too."

"Don't talk loud, boy," the man insisted in an explosive whisper. "Don't wake nobody. I got something I want you to read—something I picked up in the street last night. You looked like a boy who could read, clean clothes, shoes, and all like that. I was a mind to wake you up when they first brung me in here last night, but it was too dark for anybody to read then. Here it is." He pulled a paper out of a leg of his pants. "It must be powerful reading, son. I seen some white men reading one just like it in front of the Planter's Hotel last night, and they was carrying on something terrible. Read it to me, boy. Hurry and read it."

Caleb unfolded the paper, held it before the light of the window and began calling the words, slowly but distinctly, pausing now and then to catch his breath or to let the meaning sink in his mind, while the frizzly-whiskered man in plantation rags clung with one hand to the window sill to keep from being overcome by excitement. The fellow's mouth hung open, his eyes seemed ready to pop out of his head.

"Whereas," Caleb read, "on the twenty-second day of September, in the year of our Lord one thousand eight hundred and sixty-two, a proclamation was issued by the President of the United States, containing, among other things, the following," Caleb read. "That on the first day of January in the year of our Lord, one thousand eight hundred and sixty-three, all persons held as slaves within any state, or designated part of a state, the people whereof shall then be in rebellion against the United States shall be then, thenceforward, and forever free." Caleb took a deep breath, then launched into the part that contained the details. For another ten minutes his voice droned on. Finally he came to the powerful concluding sentences: "And upon this act, sincerely believed to be an act of justice, warranted by the Constitution upon military necessity, I invoke the considerate judgement of mankind and the gracious favor of Almighty God.

"In witness whereof, I have hereunto set my hand, and caused the seal of the United States to be affixed.

"Done at the city of Washington, this first day of January, in the year of our Lord one thousand eight hundred and sixty-three, and of the Independence of the United States of America the eighty-seventh." Again he paused, breathed deeply and then read the name of the signer, "Abraham Lincoln."

When he had finished, Caleb looked up and saw that most of his sleeping companions on the floor had opened their eyes. A few were sitting up. All had puzzled looks on their faces.

"What you say just now?" a sleepy voice asked suddenly. "Let me hear that again, son. My ears must be fooling me."

Old Frizzly Whiskers was laughing now. "Nothing ain't the matter with your ears, friend. Wake up and listen good, you all. This here's the Resurrection Day. Read it again, boy."

Once more, with more assurance this time, Caleb read the Proclamation of President Abraham Lincoln. When he finished, a slave woman who had put her head in the door threw up her hands and shouted, "Hallelujah, children. Hallelujah! We's free. Free at last!"

"Don't get happy too soon," Frizzly Whiskers warned her. "That's President Lincoln talking. It don't mean these folks down here will let us go. War is still going on. We might have to wait a long time before we can enjoy our freedom. That's how it is."

"Free, but not free," Caleb commented bitterly.

The others exchanged bewildered looks.

"That's how it is," Frizzly Whiskers nodded. "Free, but not free."

There was silence in the room for several moments. Then footsteps were heard coming up a wooden stair. Presently a guard entered the room.

"Everything's mighty quiet in here," he said. "Which one of you is Caleb?"

"I am, sir." Caleb had automatically hidden the paper behind his back. He now watched his chance to return it to old Frizzly Whiskers.

"Someone's here to see you. Come downstairs," the guard ordered.

"Yes, sir," Caleb whispered. When the guard turned his back, Frizzly Whiskers was across the room and looking the opposite way. Caleb could not get the paper to him. Instead, he slipped it inside his own shirt as he followed the guard out and down the stair.

Mr. Harvey was standing in the entrance to the building. Behind him was the man in the red vest who had produced the handful of paper money that climaxed the auction sale, where Caleb was concerned. He was a calm-faced man, wearing a gray coat and a gray derby hat. Mr. Harvey, thin and slouched and dressed in brown broadcloth, seemed to be on friendly terms with the red-vested stranger.

"Caleb," the tailor said. "I've been talking to your new owner."

"Yes, sir, Mr. Harvey," the boy answered softly.

"He wanted to know something about you, and I've told him everything I knew." Caleb's hopes began to rise, but after a pause Mr. Harvey added, "I even tried to talk him into letting you stay here to run my business for me after I join the Army of the Confederacy." The tailor's voice dropped. "He wouldn't agree to that. Like Colonel Willows said, there is some danger of Charleston being occupied by Union forces. If that were to happen—"

"I'm not as worried about that as Colonel Willows seems to be," the red-vested man interrupted, "but there's no call to take unnecessary chances. Besides, I got a little business of my own in Chattanooga that I have to think about."

"Mr. Coleman wouldn't consider selling you either," Mr. Harvey went on, "but he did promise me that he would take you out of this place where you've spent the night. I assured him that I will be personally responsible for you till he gets ready to start back to Chattanooga."

"I'm much obliged to you, Mr. Harvey," Caleb said.

"I'm glad to do that for you, Caleb," Mr. Coleman said, a little awkwardly. "I can see you're a—different from them others up there. You're clean, and you stand up straight, and you got a nice way of talking, and I like all that. I wouldn't have put you in a dirty, crowded place to sleep if I'd met Mr. Harvey sooner, but Colonel Willows got away before I had a chance to find out much about you from him."

A shadow passed over Caleb's face. He couldn't help remembering the paper in his shirt and wondering whether or not the two white men had read the Proclamation. Surely they couldn't have missed it. And Colonel Willows must have read it too. Perhaps this had something to do with his eagerness to dispose of the slave people he owned.

"Your pa and ma will be at home because this is Sunday," Mr. Harvey said, "and Mr. Coleman won't be able to start out before tomorrow."

"How will I find you at daylight tomorrow?" Mr. Coleman asked.

"I'll be wherever you say, Mr. Coleman," Caleb replied.

"You could meet at my shop," the tailor suggested.

"Fine." Mr. Coleman turned to Caleb again. "Bring what clothes you got. Anything you aim to carry along."

"Yes, sir." Caleb hurried away as the new master dismissed him with a wave of his hand.

A few minutes later he turned into the alley near the carriage shed.

Precious Jewel

They traveled by train, Mr. Coleman and the tall slave boy he had purchased in Charleston. Along the way they stopped overnight at inns and hotels, the slave sleeping on a pallet in the same room with his master. By the time they reached Augusta, Georgia, Caleb was tired of riding, but another long stretch lay between that city and Atlanta, where they spent another night. Later their train crossed the Tennessee line and came up the mountains to Chattanooga.

Only occasionally did Caleb pay attention to the red Georgia soil or to the pink clouds of dust that rose from it as the coach wheels turned in the road. During most of the journey his thoughts remained in Charleston. Somehow he couldn't forget his last hours there, especially the sad farewells in the carriage shed above the alley. His mother had wept, with her head against his chest; his father had walked the floor sorrowfully. Neither of them had been consulted by Colonel Willows before he sold Caleb, but this didn't surprise them. They had been slaves too long to expect human feelings from a man who had learned to think of people as property.

It was as an afterthought that Moses reached under the bed and pulled out the African drum, now wrapped in old paper, and handed it to his son.

"Your new master told you to bring your clothes and things," he mused. "Maybe he won't mind if you tote this drum along with you. You might feel like beating it sometime when you get where you're going. It's a powerful drum. Make people do things they didn't expect to do. And it's something from Africa, where our people came from. It's the onliest thing I can give you."

Caleb couldn't forget the shadow of suffering which at that moment passed over the masklike face of his big-muscled father. He couldn't forget Sarah's quick movements as she cut a hole in the mattress with a kitchen knife, took out a tiny sack in which gold money could be heard clinking, and began sewing it to the inside of a pair of his pants. "I never did get around to giving you that gold piece for learning to read," she whispered. "There's three or four more in there now. I'm going to give them all to you, Caleb. Put this pair of pants on before you leave. You know how to read and write and play the mandolin and sing, and I don't know what all else. This little money'll do you heap more good than it will us. I want you to have it, son."

It was a parting that free people can scarcely understand, because there was no need to say such things as "I'll come back to see you," or "Write us a letter sometime." It was a parting that left Caleb lonely and silent for days. Mr. Coleman must have realized this, because he did not make matters worse by trying to persuade the boy to talk. Once in a while, however, he would say things to Caleb about what he called the South's hour of agony, about his own hesitation to join the Army of the Confederacy, and about his fears for his business and his family if this should become necessary.

A blue twilight was falling as they entered Chattanooga. By the time they reached the entrance to Mr. Coleman's store building, it was quite dark. Everything was closed; there were no lights. Caleb could see a balcony above, reaching over the storefront.

"We live upstairs," the merchant explained as Caleb

took the luggage off the public hack and set it on the ground. "In the back of the store there's a stockroom with a cot in it. You'll sleep there. Miranda will feed you—she's our colored woman."

Caleb carried his new master's bags up a dark stair. Presently Mr. Coleman found a kerosene lamp, made a light, and returned downstairs with the tall boy. He led Caleb through a well-stocked dry-goods store with shelves and counters and tables piled with merchandise that could be seen only dimly by the small flickering lamp. The clean odor of crisp cotton materials and of floors over which fragrant sawdust sweepings had recently passed filled Caleb's nostrils.

The stock room was no less agreeable to his nose. Mr. Coleman placed the lamp in a wall bracket and pointed to the cot in a corner. The sleeping place was surrounded by unopened boxes and cases, but it was more inviting by far than any in which Caleb had slept before.

"Our kitchen is right above this," Mr. Coleman said. "When you hear Miranda walking and you smell coffee brewing, it will be time to get up. That door opens into the back yard; there's a pump out there and an outhouse. You can get yourself clean and then come up the back steps and ask Miranda for your breakfast. By that time some of my clerks will be in the store, and I'll come down and show you what to do."

Caleb sat on the side of the bed, his two bundles at his feet. "Thank you, sir. I'm much obliged."

"I'll leave you now," Mr. Coleman said. "I'm pretty tired."

Caleb did not move till after he heard the door close in front of the large store and the key turn in the lock. Then he stood up and began to explore the quarters to which he had been assigned. A few moments later he opened the bundle that contained his clothes and took out the copy of *The Columbian Orator*, which he had concealed among them. He wanted to see how well he could read the book under the light of a real lamp.

It was fine. It was going to be easy to read here. And around a store of this size there would certainly be newspapers and magazines Caleb could pick up and save for reading at night. This stockroom wasn't going to be a bad place in which to sleep either. Caleb began to consider how he could rearrange the boxes and packing crates to improve the appearance of the room. Fortunately, there was plenty of space. He wondered if Mr. Coleman would object to his saving old scraps of burlap and sewing them together to make curtains to separate the sleeping place from the rest of the room.

To ornament the room he—yes, he *would*—he would put the African drum on a small shelf just above the cot. All of a sudden it occurred to him that it would be wise not to make a secret of the drum or the book, *The Columbian Orator*. Mr. Coleman did not appear to be a man who would object to Caleb's having a keepsake from his father and to his placing it on the shelf above his cot. As to the book, that couldn't offend him either, since he had learned from Mr. Harvey that he was getting a boy who knew how to read and write. But even if the new owner were one of those men who objected to seeing such things in the possession of slaves, Caleb felt that there would be something gained by putting him to the test as early as possible. Uncertainty was always a strain; it was better to know where you stood.

He began to yawn. His eyes became heavy. Caleb undressed quickly and blew out the lamp.

The plans he made that first night in Chattanooga were realized sooner than Caleb expected. Instead of being offended by Caleb's rearrangement of the stockroom, Mr. Coleman was pleased. He mentioned it to one of his clerks in a tone of approval. Two young white men who waited on customers in the store came back among the boxes of stock to see what the new slave boy had done. They exchanged nods that clearly meant no offense.

When Caleb put up the drum, it drew curious looks, but nothing else. *The Columbian Orator*, which he purposely left on the shelf beside it, was ignored by all.

He was put to work cleaning the store. Before noon the first day he was helping customers with their purchases, carrying parcels out to the hitching posts and handing them to people who sat in carriages. By evening he had been called on to open a box of stock and bring in the material and place it on a shelf. And he had seen a steady stream of people coming and going in the store all day, but they didn't pay much attention to him.

It was not like the little two-man tailor shop of Mr. Harvey's on a Charleston side street. This was an active business, with many customers, in the heart of Chattanooga, and it kept Caleb so occupied that a whole week passed before he found an opportunity to walk around the city and get a view of the surrounding mountain ridges. It was two or three weeks before he had a chance to feel lonesome for the people he had left in Charleston. Disturbing things had begun to happen right in Chattanooga.

Mr. Coleman came down from breakfast one morning and called his clerks to a conference around the cash drawer. Caleb did not stop his sweeping, but he arranged to stay near enough to catch a part of the discussion.

"It's a draft," Mr. Coleman said. "The South's scraping the bottom of the barrel for man power. Our time has come. Every one of us is apt to be called. If that happens, the only one left to run the store will be—Caleb." There was a good bit of buzzing after that statement, and Caleb discreetly turned his back. When this subsided, however, he distinctly heard Mr. Coleman say, "I haven't had Caleb very long, but I trust him. I'd trust him with anything I have. And I want all of you to see that he's prepared to carry on the business if the rest of us have to go."

Caleb gave no indication that he had overheard, but a few hours later, when he was asked by one of the young men to measure off seven yards of cloth for a woman customer, he knew what was happening. And the next day, when Miranda was asked to come down and do the sweeping, so that Caleb could take his place with the clerks behind the counter, he understood. When Mr. Coleman sat with him under a lamp the following evening, running through price lists and inventories, Caleb didn't have to be told that the outlook for the South was dark.

This brought to his mind the Proclamation of Emancipation by President Lincoln, which he had read in the slave prison in Charleston. Was it possible that freedom was nearer than he realized? If the South was near the end of its man power, how about the North? Could it keep on moving? Where were its armies now? Caleb kept his mind on the price lists and the inventories, but it was all he could do to keep these other thoughts from crowding in.

"I understand, sir," he said when Mr. Coleman closed the book.

"My wife would help if she could, Caleb," the merchant explained, "but she can't leave her room. She's an invalid, and the children are too young." He rested his chin on his hand, and his eyes were troubled. "Do you know what's happening, Caleb?' he asked suddenly.

"It's the war, I reckon, sir."

"The South's got its back to the wall, boy. We're still fighting, mind you, but we're backed up against a wall.

Every able-bodied man has got to fight now. That leaves it up to folks like you and Miranda to keep our businesses for us and our homes while we're away. You understand that, Caleb?" His voice shook with feeling. "We've got to leave our families and our property in the hands of our slaves. And you—you've got to stand by us in our trouble, Caleb."

Caleb's forehead wrinkled. Of course he would stand by Mr. Coleman and his business. But he wondered if this merchant, this man of wealth, this owner of slaves, realized that this war did not mean the same thing for Caleb. He wondered if Mr. Coleman understood that to a slave, freedom was the sweetest dream of all. It was putting a slave boy in a hard spot to ask him to look after his owner's interest while the owner was off fighting against the one who was trying to set the slave free. Caleb knew he couldn't explain this to Mr. Coleman, so he didn't try. Instead, he went back to the stockroom and sat on the cot.

Later, after Mr. Coleman returned to his apartment upstairs, Caleb opened the back door, slipped through the yard and gate and came out on a back street. He walked down a footpath with trees hanging over it. There was no place he wanted to go, nothing he wanted to do except walk and to think. As he walked, however, he began to feel strangely lonely, and he wondered what caused it.

Was it the way Mr. Coleman had talked to him about the South and its troubles? Was it the freedom Abraham Lincoln had proclaimed—the freedom Caleb was waiting for? Or was it just the wind rustling the leaves of the trees?

By the time Mr. Coleman was drafted, his clerks had already gone to the Army of the Confederacy in Tennessee. By that time the people of Chattanooga were so upset by war experiences that they had little time for shopping in dry-goods stores and less money with which to buy. Caleb found that he could easily serve them all; there were even times when he could sit and read.

The reduced stocks of materials in the store may have had something to something to do with this. Nothing new had been obtained by Mr. Coleman in months. Aside from buttons, remnants, odds and ends, there was little a customer could expect to find anyhow. Still a certain few kept returning to inspect the nearly empty shelves and to finger pieces of cloth they had formerly rejected. Sometimes they actually bought.

One of those who came to buy in those days was a girl who had been looking all over town for a kind of golden thread she required for needlework. When Caleb was unable to supply it, she sighed deeply, "Oh, I'm so disappointed."

Caleb looked up and discovered that the face under the carefully knotted bonnet was a soft brown, that the eyes were large, the curls all in place. He couldn't hide his surprise. "Does it have to be gold thread?" he asked.

She seemed to become embarrassed as he looked at her. "Yes." She hesitated another moment, then hurried out of the store.

Caleb couldn't take his eye off the door when it closed behind her. Never before had he seen a girl quite like that. In manner and in looks she reminded him of the Sazon family in Charleston, but the Sazons had no girl of this age. The daughter in that family was a young woman of perhaps twenty-five. This girl seemed younger than Phillip Sazon—younger than himself, perhaps. And what eyes! What honey and cherry cheeks! Caleb sat on a stool behind the counter and rested his chin in his hand.

Had this girl ever been in the store before? If so, how had he failed to notice her? Surely she wasn't a slave. Her way of talking made that plain. Her clothes set her apart too. That big bow with which her bonnet was tied under her chin—what slave would be allowed frills like that? And what did she want with gold thread? Why was she disappointed?

Caleb stood up again, shook his head in confusion, and began walking up and down the aisles of the store. Soon another customer entered and he had to attend to business again. But he did not stop thinking about the honey and cherry girl who wanted to buy gold thread. He thought about her again that night as he read about the war in a newspaper a customer had left on the counter. He thought about her the next evening when he went for a walk in the city after closing hours and climbed to the top of a hill at the edge of the town.

The following Sunday, with his clothes as clean as he could make them, he thought about her as he wandered down a side street and heard slave songs coming from a carriage shed like the one over which his parents lived in Charleston. He thought about her as he was drawn toward the singing, but he did not expect to find her among wailing slave people crying out about the trouble they'd seen.

He reached the old carriage house and stuck his head in the door. She wasn't there, but the singing soothed his feelings. The leader was a barefoot man in overalls. "My ship is on the ocean," he cried. And all the others answered together: "We'll anchor by and by."

> "We'll stand the storm it won't be long,
>   We'll anchor by and by.
>   Stand the storm it won't be long,
>   We'll anchor by and by."

"She is making for the harbor," the leader added, his voice breaking with pathos.

The chorus of voices replied:

> "We'll stand the storm it won't be long,
> We'll anchor by and by."

After this chorus the leader hesitated and Caleb stepped forward. He began to sing, "King Jesus is our Captain." His voice was mellow and clear, and he held the high notes till they echoed among the rafters. An old woman shouted; the rest of the voices blended together afterwards as they had done before:

> "We'll stand the storm it won't be long,
> We'll anchor by and by."

The leader came over and shook Caleb's hand to welcome him, and the singing and preaching continued. It was a slave church in session, and there was no coolness whatever toward a stranger. The members threw their arms around the boy with the fine singing voice and asked him to lead another song. This Caleb did without hesitation, starting out with the words, "Keep your hand on the plow; hold on, hold on," and everybody sang with him, and all of them knew as he did that what they were thinking about and striving for was freedom in this world as well as heaven in the next. The slave songs had double meanings.

After the meeting was over, the group broke up quietly, almost secretly, with some of the worshipers slipping down alleys, and others finding quiet streets on which their passing would not be noticed. A small group put their arms around Caleb and invited him to come with them over a hill into the woods. He went along.

When he reached the secluded spot they had selected under the trees, he understood the reason for their invitation. A pig that had been barbecued the night before was still hanging over live coals in a pit camouflaged by green twigs. Jugs of sweet cider and food were found hidden nearby. The group sat on the ground and feasted, then stretched out on a grassy slope, their hands under their heads, and fell asleep.

It was nearly dark when Caleb reached the back gate, let himself into the stockroom by the rear door and lighted the lamp. Miranda must have been listening for him, because she immediately came down the steps from the kitchen above and knocked on Caleb's door.

"Yes'm," Caleb said, opening the door.

Miranda was a stout woman with a white apron, a white cap and stern little eyes. Her dark face was glossy in the lamplight. "I don't know how long you expects me to keep your Sunday dinner hot," she greeted him, "but I'd like to find out."

"I went to a church meeting," Caleb apologized. "I couldn't get away."

"Keep on doing that," Miranda warned, "and you'll knock on the kitchen door sometime, and I won't have nothing for you."

"I was looking for somebody," Caleb confessed.

"Did you find them?"

He shook his head. "Ever see a right pretty girl with a bonnet tied under her chin?" he asked.

Miranda paused. After a moment, she said, "Yes, I seen a gal like that, but you better not be cutting your eyes at her."

Caleb's face burned with anger and humiliation.

"I don't know what you mean," he said sharply. "It was about some thread."

"On Sunday!" Miranda exclaimed, turning it into a

laugh. "Looking for a gal with a bow under her chin about some thread on Sunday! You must be don't feel good. Come on up and get your plate," she ordered.

Caleb went without protest, though he really wasn't hungry, and it was several hours before he ate the food he brought down to his room on the plate.

The city of Chattanooga was in a fit of excitement when he finally found the girl with the bonnet again, the girl whose cheeks reminded him of cherries in honey. Horses galloped through the streets. Women leaned out of upstairs windows. Some spectators stood on balconies. Others went to the tops of brick buildings to get a better view. Across the town and beyond the nearest hills there was a steady roar of cannon and musket fire.

The newspapers that occasionally fell into Caleb's hands had been speaking of drives by Union armies in the west, but Caleb knew little about geography and had not guessed these would reach Chattanooga so soon. How the battle had been going beyond Missionary Ridge had not been revealed to him. He stayed inside the dry-goods store as if nothing unusual was happening, but he couldn't fail to notice the lumbering supply-wagons passing through the city, the detachments of wounded men in tattered gray uniforms withdrawing from the lines of battle.

The climax came with the swiftness of a hurricane, with large masses of troops pouring down the hillsides and through the city streets. While all this was happening, Caleb sat behind the counter trembling with anticipation. Was this the deliverance? Was this the coming of Abe Lincoln's armies to put down slavery? Was there anything he could do besides just sitting and waiting? Was there any way he could reconcile a feeling of loyalty to a master who had put trust in him with the gratitude

he felt toward the soldiers who were fighting to end
slavery, whose marching song was:

"Mine eyes have seen the glory of the coming of the Lord;
  He is trampling out the vintage where the grapes of
        wrath are stored;
  He hath loosed the fateful lightning of His terrible swift
        sword;
      His truth is marching on.

"I have seen Him in the watch-fires of a hundred circling
        camps;
  They have builded Him an altar in the evening dews
        and damps:
I can read His righteous sentence by the dim and flaring
        lamps;
      His day is marching on.

"He has sounded forth the trumpet that shall never call
        retreat;
  He is sifting out the hearts of men before His judgment
        seat;
  Oh, be swift, my soul, to answer Him! be jubilant, my
        feet,
      Our God is marching on.

"In the beauty of the lilies Christ was born across the sea,
  With a glory in His bosom that transfigures you and me:
  As He died to make men holy, let us die to make men
        free,
      While God is marching on."

  The troops were still moving when the brown girl in
the bonnet suddenly opened the door and hurried to the

counter where Caleb was absent-mindedly turning the pages of the inventory book. He noticed a small round basket on her arm.

"I can't get home," she cried. "The roads are jammed with soldiers."

"Maybe—maybe if you wait a little while."

"I've been waiting most of the day. My mother will be worried."

"Where is your home?" Caleb asked.

The girl pointed. "That way. It's a good piece."

When he could think of nothing else to say, Caleb asked instead, "Did you find the gold thread?"

The girl shook her head slowly. "No, I had to change the pattern." She opened the basket and brought out a folded cloth. "Here it is."

The embroidered design showed two lovely blue birds in a bower of leaves.

"That's powerful pretty," he whispered. "Don't know as I ever saw anything that pretty before."

She shrugged her shoulders. "It's something to do while we're waiting."

"Waiting? Waiting for what?"

She looked surprised. "For the war to end." She turned impatiently. "I must get home—my mother—"

Caleb pondered. "Maybe the war won't end right soon," he reasoned. "Maybe the South will win out."

"My mother didn't want me to come over on this side of town. I thought I could get back in plenty of time. The old white lady that was helping with the pattern lives near here. She kept me too long."

"Maybe Miranda will take you upstairs," Caleb offered. "You could wait there long as you need to."

The girl continued to shake her head slowly. "I know my mother will worry."

"What's your mother's name?" Caleb asked.

"Same as mine." The girl tossed her head in a way that seemed to Caleb a little impolite. But a moment later she added, "Precious Jewel Thomas."

He forgave her instantly for the first curt remark, but the fact that she mentioned the name of Thomas along with the given name of Precious Jewel struck him with even greater force. Slaves did not ordinarily use surnames. Precious Jewel was obviously free. Having known Phillip Sazon in Charleston, he knew what that meant. He began to wonder how great the gulf would be between a free girl and a slave boy who thought she was mighty pretty. But all he could think of to say was. "That's a fine-sounding name. I like that name, Miss."

Precious Jewel put the embroidery work back into the little basket. "I can't let my mother worry any longer," she said. "I'm going home now."

"Would it make any difference if I walked along with you?" Caleb asked.

She thought about this a moment. "Maybe—if you want to—"

Caleb planned. "I'll lock the store. If we go a roundabout way, we might stay out of the streets where there are so many soldiers." He quickly locked the front part of the store and led the girl through the back quarters and through the little yard to the wooden gate opening on the side street. They began to walk fast.

"You don't know much about the war, do you?" she asked, taking two short steps for every one of Caleb's long strides.

"I can read. I read the Emancipation Proclamation before I came here from Charleston. Sometimes people leave newspapers lying around and I read them."

"Seems like you'd be more anxious for the Union Army to get here."

"Do you think that will be the end of the war?" he asked.

"Whether it's the end or not, it will be the end of slavery here. First thing the Union Army does is set the slaves free, like President Lincoln proclaimed."

Caleb paused to look around. "Where will this road take us?"

"It doesn't go too far out of the way," she said.

A group of Confederate cavalrymen had tied their horses under the trees in the yard just ahead. The soldiers were drinking out of canteens while servant boys brought water to the horses in buckets. Caleb and Precious Jewel passed on the opposite side of the street.

Farther along Caleb asked, "What happens after the Union Army sets the slaves free?"

"Behind the Union lines they're already starting schools for the freedmen," she told him. "The emancipated slaves have to start looking out for themselves. Somebody has to teach them; so teachers come right along with the Union Army. When they can find free colored people and others who are educated and willing to help, they use them. That's why I don't expect to have time for needlework after Chattanooga changes hands. I intend to help."

A column of dusty, gray-clad boys was passing at the next turn, but Caleb pointed to a path that crossed open lots and led to another neglected side street. He continued to walk rapidly, and Precious Jewel struggled to keep pace. "I been wanting to be free a long time," he confessed. When she did not comment, he explained, "I tried to run away once. The patrollers brought me back." His voice broke with deep feeling as he told her, "I can't hardly wait for freedom."

"This is where I live," Precious Jewel answered.

Caleb noticed the small cottage surrounded by a picket fence. They were at the gate. "I'll hurry back to the store now," he said. "I wouldn't want Mr. Coleman to drop in and find me away on a day like this."

The girl seemed puzzled by his tone. "Don't forget, this may be your emancipation day," she said.

A smile began to spread on Caleb's face. He felt like singing, but he knew that was not the thing to do. Instead, he bowed his head and hurried toward the dry-goods store.

Good News
And Bad

"I'm free. I'm free," he repeated as he walked back to the dry-goods store. "I'm not a slave no more. I'm what they call a freedman. Caleb Willows, freedman. That sounds good to me."

Nothing had happened at the store during his absence, so he opened the doors and blinds and began checking Mr. Coleman's account books again. No customers entered the shop that afternoon, and none came the following day. The city grew strangely quiet after the occupation by Union troops. Several more uneventful days passed, and Caleb began to feel restless behind the counter of the deserted store. He began to wonder how things were with Precious Jewel and her mother in the cottage with the picket fence.

Before he could find out, however, a commotion started in the rooms overhead, where Mr. Coleman's family lived. Miranda seemed to be taking down beds and dragging furniture across the floor. This continued for two days, then about midnight of the third day, Miranda came down the back steps and knocked on the door of the stockroom.

Caleb jumped out of bed, lighted the lamp and slipped on his pants.

The big dark woman's head was tied in a white kerchief. Over her kitchen dress and apron she wore a man's coat, which may have belonged to Mr. Coleman. Her eyes were bright with secrets.

"Mrs. Coleman and the two young ones is fixing to leave it with you, Caleb," she announced. "We got a horse and wagon out front all loaded. Mrs. Coleman is feeling poorly. I'm taking her and the children back to her people in Virginia. We don't know what's become of the master since he joined the Confederate Army. If he comes back, you can tell him about us. Here's the keys to the upstairs. You can cook yourself something to eat in the kitchen."

"I'd like to say good-by to Mrs. Coleman," Caleb offered.

Miranda shook her head. "Never mind about the good-by; Mrs. Coleman don't feel like seeing nobody. That's how come we leaving at night. Just remember what I said. I'll go out the back gate and meet them round front."

She disappeared in the darkness, but for several moments Caleb did not close the door. As he stood there, slowly recovering from the shock of this unexpected scattering of his master's family, he began to realize that suffering was not confined to slaves. He could have cried if he had let himself, but he had learned to hold tears back. Instead, he put on his shoes, followed Miranda through the back gate and walked slowly around the store building. When he reached the front, the wagon was already on its way. He saw the high-piled load wobble a little as it vanished down the street.

In his heart a song began to swell, one of those double-meaning slave songs that seemed to fit so many situations: "Stay in the field," it said, "stay in the field till the war is ended."

"If religion was a thing that money could buy,
The rich would live and the poor would die.

"Stay in the field,
Stay in the field
Till the war is ended."

After the song he slept. He slept many nights thereafter with only a song for company and consolation. The war was not over. The strife was still bloody. Caleb knew he was free. Union troops held the city, and now homeless freedmen, former slaves who had lost their homes and didn't yet know what to do with their new freedom, began to crowd the streets. He knew it would be better for him to remain in the stockroom at night and to keep the store during the daytime than to join the miserable crowds he saw on the corners. More important still, it was unthinkable that he should leave his post in the store before Mr. Coleman or one of his regular clerks could come to relieve him. Freedom or slavery had nothing to do with this responsibility.

Caleb decided to wait for some definite word, no matter how long it should be in arriving. While he waited, checking and rechecking the almost empty shelves and running through the account books time and time again, he gave thought to his own affairs. What could he do with himself after the owner of the store returned? Would Mr. Coleman be willing to keep him as a helper and pay him a salary?

Perhaps that was a possibility, but Caleb rejected it. There was something else he wanted to do first. Although he liked Chattanooga and had enjoyed the work in the store, he had missed the evenings in Charleston with his mother and father. He had begun to wonder how they were getting along. And he wasn't sure he would have a better chance in Mr. Coleman's dry-goods store when all the former clerks returned than he would have in Mr. Harvey's tailor shop if he were to present himself there and ask for work as a freedman. It all added up to one thing. He would return to Charleston as soon as he was at liberty to do so.

Fortunately, he had never found it necessary to use the gold pieces his mother had given him as a reward for teaching himself to read. They would pay his way to Charleston, and there would be money to spare.

That much was easy. The part he didn't like to think about concerned Precious Jewel Thomas. Not seeing her in the store again with the bow of her bonnet tied under her chin was already troubling him. Not even emancipation seemed as important at this moment as meeting Precious Jewel again. And the thought of going to Charleston, which was in another state, and seemed almost in another world, was terribly confusing.

Sundays came and went while Caleb waited for the war to end and for somebody to come and relieve him of his duties in the store. Each week he returned to the meeting in the carriage shed and with the group of ex-slaves sang songs like "I' Ain't Gonna Study War No More," "Freedom After Me" and "Swing Low, Sweet Chariot." And sometimes he lingered after the meeting to talk to the other young people and try to learn what they were doing with their freedom. Most of them had been less fortunate in slavery than had he and were just now ready to begin to learn to read and write.

Caleb agreed to help a few of them with their learning at night if they would come to his room. Their eagerness became a problem. Young and old came. Their number increased so rapidly that the stock room was crowded in a week. Some of the folks found old slates on which to practice writing. Others brought sticks of charcoal with which to make marks. Caleb began teaching the alphabet.

One morning in the week that followed he was sweeping out the store when Precious Jewel and her mother entered. "Of course you've heard about it!" they almost shouted. Caleb shook his head, but he could not keep from smiling. "But we didn't come to bring the news," the mother added.

"No, we came to ask about the class you're teaching," Precious Jewel explained.

"But since you haven't heard, you might like to know the news." Again they seemed to be talking together.

"I would. What's happened?"

"The surrender. The war's over. Aren't you glad?" the mother and daughter cheered.

Caleb tried to hide his mixed feelings. "I'm glad," he said. "Yes, indeed, yes, indeed."

There was a pause before Precious Jewel remembered, "You don't know my mother."

Caleb and Mrs. Thomas exchanged smiles. "You look just like your mother," he commented, turning again to Precious Jewel.

"I heard about your teaching," Mrs. Thomas said. "We're trying to help a little too, but we don't have slates, books, paper—not anything. And there are so many who want to learn, young and old. We can't handle them. How are you managing?"

His experience, he told them, was about the same as theirs. In a way it was not so favorable. He could only continue the little he was doing till someone came to claim the store. Then he would have to find another place to live. Perhaps he would return to Charleston. His life, too, was complicated by freedom.

The girl looked at him critically. "Those of us who have had a few advantages can't think too much about ourselves now," she reproved. "The others, the ones who are almost helpless, need us." She hesitated a moment. "You could do a lot of good here."

"Those you've been helping seem to have confidence in you," Mrs. Thomas agreed.

"I'm not a teacher," Caleb protested. "I don't know much myself yet. And I couldn't help anybody, not even a little bit, if I didn't have some way to make a living for myself."

"Of course that's true," Mrs. Thomas agreed, "but maybe Mr. Coleman will have some plans for you when he comes home. We like Mr. Coleman. He has always been very nice to us. That's saying a good bit, you know. Some Southerners who are very kind to their slaves are very ugly in the way they treat free colored people."

"I hope he gets here soon," Caleb said.

"Where do you do your teaching?" Precious Jewel asked.

Caleb led the girl and her mother into the stockroom, which now contained only empty crates, boxes and cases, except for the corner in which his cot was placed. "Mr. Coleman put me in here to sleep. He never told me I could bring the others in," Caleb apologized.

"I don't think he'd mind," Mrs. Thomas said, "not if he were here and saw how things are. Besides, I'm sure Mr. Coleman will want to do everything he can for you when he comes back, after the way you've attended to his business."

Caleb didn't smile, but there was humor in his eyes as he confessed, "All I really want him to do is to come here and take his store off my hands so I can leave."

"You're thinking about going away?" Precious Jewel asked.

"I left my ma and pa in Charleston." He turned to Mrs. Thomas. "Charleston ought to be a right nice city to live in—without slavery."

"Without slavery, Chattanooga will be mighty nice too." She almost seemed to be inviting him to remain.

"Maybe I'll come back sometime."

Mrs. Thomas smiled pleasantly. "But what is that curious thing on the shelf above your bed?"

"It's an African drum, ma'am."

Precious Jewel went over and took it in her hands. "Where in the world did you get a thing like this?"

"Bring it out where the light's better," Mrs. Thomas suggested, leading the way back into the store and toward the open windows in the front.

Caleb stepped behind the counter, and Precious Jewel and her mother seated themselves on stools provided for customers who wished to rest while examining catalogs or yard goods.

"It came from Africa," he told them, leaning forward and resting his hands on the instrument. "It belonged to my pa. He got it from a sailor on a boat. Our folks could do a lot with drums—I mean back in Africa."

"That was a long time ago," Precious Jewel said.

"We can all afford to forget about Africa now," her mother suggested.

Caleb disagreed politely. "Now's the time I want to start remembering Africa," he said. "When I think about the place where my people came from, way back yonder two hundred years ago, it helps me to feel free. Now the war is over, I think I'd like to beat the African drum."

Mrs. Thomas laughed. "If that's how you feel, go right ahead. Beat it all you please. You have a good reason to beat any kind of drum you can get your hands on today. You're free, Caleb."

"I always wondered how it felt to be a slave," Precious Jewel said softly. "Now I wonder how freedom feels when you first get it."

Caleb began to tap the surface of the drum with the tips of his fingers. The sound was muffled and dim at first, but it grew and grew till presently it filled the room. Caleb turned to the girl, the tips of his fingers still pounding rhythmically. "Let me tell you a secret," he whispered above the tom-tom. "I never did feel like a slave. Not really. In my mind I was free all the time."

"I like your attitude, Caleb," Mrs. Thomas approved, "even though we don't have the same idea about the drum."

She and Precious Jewel rose to leave. "I wish you were going to stay here so that you could help, but maybe it's just as well. I suppose there's as much to be done in Charleston as here." They turned toward the door.

The two went out and the store door closed.

The war had been long and bloody, and the South had been defeated at great cost. Much of the region had been a battlefield. Now it was in ruins. People of all classes were humiliated and poverty-stricken. Where to go and what to do were questions thousands of people had to ask. But to none was the situation more difficult than to the freedman—the ex-slave who had just been emancipated into a world that was almost completely destroyed.

To the defeated South the War Between the States had been a catastrophe so great it can scarcely be described. In such a place and in such a time suffering people are always inclined to look around for someone to blame for their troubles. To blame the enemy with whom one has been fighting wouldn't do, because that would be to blame oneself for not defeating the enemy. Suffering people, in a case like this, are apt to look for a third party on whom to place blame for their miseries. The suffering South turned on the slave people who had tilled their land, served in their homes and cared for their children without wages for two hundred years. The slaves, they told themselves hysterically, were the cause of their impoverishment and ruin. The people who questioned this attitude and wanted to know whether or not it was based on truth and whether or not it was fair to the slaves became unpopular.

In Mr. Coleman's dry-goods store Caleb saw only a

small part of the whole picture, but he learned something about the havoc of war when two deputies came into the store one morning and announced that the store and stock were being offered for sale immediately.

"You'll have to wait till Mr. Coleman gets back from the war," Caleb protested.

"We won't wait for that," the first deputy said curtly.

"*You* better not wait either," the second remarked. "He ain't coming back. He's missing in action."

Caleb bowed his head. After a moment he asked, "What do you want me to do?"

"Let us see all the records you got—the account books, everything."

Caleb led them back of the counter and opened the drawers in which the records were kept. The deputies squinted as they opened the volumes and turned the pages.

"Most of these accounts are no good now," one of them concluded eventually.

"I doubt that an auction will bring anything like enough to pay the owner's debts," the other added.

They went out grumbling. Caleb began thinking about Charleston and the peaceful loft in which his mother and father lived above the carriage shed. When the deputies returned a day later, accompanied by several men, his few belongings were already packed in a small bundle. "I'm just fixing to leave," he told them.

A deputy spat tobacco juice on the floor. "Good thing you are. The new owner might not have any use for you." He turned to one of the others. "Let's move some counters and tables around here and make a place for the sale."

Caleb went into the stock room and picked up his bundle. He continued out the rear door and through the gate to the side street. He did not look back.

CHARIOT IN THE SKY

He arrived in Charleston nearly a week later and hurried immediately to the alley on which he had lived with his parents while there. As he approached the carriage shed, he noticed that the loft door was hanging open. The honeysuckle and columbine had not been trimmed recently, they almost covered the entrance. This seemed strange. Sarah and Moses had always kept the doorway clear in the past. Caleb reached the shaky steps and climbed them slowly. At the top he pushed the tendrils of the vines aside and entered.

The loft was filled with spider webs. The bed and table were gone, the boxes overturned. A bat, startled by Caleb's presence, began to flutter dismally from one side of the place to the other. Caleb didn't have to be told that nobody had lived here in a long time. But what had become of his parents? Where should he look for them? Who could tell him? His forehead wrinkled. His thoughts began to spin. His hands became moist. His throat felt dry. Where? What?

A moment later he found himself rushing down the alley, scarcely aware that he was headed toward Mr. Harvey's tailor shop. Somehow, in spite of the widespread destruction and misery caused by the war and the scattering of people, he had never even dreamed of Sarah or Moses being any place but where he had left them. During the days of train travel, when there had been time for much thinking, the only thought that had never once come into his mind was that his parents would not be in their loft above the alley when he reached home.

The door to the tailor shop was unlocked, and the bell tinkled in the back when he opened it, but no one was there. Caleb looked in the reception room, in the big work room and outside in the yard behind the building. There was some evidence that someone had been there, but there was no indication that any work was being done.

Caleb left his bundle by the table where he had worked in the past and ran through the shop and out the front door. "Mr. Harvey," he called. "Mr. Harvey."

A strange woman leaned her head out of a window across the street. "Ask the jeweler," she said. "He might know where Mr. Harvey is."

Without pausing to acknowledge her help, Caleb turned and entered the shop next door. The cross-eyed jeweler was sitting in a chair playing checkers with a shrunken little man in the worn-out uniform of a Confederate soldier. Both men needed haircuts; both seemed old and tired and worn out. Caleb had to look three times before he identified the soldier as Mr. Harvey, and by that time he felt such a pity for the little man he scarcely knew what to say.

"As I live and breathe," Mr. Harvey greeted him, trying hard to bring a cheerful note into his voice; "it's Caleb."

"I wouldn't of known him," the jeweler echoed.

"I'm proud to see you, Mr. Harvey," Caleb whispered. "I was worried when I didn't see anybody in your shop."

"The shop's still there," the tailor smiled wanly, "but that's about all. There's no work—no business. Who wants dress clothes now?"

The jeweler raised his eyes in despair. "What would they buy them with?"

"The South is ruined, Caleb. There's nothing left for any of us," Mr. Harvey lamented. "I can't give you a job. God only knows how I'm going to feed myself."

Caleb paused, trying to comprehend the full meaning of what he had heard and seen. When he spoke again, his words came slowly and in a dull tone. "I was going to ask you about my ma and pa. What's come of them, Mr. Harvey?"

The tailor pushed the checkerboard aside. "Colonel

Willows sold all his slave people, Caleb. After he let you go, he came back and disposed of the rest. Sarah and Moses left Charleston soon after you did." Mr. Harvey went to the window and looked out on the quiet street. Caleb noticed that there wasn't much hair left on the top of his head.

"Do you think I'd be apt to find them on the plantation?"

The jeweler shook his head vigorously. "That's just where you'd be sure not to find them," he said. "Somebody else is on the place now. No Willows people are left. Not even a Willows' mule."

The two men shook their heads. "The South is ruined," they chanted somberly.

"You wouldn't know anything about the Sazon family, would you?" Caleb asked.

"The womenfolk are still around, I believe. I don't know what became of the men," Mr. Harvey said. Another long pause followed, the two men looking out of the window dejectedly, Caleb towering above them, his head bowed. Finally Mr. Harvey spoke again. "What do you think you'll do with yourself, Caleb?"

"I think I'll go somewhere else, sir. Charleston don't seem like it used to."

"It's the same all over," the jeweler said. "It ain't just Charleston that's changed."

"I know," Caleb agreed. "I wouldn't have come back if I'd known my pa and ma weren't here. I'd have stayed in Chattanooga if I'd known business was like this with you."

"You can sleep in my shop if you don't have no place else to stay," Mr. Harvey offered. "You can cook yourself something to eat over the fireplace in the back yard. That's the best I can do for you, Caleb."

"Thank you, sir. If there's anything I can do to help

around, I'll be proud to do it. But I won't stay long, Mr. Harvey. Just about a week maybe."

"That's up to you. I know you must feel bad, not finding your ma and pa in town after you come all the way from Chattanooga. But you're your own man now. You come and go as you like, Caleb."

"I'm much obliged to you, Mr. Harvey. I'll always be much obliged to you. I believe I'll walk around town a little bit now. I been riding too long, my legs need a stretch."

A week later Caleb was still stretching his legs on the streets of Charleston. His heart was still heavy with disappointment after asking questions of everybody who might by any chance know what had become of his parents after they were sold at auction by Colonel Willows. But there had been so much tragedy in Charleston, so many families had been broken and scattered that the case of Moses and Sarah Willows made very little impression on anybody.

As days passed, Caleb found that his wanderings through the city became more and more aimless. He no longer hoped or expected to find his parents. Still he walked. And finally, on an afternoon that was especially quiet, he found himself standing at the gate of the Sazon house. He had been there several moments when he saw the door open and Mrs. Sazon come to the porch.

"I saw you from the window," the handsome buff-colored woman called. "I thought you looked sort of familiar."

Caleb entered the yard and approached the steps. "I don't know what brought me here," he said. "I was just walking."

"You do look kind of lost," Mrs. Sazon smiled. "You were with Mr. Harvey, I believe."

"I'm Caleb—Caleb Willows, ma'am. Your son—"

"Of course. Phillip told us about the blue-back speller he let you have when you came to deliver that suit. That was a long time ago."

Caleb nodded. "How is your family, Mrs. Sazon?"

"My daughters are well. We've lost track of Phillip. But I hope we'll hear something, now that the war is over."

"I've lost track of my people too," Caleb told her. "I thought sure I'd find them here. Otherwise I wouldn't have come back."

"Do you have a place to stay?"

Caleb explained the situation at the tailor shop. "But I don't want to stay in Charleston," he added. "I want to go back to Chattanooga. That's what's bothering me."

"How much money do you need, Caleb?"

"I can make out with the little money I've got, thank you. What I'm worried about is my pa and ma. They might come here looking for me after I'm gone."

"Don't let that worry you," Mrs. Sazon said. "You can leave word with Mr. Harvey. They'd be sure to ask him about you if they came to town. And you can take my address and keep in touch with me. What do you have in mind to do in Chattanooga?"

Caleb showed embarrassment. "I was teaching some folks how to read," he confessed. "Of course, I don't think my teaching was so good," he added quickly, "and I'd like to learn considerable more myself, but I was doing my best."

"I'm sure you were. My daughters are both teaching freedmen. Won't you come inside and let me fix you something to eat?"

Suddenly it occurred to Caleb that he had eaten almost nothing all day. He couldn't resist the invitation. "Thank you, ma'am. I'd be much obliged." He smiled gratefully as he entered the house. "I wonder if you would do me another favor too?" he asked.

"What's that, Caleb?"

"I've got a drum my pa gave me. It's at the tailor shop now, but I'd be mighty happy if you would let me leave it here with your family."

"Of course." She left him in the front room. "I'll have something warm in a minute."

Lonesome Road

Back in Chattanooga again, his clothes dusty and worn and his untrimmed hair looking like a cuckoo's nest indeed, Caleb decided not to call on Precious Jewel Thomas and her mother till he could do something about the way he looked. In this he was helped by a middle-aged man whom he did not immediately recognize. The man was cutting hair in one of the better barber shops in the heart of the city, serving white customers.

It did not surprise Caleb that all the barbers in this shop were Negroes, for that was customary, but when one of them saw him through the window and waved his hand, he was puzzled. The brown man had mixed-gray hair and looked clean and neat in a white starched barber's jacket. He nodded and smiled as Caleb peered through the window of the shop. A moment later he removed the mantle from the customer on whom he had been working and came outside to speak.

"You don't remember me?" he asked.

The barber's voice had a familiar sound, and Caleb recalled presently that this man was one of those who had come to his room behind Mr. Coleman's dry-goods store, to be taught the alphabet and the first steps in reading.

"I didn't know you could barber."

"I been barbering right here since I was young like you," the man said. "My master owned the shop. Now that freedom's here, they're talking about taking our jobs away from us and giving them to white barbers, but they ain't done it yet, so I'm still working. That's how come I want to learn how to read and write. Times is hard, and they're apt to get worse."

"I been out of town," Caleb explained. "I been back home looking for my people."

The expression on the barber's face showed that he understood. Half the emancipated slaves, it seemed, and a good many whites of the South, were looking for lost families, relatives and friends. "You're kind of wore out, son," he observed.

"Sometimes I was walking and sometimes I was riding," Caleb told him. "Sometimes I had a place to sleep and sometimes I didn't. Sometimes I ate and sometimes I just drank water. But my mind was set on coming back here to Chattanooga—when I didn't run across my people."

"If you'll start teaching us again, I'll get the folks together," the barber suggested.

A humorous smile twisted Caleb's lips. "I don't think I could teach nobody nothing till I get washed up and get on some clean clothes. My hair needs cutting too. Looks like a cuckoo's nest, I reckon."

"Never mind about that," the barber laughed. "You teach *us* and we'll scrub *you*. Wait around till closing time; I'll take you home with me."

"I couldn't just wait here, doing nothing," Caleb said.

"Come inside. I can fix that." Caleb followed the barber through the shop and into the room behind. "Here," the man said, handing him a broom, "you can sweep the shop."

"That's more like it."

"I'm the number one barber here. My name's Joel Burton, if you don't remember it. The boss lets me hire a boy to sweep out and keep things clean. So you're it, now."

Caleb was so pleased he sang as he swept. And he almost forgot that he was hungry and that his clothes were in bad shape and that his hair needed cutting. Customers in the chairs turned their heads and listened as his rich, deep voice raised the words:

> "Do you see that good old sister
> Come a-wagging up the hill so slow?
> She wants to get to heaven in due time
> Before the heaven doors close.
>
> "Go chain the lion down,
> Go chain the lion down,
> Before the heaven doors close."

After the shop closed, Joel Burton locked the doors, pulled the blinds and gave Caleb a good haircut free of charge. Then they left together. Half an hour later they came to the narrow, dusty street in which the barber lived with his plump, smiling wife. The house was small, but the yard was swept, and odors of boiled greens and ham hocks and baking yams poured out of the doors and windows. There were lilac bushes on each side of the doorsteps.

"Come meet the company, Viney," Joel Burton called as he and Caleb entered the front door. His wife was drying her hands on her apron as she emerged from the kitchen. Her face was as round and bright as the moon of May, her smile was friendly. "This here is the young professor," her husband announced proudly. "The one that was teaching us; remember?"

"Where'd you find him, Joel? I thought he went away."

The barber's tone became sympathetic. He lowered his voice. "He was looking for his people, Viney. That's how come he left us like he did. But he's back now. And right now Caleb would rather see a plate of victuals than anything else you can name."

"Well, there's plenty here for him," she said. "All he can eat. I'll have it on the table directly."

"I'm much obliged to both of you. I thought I was at the end of my string. I needed somebody like you all."

A few moments later the three of them took places around a small table with a checkered cover and drew up their chairs.

"Think you'll stay in Chattanooga this time?" Mrs. Burton asked as she served Caleb's plate.

Caleb shook his head. "Something tells me I'm just starting to travel," he said dreamily. "Where I'll end and what will become of me I don't know. But if I keep moving, maybe I'll find out. The world's big, and everywhere is not the same. I got to find out more about it. I'd like to go up North and see where the Yankees come from. I'd like to cross the water and find out where the boats go. I'd like to study and learn—"

"But you already know how to read," Mr. Burton reminded him.

"I don't know enough," Caleb said. "If it hadn't been for you, I'd be walking the streets hungry right now. That's not the way I want to live. That's not the way for anybody to live."

All three of them became thoughtful. Presently Joel Burton put his fist down on the side of the table for emphasis as he muttered: "This freedom ain't working out so good, Caleb. All of us is free now—like we wanted to be—but most of us is walking the streets hungry. Free but hungry. That don't make sense. What you say about traveling is all right, but you need to know where you going. And you need to know how come. What the freedmen need now is somebody to show them how to get out of this fix they're in. They ain't slaves no more, but nobody has learned them how to walk like men and look after themselves and make a living. If I could read good, I might help, but I don't know my letters. Why don't you start a little school here, Caleb?"

There was another silence, and Caleb pondered the words of the barber. Finally he raised his eyes from his plate again. "Mrs. Thomas and her daughter, Precious Jewel, can teach the letters to the folks. What I want to do is like you say, Mr. Burton. I want to learn how to walk like a man. Where do you think I could learn that?"

Mrs. Burton interrupted. "That girl you mentioned— Mrs. Thomas' daughter—she ain't here no more."

Her husband ignored the interruption. "I hear a lot of talk about a school some soldier-teachers in the Union Army is trying to start in Nashville," he replied. "They're calling it the Fisk school."

Again Mrs. Burton cut in. "That's where she's gone, Precious Jewel. Mrs. Thomas is doing all the teaching herself now."

Caleb found his head bobbing from one side to the other as he tried to grasp what was being said by both the wife and the husband of the Burton family. They were almost talking at the same time, and both were saying things of interest to him. A school for freedmen in Nashville—a school to which Precious Jewel Thomas had gone—Fisk school. Certainly that was the place for him. When Mr. and Mrs. Burton had finished talking, he stood up suddenly.

"I just made up my mind," he announced. "I'm going to Nashville."

"But you're not through eating!" Mrs. Burton exclaimed. "You're not ready to go anywhere."

"You just got here," her husband added. "You can't be in that big a hurry."

Caleb sat down again. "I don't mean right now," he added sheepishly. "I mean, soon as I can."

As it turned out, *soon* meant a little more than a week. First Caleb had to borrow a needle and thread from Mrs. Burton and repair the clothes he was wearing. He washed his shirts and underwear in the tub in the back yard and did his pressing and ironing on Mrs. Burton's board with her iron. By the time he got around to calling on Mrs. Thomas, he was as clean and well-dressed as it was possible with the clothes he owned, and Mrs. Thomas stood back in surprise as she opened the door to him.

"We didn't expect you back this soon, Caleb. A little more, and you'd have been here before Precious Jewel left."

"Precious Jewel is gone?"

"That school in Nashville," Mrs. Thomas confirmed. "Some of our young people will have to learn more than just reading and writing if they are to make good teachers and leaders for the children of the freedmen. We have to look ahead. We'll need high schools and colleges. Don't you agree?"

"Yes'm, I agree," he said. "But it's kind of funny too."

"Funny?"

"I mean I'm just fixing to go to Nashville myself. Maybe—maybe I'll meet up with Precious Jewel up there at Nashville."

Caleb noticed a strangely clouded expression coming over Mrs. Thomas' face. "No doubt you will," she said coolly.

Caleb felt suddenly crushed. He was sorry he had mentioned the name of Precious Jewel to her mother in that tone of hopefulness and expectancy. He was sorry he had talked about the girl at all. He was displeased with himself and disappointed in Mrs. Thomas. Didn't she like the idea of his seeing Precious Jewel in Nashville? What was she thinking about?

He felt so unhappy he wasn't even sure he wanted to make an effort to reach the school in Nashville. Why, Caleb wasn't sure. He didn't want to believe that this free-born colored woman felt that slavery marked a person for life. She had tolerated him at first; she had even seemed to admire what he had taught himself and achieved as a slave. But as soon as he betrayed by the tone of his voice and the sparkle in his eye that he admired Precious Jewel, something seemed to happen in Mrs. Thomas' mind.

Walking across town to the drab little street in which Joel and Viney Burton lived, a still greater question arose. Would Precious Jewel herself think him not good enough for her if it ever came to that? Was it wise for him to go on to the school in Nashville, in the face of all this, and take the chance of being humiliated and disappointed. Joel and Viney Burton were proving themselves kind friends who treated him almost like a son of the family; they would help him find work and make himself useful in Chattanooga if he decided to remain in the city. Wouldn't that be the safest thing to do?

But Caleb quickly dismissed it from his thoughts. He clenched his fists as he walked. Now, more than ever, he was determined to go to Nashville. Before, he had thought of going there solely out of his desire to learn; Precious Jewel's rosy-brown face had scarcely been in the picture. But now there was something else he had to find out.

So Mrs. Thomas thought that the marks of slavery

were still on him? So she had made up her mind that he wasn't good enough for her free-born daughter? He would—he would show her something, by George.

Suddenly he realized that the sun had dropped out of sight as he walked. A blue twilight had come to the city.

Nothing else mattered now. Not even the lack of money seemed important to Caleb as he watched his chance to strike out toward Nashville, in middle Tennessee, the city in which soldier-teachers of the Union Army were trying to start a school for the education of Negroes. Of course, public transportation was out of the question. The gold money his mother had given him had run out halfway between Charleston and Chattanooga on the return trip. But he had completed the journey by walking when he had to, and riding on cotton wagons and such vehicles as would give him a lift when he could. He was sure he could make Nashville the same way.

Meanwhile, he worked in the barber shop, sweeping the floor, dusting the coats of the customers with a whisk broom and accumulating a few small coins which he knew would come in handy on his trip. Then one Saturday night, when the shop remained open very late, a nervous-looking stranger, a white man, entered just before closing time. He wore a beard, but he wanted it shaved off clean—in a hurry.

"My horses are tied outside, and they're fretful," he said. "I'll be much obliged to you if you get finished as fast as you can."

Caleb knelt down and brushed the dust from the man's boots. Joel Burton went to work on the heavy beard, pausing every few moments to strop his razor and to freshen up the lather. "Do you come from far, sir?" the barber asked at one point.

"Right good piece," the man replied vaguely.

"Which way you headed?" Joel Burton prodded.

"West." The stranger had neither words nor time to waste. "My horses are fretting," he repeated significantly.

The barber could take a hint. He said no more. But Caleb began itching to put in a word. Finally he got up his nerve. "I'm headed west myself," he ventured.

At first the man appeared not to hear the remark. But presently he cleared his throat and asked, "How you traveling?"

"I'll have to walk," Caleb told him, "till I can get a lift."

The stranger opened his eyes in the reclining chair and looked the erect young porter up and down. When Joel Burton removed the mantle from around his neck, the man added, in a sort of musing tone, "Too bad you're not ready to go now."

"But I am," Caleb assured him quickly. "I *stay* ready."

The clean-faced white man shrugged. Caleb could now see that he was a pale, gentle man. "My horses are fretting, and there ain't nobody in the wagon but me."

"I understand," Caleb whispered, suppressing his excitement. "My bundle's in the next room. I keep it with me."

In less than thirty seconds he was on the wagon seat beside the stranger, and the fretful team was moving. There was not time to say good-by; Caleb was sure Mr. and Mrs. Burton would understand. When he had carried his small bundle of clothes to the shop to be ready for just such an abrupt departure, he had paved the way. He looked back now and saw Joel Burton blowing out the kerosene lamps on the wall brackets.

The horses seemed to have caught their driver's uneasiness and fear. They hurried through the business section of town as if they were escaping from something.

When they reached the pike that led across the mountains they settled down to a more reasonable gait.

The stranger let the reins go slack. "I figure you're trying to get to that school they're starting in Nashville, for the colored and white both," he said suddenly.

"How'd you know, sir?"

"You couldn't hide it if you tried. I can tell by the look on your face. Me, I'm trying to make Memphis."

A pause followed, the wagon rocking and jolting on the rough road.

"Don't know as I've seen anybody start out on a trip like this at night before," Caleb observed finally.

The man chuckled softly. "You want to know what I'm running from, don't you?"

Caleb was embarrassed. "I don't mean to meddle," he apologized.

"But you'd like to know how come I was in such a hurry to shave my beard off and leave town, wouldn't you?"

"I couldn't help noticing, sir."

"I'll tell you," the stranger said, "but it might not ease your mind none. Up in my county, I was one of them Southerners that favored the Union. I was against slavery. I laid low while the war was on, and nothing much came of it, but now that everybody's having fits about the Union Army staying down here, and nobody seems to know just which way to turn, folks have been giving me trouble. A few nights ago somebody told me that a crowd of the neighbors was planning on horsewhipping me and giving me the tar and feathers."

"What made them want to do you like that?" Caleb asked.

"A fellow came in there to start a school. The folks thought he was meddling in our affairs. I didn't see it that way, and I helped him out. I let him stay at my

111

place. I told him he could build his school on my land.
After the country folks banded together and ran him
away, they turned on me."

"You don't think they're following, do you?"

"You see, when they came threatening me with their
buckets and their brushes and their torches, I gave them
something to threaten about. When they stood under the
trees hollering and swearing and calling me out of my
house, I came out all right, but I came out shooting.
They scattered like a pack of rabbits, but I figure I must
have nicked one or two. So when I heard that they were
getting together again, I decided to call it a day. They
might want to charge me with murder. I may have to sell
the team and wagon in Memphis and catch a riverboat.
Something's starting up around here that's apt to make
it kind of hard for people like you and me, young fellow.
It's kind of savagelike."

"What do they want? What are they trying to do?"

"Same old thing—slavery. Them that owned slaves
hate to give them up. They were worth money to them.
Slaveholders are poor as Job's turkey now. If they could
stir up enough trouble to make the Union willing to let
them have their slaves back, just for peace sake, they
think that would put them straight. Others got a different idea."

"Which others, sir?"

"Some of the others never owned a slave in their life.
A lot of the poor whites were worse off than slaves during slavery. The masters owned the slaves and looked
after them. The poor whites and the free Negroes had to
scuffle for themselves. Plenty times they went hungry
while the slaves were eating fine. Now that freedom's
here and the war's over, everybody's grabbing. And the
ones that are grabbing hardest don't want to divide.

112

They don't want to see the freedmen get educated and start asking for their share. Understand?"

Caleb peered into the darkness. "Looks like a lonesome road we got to travel," he said.

"Lonesome road! That's it," the stranger agreed.

In the same instant there was a burst of musket fire about four hundred yards away. The horses started nervously. The stranger tightened the reins and held the team on the road, but he didn't try to slow it down. The horses were galloping hard when Caleb looked beyond a ridge and saw a cross burning on the side of a hill. Why it was there and what it meant he could not imagine. But he asked no questions. He was glad the stranger's horses were fast; he hoped they would not tire.

"Tell Them We Are Rising"

Two men in blue uniforms stood in the front of the room. One of them raised his hands and asked for attention. "Some of you are looking for the Freedmen's Aid Society, where they try to help former slaves who have no place to go, who are hungry and need clothes," he said. "This is *not* the Freedmen's Aid Society. That's down the street about three squares. Go there, and they will help you. We are trying to hold school here, but the room is too crowded. If those of you who are looking for the Freedmen's Aid Society will do as I say, maybe we can go ahead with our classes."

Slowly the thought penetrated bewildered minds. One by one grown men and women left the room in the wooden building that had formerly been a hospital barracks for Union soldiers, stumbled down the steps and started toward the offices of the Freedmen's Bureau. Among those who did not leave was a young man who stood tall and erect in the back of the room, an open book in his hand. His clothes were worn, but they were clean, carefully mended and neatly pressed. There was a serious expression on his face. He did not look like one who had been a slave.

"Thank you, Mr. Willows," one of the soldier-teachers said. Caleb beamed. It was the first time in his life Caleb had been called *mister*. "That was well read. You may be seated."

Caleb passed the book to the individual in front of him. The student attempted to read. Then the next, and the next. Some of them stumbled over words which seemed easy to Caleb. At the end of the period the teacher asked Caleb if he would remain. He wanted to talk with the newcomer.

As soon as the others could file out, Caleb went to the front of the room, where the two men were now seated at opposite sides of a small desk. The younger soldier, who appeared to be in his middle twenties, had a thin sensitive face covered with a silky beard. His companion was perhaps ten years older, his beard brown and heavier. It was the older man who had conducted the reading tests that had just ended. Both were remarkably different from the picture of zealous Yankees that Colonel Willows' remarks had conjured in Caleb's mind. There was no mark of fanaticism on either of these.

"Yes, sir?" Caleb's voice had grown so resonant that even his whisper was clearly audible.

"I'm Professor Ogden." The older man rose and extended his hand.

Caleb shook it firmly. "Yes, sir. I know."

"Mr. Willows, I want you to meet an important member of our staff, Mr. George L. White."

Though he seemed pale and thin beside the other man, George L. White's features were not weak. His glossy hair was parted on one side and neatly turned back from a strong forehead, his handclasp was quick and friendly. "We're going to know each other better soon," Mr. White smiled, "much better."

"I hope so," Caleb answered.

Professor Ogden laughed pleasantly. "You don't know what Mr. White means. You see, among other things,

115

he's treasurer of the Fisk school. He's the one to whom you pay your fees."

Gradually the smile vanished from Caleb's face. "I don't have no money right now, sir," he confessed promptly. "But if there's any other way, anything I can do—"

When Caleb's voice suddenly broke off, the two schoolmen exchanged glances. Apparently they understood.

"Your story is a familiar one, Mr. Willows," the young treasurer told him. "But an education will cost you something; it's not free."

An uncomfortable silence followed.

"Sometimes I think we're trying to get blood out of turnips," Professor Ogden complained. "So few can pay —not one in ten."

Caleb thought of Precious Jewel, whom he had not seen since reaching the school. She was probably one of the elect—the one in ten. With a mother like Mrs. Thomas, who lived in her cottage and worked as a teacher, there was perhaps no question as to how her fees would be paid. He wondered how this problem of paying school expenses had escaped his mind so completely, while he was dreaming about the school in Nashville and while he was making the journey from Chattanooga in the wagon with the stranger.

"What happens to the rest of us?" Caleb asked nervously. "The nine out of ten?" He was genuinely disturbed. If school was denied to him, he would be disappointed, terribly disappointed, but he couldn't believe that he could come this close to his goal and then fail. He would find a way—he would have to find a way.

Mr. White stroked the young beard on his pale face. "I try to advise the students who can't pay, Mr. Willows. One way and another, we've been able to work out plans for self-help in a number of cases. It's not always possible, of course, and it's never easy. To a large extent it depends on the student, his special skills, if any; his determination and his ingenuity."

"You read very well," Professor Ogden recalled. "That's something."

George L. White nodded. Suddenly he dropped his official manner. "This has no bearing, but I've been noticing your speaking voice. Do you sing, Mr. Willows?"

"Sometimes," Caleb told him. "When I have something to sing about."

"Do you know a good many songs?"

"Just the—the slave songs, sir. I know a right smart number of them."

Again the two teachers exchanged smiles.

"Mr. White likes music, especially singing," Professor Ogden explained. "Sometimes I wonder if he isn't more interested in music than he is in his work."

His companion seemed to take this as reproof. "Your case, Mr. Willows," he said, getting back to the issue, "will have to be studied like the rest. I'll sit down with you in the morning and you can tell me about your life, your work experience and such things, and we can start exploring after that if we feel encouraged."

"We can keep you tonight anyhow," Professor Ogden remarked.

Caleb's bundle was in the back of the room, tied in a maroon table scarf with a fringe, an article he had salvaged from the stockroom of the dry-goods store. "Thank you, sir," he murmured.

"You'll find the young men in the unit to your right, as you go out," Professor Ogden added.

"If Professor Ogden will close his ears a moment," Mr. White said, blushing a little, "I'll tell you a secret, Mr. Willows. Some of us are going to meet in this room and do a little singing after supper. We'd be glad to have you come if you feel like it."

"Thank you, sir."

The cluster of one-story wooden buildings was located in Nashville, Tennessee, a city which still remembered the invading Army of the Cumberland, and where now General Clinton B. Fisk, Assistant Commissioner for the Freedmen's Bureau in Tennessee and Kentucky, had his headquarters. Caleb's eyes explored the grounds as he emerged from the unit that had formerly served as a reception center. His bundle under his left arm, his right hand stuffed in his pocket, he was a picture of utter dejection.

So this was the school about which he had heard so much talk; Fisk school, as it was called. And here he was, after a long and wearisome journey. But nothing was as he had expected. Reaching the school was one thing; being admitted as a student was quite another. His hopes began to slip. Perhaps it was partly because he now realized how careful both Professor Ogden and Mr. White had been not to promise him anything; and partly, perhaps, it was because it was nearly evening, and he was beginning to feel worn out as a result of his days of wagon travel.

He had been standing in one spot several minutes when he became aware of two well-fed Negroes in derby hats and with gold watch chains suspended across their vests. They stood in the street beyond the school grounds, both smoking cigars. One man was short and dark, the other slender, freckled and lemon-colored. They had been watching Caleb, and now began to beckon to him with their hands.

"How did you make out, partner?" the freckled face inquired insolently.

Caleb was now sorry that he had crossed the street, but he couldn't make himself turn away and ignore their question. "I don't know yet."

"Don't let them white folks trick you," the short man giggled.

"We your friends, partner," the freckled man spoke again. "Let me tell you about them Yankees."

The high-pitched giggles of the stubby individual kept punctuating the remarks. "I can tell you what side your bread's buttered on."

"I got to go over here now," Caleb excused himself, pointing toward the boys' quarters to which he had been directed. He turned to leave.

"Wait a minute. Let's get acquainted. I'm Pinky. This here's my buddy; we call him Blue. Ask anybody about Pinky and Blue. We know this town like a book." One of them had caught the lapel of Caleb's coat; the other was trying to get a grip on the bundle.

"Some other time," Caleb said firmly. "I got to go now." He brushed the hand from his lapel, pulled his bundle away from the other. "When you want to talk to me, I'll thank you to stand over there and let me stand over here."

"Mind what I tell you," Pinky shouted. "Yankees is white folks too. They all the same. Working for one ain't no different from working for another. You just like the rest of the freedmen. Like me and Blue. And you was better off when you was with your old master, eating them good collard greens and ham hocks and corn bread. I bet you don't know where your next meal's coming from. Some freedom!"

"Some school too," Blue chirped, "if you can pay for it!"

"If your own old master ain't got no more use for you, partner, I know somewhere you can go. You won't get no money—nothing like that—but they'll feed you good."

"You'll get your grub at the commissary. It beats nothing."

"That's just slavery," Caleb asserted angrily. "You two are trying to help somebody put Negroes back in slavery again." He turned his back and started toward the young men's quarters.

Blue giggled. "It's all in how you look at it."

About twenty young people came to the assembly to sing. Caleb took a seat by himself removed from the group; he was a visitor, and he had come to listen rather than to take part. Mr. White entered the room and began passing out music. "I'm sorry I can't offer you a copy to follow, Mr. Willows," he apologized, "but there aren't enough to go around, there's just one for a section."

"I'll start out by listening, if you don't mind, sir." Actually he was already confused by the language of the rehearsal. He wasn't sure what Mr. White meant by *section*, and he had only the vaguest idea of the distinction between bass and the other voice parts. His own voice had once been described by his parents as bass, and in the group singing of the slaves in Chattanooga he had been aware of a difference between voices. Some were called leaders, some followers, some voices were high-pitched, others were low. He had vague impressions about such matters, but no exact knowledge; he had never examined a page of music.

Mr. White was most agreeable, "As you prefer." Caleb could see from the first that this singing session was not a part of the treasurer's regular work; it was just something he liked to do. It was like playtime. He rubbed his hands together in pleasant anticipation as he turned to the group. "Didn't I see Ella Sheppard a moment ago?" he asked.

A bright-eyed brown girl stood among the sopranos. She was delicately thin, but erect and energetic, and her hair was simply arranged on the top of her head. "I'm ready, Mr. White," she answered.

"Thank you, Miss Sheppard. Let's start with 'There's Moonlight on the Lake,' please."

Ella Sheppard went to the piano. She struck the chords and played the introductory accompaniment with an ease and assurance that filled Caleb with astonishment. What rippling, bell-like miracle was this! When the singers were given the pitch and struck a firm chord of harmony, he was fascinated. He leaned forward, mouth and eyes rounded, as they went into the song. It was all strangely wonderful.

Another thing was equally strange and wonderful. Why was Mr. White so careful to call the pianist *Miss* Sheppard? Why had he and Professor Ogden kept calling Caleb *Mr. Willows?* Before long, Caleb mused, he would have to know the meaning of that. Yes, and he would have to understand the secret behind the music that filled the assembly room at this very moment.

They sang "Annie Laurie," "Patrick McCuishla," "Home, Sweet Home," and "Battle Hymn of the Republic." Then Mr. White gathered up the music. "All right," he said. "That will do for tonight." He paused. "But don't go yet. Remember what some of you promised me last week?"

Caleb detected an undercurrent of embarrassed whispering among the young people. A small cream-colored girl with lovely curls laughed out loud. "Oh, not before company, Mr. White," she protested. "We promised we'd sing some of those slave songs just to *you* sometime."

Mr. White rested one foot on a chair. "You're right, Miss Tate," he agreed. "But Mr. Willows said something to me today which caused me to think he wouldn't mind."

"They're the only songs I know, sir," Caleb spoke up honestly.

"Maybe I should tell you something, Mr. Willows." Mr. White lowered his voice confidentially. "There is a difference of opinion around here about singing the slave songs. Some of our teachers as well as students consider these songs a reminder of slavery. They recommend that we forget them. Professor Ogden and I thought about this debate when you mentioned them today. And since the lady members of the Fisk faculty outnumber the men, and most of them are against the songs, that side is winning. But I think the songs are wonderful music, Mr. Willows; I never hope to hear anything more beautiful. That's why you see me trying to bribe the group into singing a few of them before we break up."

"Well," Ella Sheppard smiled, striking a chord by ear, "close all the doors and windows."

Mr. White sat down and folded his arms, and the young people began to blend their voices in "Roll, Jordan, Roll." Caleb caught the rhythm. His shoulders swayed back and forth, and when it came to the point where the leader takes the melody alone and cries out musically, "Oh, brothers, you ought to've been there, a-sitting in the kingdom, to hear old Jordan roll," he forgot himself. He imagined he was with the group in the carriage shed in Chattanooga, and before he knew it, he had opened his mouth and sung the line. Then he felt ashamed. Nobody had asked him to lead the verse. Maybe he shouldn't have done it.

"What a voice!" Mr. White exclaimed when the harmony died away. "What a song! The only word for it is majestic." He turned directly to Caleb. "Mr. Willows, you've been holding out on us tonight. With a voice like that, why didn't you join in right away? But you can't stop now. Sing another song. And you take the lead, Mr. Willows. Come in a little closer."

"What will it be, Mr. Willows?" asked Ella Sheppard.

"How about 'Swing Low, Sweet Chariot'?" Caleb suggested.

They took it up, and the song poured forth.

> "Swing low, sweet chariot,
>   Comin' for to carry me home,
>   Swing low, sweet chariot,
>   Comin' for to carry me home.
>
> "I look'd over Jordan an' what did I see,
>   Comin' for to carry me home,
>   A band of angels comin' after me,
>   Comin' for to carry me home.
>
> "I'm sometimes up and sometimes down,
>   Comin' for to carry me home,
>   But still my soul feels heavenly bound,
>   Comin' for to carry me home."

A door closed sharply in the back of the room as the last line ended. Caleb looked around and saw a stern-faced woman standing with folded arms. Even Mr. White became uncomfortable in her presence. He rose apologetically. She was nearly twice his age.

"I take the blame, Miss Priddy," he said. "They were just singing for me. You weren't supposed to hear those last two songs."

"If that's what they come to Fisk school for, who am I to stand in the way," she said hopelessly. "But I'm here to remind several of you," she added, her eyes flashing, "that slave songs will not help you pass my Latin examination tomorrow. I hope that's plain."

Ella Sheppard closed the piano and started toward the door. "Yes, Miss Priddy," she whispered.

Minnie Tate followed, and in another moment there was a general exodus. Caleb waited for Mr. White.

"I'll walk to the men's building with you, Mr. Willows," the young soldier said.

When Caleb entered the treasurer's room the next morning, Mr. White was fingering a small stack of papers. He seemed brightly alert at this hour. "Have a seat, Mr. Willows; I think I've found something here."

Caleb drew an empty chair a little nearer the desk. "Would you mind if I asked you something first?" he smiled.

"Of course not."

"It's been on my mind all night," Caleb said. "You and Professor Ogden and Miss Priddy and the other teachers call all the students *Miss* and *Mister*. I wonder how come."

"Would you rather be called just Caleb?" Mr. White asked.

"I don't know, sir. I was just wondering. Nobody else ever called me *mister*."

Mr. White nodded. "That's the reason. Because nobody else calls you *mister*. When you call a young man by his first name only, you make him feel like a boy. When you call him by his last name and use *mister*, you make him feel like a man. Those of us who have decided to stay in the South and help the freedmen rise know that our first job is to make the former slaves feel like people and believe in themselves. We believe that if we call a colored boy *mister*, he will become a gentleman."

It took a minute for all this to sink in, but finally Caleb raised his eyes. "I see, sir."

"Now about your expenses at Fisk," Mr. White added

quickly, removing one sheet of paper from among the others. "I've had another talk with our principal, and I told him your story as you told it to me last night. He thinks as I do that you are one we should encourage. That's where the matter stands as of this moment, Mr. Willows."

Caleb wasn't sure what that meant, but he supposed that it called for an expression of gratitude. "I'm much obliged to you," he murmured, "to both of you."

"But it will take more than our encouragement to keep you in Fisk," Mr. White cautioned.

"Yes, sir," Caleb agreed vaguely. "I reckon it will."

"These letters are answers I have received from people to whom I have written, to ask about work opportunities for promising young people who need some means of support while attending school. I don't mind telling you that this has turned out to be the biggest part of my work as treasurer of Fisk school." Mr. White's tone became confidential. "Your case is like many others, Mr. Willows. There are so many like you, in fact, that I can't see for the life of me how we're going to keep the school going—unless a miracle happens."

"I can do most any kind of work," Caleb reminded him.

"That may help. Especially the tailoring you mentioned. This letter is from a tailor. He can use someone weekends."

"That would suit me fine, sir."

"But you may need more work than that. I've been able to find jobs for a number of students in rural day schools of this county and adjoining ones. Such schools are springing up all around, and they don't depend on trained teachers. Anyone who can help the people learn to read and write is appreciated."

Caleb's forehead wrinkled. "That would keep me from going to school here, wouldn't it?"

"Not exactly. These schools don't try to run more than two or three months in a year. If you could be placed in one of these country schools for a term, you might be able to make sufficient money to start you at Fisk. The weekend tailoring could be added."

"I'd like that fine, sir."

"General O. O. Howard, of the Freedmen's Bureau, told us recently how he had visited one such school and asked the young folk what message they'd like him to carry to their friends in the North. One little fellow stood up in the back and said, 'General, tell them we are rising.'" Mr. White spoke warmly. "I think that says everything. My own experiences—" he went on eagerly, "But I mustn't waste time on my life story now."

"I'd like to hear it, Mr. White," Caleb said.

Mr. White looked embarrassed. "It really isn't important. You'll hear me tell it often enough, I'm sure, if we can find some way to keep you at Fisk." When he laughed, Mr. White's voice betrayed his youth. He was as excited as a boy over the adventure on which he was launched. He reached over his desk and handed Caleb a slip of paper. "Anyone can tell you how to find this tailor's shop. You may stay in the young men's building for the present. I'll be able to let you know in a week or two what the chances are for teaching work; in the meantime, I hope you'll continue to sing with us."

Caleb's smile kept broadening. "I'll be sure to do that, Mr. White," he promised.

Outside the treasurer's room students were passing. Caleb was so encouraged by his talk with Mr. White that he took time to watch them for a few minutes. They were excellent in appearance, the cream of the emancipated youth of the region; it was hard to imagine any of them as slaves. Some had been born free, of course, but looking at them as they passed from one of the barracks buildings to another, Caleb couldn't possibly tell which were which. He was amused by this fact. But he suddenly realized that he *could* tell the difference—in one case at least. Precious Jewel Thomas was looking at him and waving her hand, and he knew she was one who had been born free.

He crossed over to where she stood.

"I thought that was you, Caleb," she said. "Are you in school here?"

He didn't know how to answer. "I am and I ain't," he replied. And before it was out of his mouth, he began to worry about that word *ain't*. Somehow it didn't sound right, here at the Fisk school.

The girl laughed pleasantly, however. "Say, what kind of mystery is this?"

"I'll be here a little while anyhow," he explained.

She was on her way to the classroom with a book and some writing materials in her hand. "Then I'll see you again," she said.

Caleb didn't take his eyes off her till she entered an adjoining building. Then he remembered the slip of paper in his hand. He had unconsciously rolled it into a round wad. Now he had to unroll it before he could read the tailor's address.

Who Is That Dressed In White?

The shop was stuffy and small, and the tailor was finicky and unpleasant, but to Caleb these were details of no importance. His first aim was to enter school at Fisk, and he was grateful for any job that helped him toward that end. The hours he worked between Friday noon and Saturday night passed so quickly he scarcely gave a second thought to the cramped quarters, the steamy air over the pressing board, or the hunched individual with the black apron, the green eyeshade, and the whiskers stained by tobacco.

Nor did he have any trouble keeping himself busy during the following week. Though not yet enrolled in school, he went twice to Mr. White's music class and listened without participating while the other singers rehearsed choral numbers from a cantata called *Nicodemus the Slave*. On one of these nights Mr. White took a moment to make an explanation for Caleb's benefit.

"I don't think I mentioned the cantata to you last week, Mr. Willows," the leader said. "It's another of my pet ideas. But I did tell you, I believe, that Fisk is hard-pressed for money. As treasurer, I'm the one who has to pay the bills. Sometimes I feel pretty discouraged. The singing group helps me to forget this problem for a few hours each week. But since we started singing together like this, we have been invited to sing on programs in the city and in near-by towns like Lebanon and Gallatin and always the response has been gratifying. That suggested the cantata. About a month from now we expect to present it in one of the local auditoriums. We hope to raise some money for Fisk in this way."

Caleb wondered if Mr. White's hope to raise money for the school was more of a hope than an expectation. Mr. White added, "Anyhow, if I were sure you would be with us at that time, Mr. Willows, I would ask Miss Sheppard to drill you on the bass parts."

The slender Ella turned on the piano stool. "I think I could find time to go over the bass parts with you, Mr. Willows."

So Caleb borrowed a score, returned to the assembly room the next day at an hour when it was unoccupied and tried to find on the piano the bass notes he recalled from the rehearsal. But the music of the cantata was strange; he couldn't follow the harmony. Every time he started off on a bass note, he ended up by singing the melody. It didn't take him long to realize that he wouldn't be much help with the cantata even if he should be admitted to school in time.

While he was unable to learn musical notations and part singing without help, Caleb was less handicapped in other ways. He turned the pages of the textbooks he found lying on tables or desks when they were not in use and began to make little discoveries. In one of them he learned that in addition to Abraham Lincoln, George Washington and Thomas Jefferson, there had been a good many other Presidents of the United States whose names he had never known. In another he found information about the physical world. Another was devoted to ancient times and to countries called Greece and Rome and Egypt; while still another showed numbers and figures in strange arrangements.

CHARIOT IN THE SKY

Wandering about the grounds and buildings while he waited for Mr. White to give him another definite word, Caleb had no trouble filling his time. His only problem was to keep out of the way of the classes. He even attended the devotional periods and assemblies. Here, too, he learned fascinating things. He discovered that it was the American Missionary Society of the Congregational Christian Church that had taken the lead in establishing this school for freedmen at Nashville, that this organization had been engaged in adventurous educational pioneering in Africa, the West Indies, and the islands of the Pacific Ocean as well as in the southern region of the United States and on this country's undeveloped western frontier. He learned that at Fisk its work was associated with the Freedmen's Bureau.

Another weekend; he returned to the part-time work in the tailor shop. And again a week of waiting and a weekend of tailoring passed before Mr. White called Caleb to his office. The busy treasurer was fingering papers as usual. Caleb had waited so long for this interview that he was taken completely by surprise when Mr. White suddenly put his papers aside and said, "I've seen you talking to Miss Thomas several times."

"Yes, sir."

"Perhaps someone neglected to tell you that that's not permitted on the school grounds, Mr. Willows." Caleb's eyes fell. What blunder was this he had made? "Courtship and studies don't mix, you know."

Caleb was startled by the word *courtship*. He didn't consider his short conversations with Precious Jewel as having any such meaning. He was sure she would have been offended by the idea. While it was not an unpleasant thought, it just wasn't true.

"I didn't aim to do anything out of the way, sir."

"Did you know Miss Thomas before you came to Nashville?"

"Yes, sir."

"Maybe that excuses you—since you're not yet a student—but one of the lady teachers may reprove Miss Thomas."

"I hope not," Caleb protested. "She wasn't—" Suddenly he put two things together. Did this rule about talking to boys explain Precious Jewel's coolness toward him at Fisk, her eagerness to get away when she talked to him on the school grounds? Was it this rather than her mother's changed attitude? He wondered—and hoped. "I reckon I was the one to blame, sir."

"Miss Thomas is one of our good students," Mr. White added. He hesitated a moment. "But that wasn't why I sent for you." Caleb relaxed with a sigh. "What I wanted to say, Mr. Willows, was that we have found a situation for you. It's in a country school about thirty miles from here."

Eagerly Caleb waited to hear the details.

Two mornings later he crossed a small creek, walked through a grove of cedar trees, and came to a log cabin in a clearing. A bent old colored man was waiting at the door with a hickory stick in his hand. As Caleb approached, the old fellow looked puzzled.

"You ain't the new teacher?" he asked skeptically.

Caleb began to feel uneasy. "I'm the one they sent."

"You?" The man threw up his hands in laughter.

"I don't know what you're laughing at," Caleb answered sharply. "I can read reading and writing too, and if anybody around here wants to learn, I'll try to show them how."

The tone of his voice promptly sobered the old man. "I didn't go to make you mad, son," he said. "I'm glad you come. I'm mighty glad to see you. But you don't favor the last teacher we had here."

"How's that, sir?"

"He wasn't no more'n twelve years old and scrawny as a sparrow. I had to come down here every day with my stick and stand in the corner to keep the young ones quiet whilst he called out the letters and showed them how to make figures on a slate. But it looks like I'm out of a job now. Great big somebody like you won't have no trouble making folks listen to you." The old man couldn't hold back his laughter any longer. He threw his hands into the air and giggled again.

It was obvious that he meant no disrespect by this behavior; it was just his way.

"I'd like to have you stay just the same," Caleb told him. "I don't know much about teaching school, I might need you."

This seemed to be just what the old fellow wanted to hear. "Sure 'nough?" he cried. "You mean that?"

Caleb suppressed a grin. "What's your name, sir?"

"They call me Uncle Ephraim, son."

"My name is Caleb Willows," Caleb volunteered.

For no apparent reason, Uncle Eph had to laugh again. He just couldn't help it. "Now ain't that the finest name! I know you going to be a powerful schoolteacher, and I aim to help you out all I can."

"Is the door unlocked?"

"The door? It *stays* unlocked," Uncle Eph giggled. He shoved it open, and Caleb followed him inside.

Several rough boards had been placed on stumps sawed from logs; these formed the benches on which the pupils would have to sit. In the front of the room there was an old chair and a small table for the teacher. Uncle Eph began lifting the board flaps that covered the window openings at each end of the room. These were as crude

132

as the pupils' benches, but they served to keep out rain when the schoolhouse was closed and to let in light and air when it was open. Caleb walked from one side of the room to the other, inspecting everything carefully.

"Where are the books?" he asked finally.

Uncle Eph showed surprise. "We ain't got no books, son. We ain't never had none. Some of the young ones got pieces of slate to write on, but books is scarce as hen's teeth out here."

"I don't see how they can learn much without books."

"Ain't you got no books, professor?"

Caleb could no longer be irritated by Uncle Eph. That word "professor" sounded ridiculous, as if the old man were making fun of him, but Caleb now knew that Uncle Eph was trying to show respect. He put his hand in his pocket and brought out the old worn copy of *The Columbian Orator*. "Just this one," he said.

Uncle Eph squinted. "It don't look like the blue-back speller."

"I used to have a blue-back speller," Caleb recalled. "I gave it away when I got this book."

"You should of kept it." Uncle Eph shook his head sadly. "Down here everybody wants to learn out of the blue-back speller."

"I don't blame them a bit, and I'll teach it to them if I can get my hands on one," Caleb said. "But this is a good book to learn out of too."

"It ain't blue."

"No, it ain't blue," Caleb admitted. After a pause he asked, "Where am I going to live while I'm down here, Uncle Eph?"

"Me and my wife keeps the teacher with us," the old man chuckled. "We got a extra room. The other folks bring us a piece of meat now and then and a few vege-

133

tables to help out with the victuals. We won't let you starve, son."

"I'm glad to hear that," Caleb smiled. "The gentleman in charge of the country schools said they would pay me a hundred dollars for the school term. He didn't tell Mr. White or me when I'd get my pay or how I'd eat and sleep till the pay day comes around."

Uncle Eph slapped his knees and crowed as if it were a joke. "Ain't it the truth! Them white gentlemens in the county seat ain't telling us country folks much of nothing these days. But a hundred dollars sound like a heap of money for just sitting down and teaching school."

"It'll take that much and more to pay my expenses at the Fisk school," Caleb explained. "That's why I'll have to go back to Nashville every Friday afternoon and work in the tailor shop. But I'll be here bright and early every Monday morning."

"When you aim to start studying at Fisk?"

"I hope I can begin next year."

"H'm," Uncle Eph mused. "Well, I hope you make it, son. I hope you make out good here, and I hope them county gentlemens don't disappoint you neither. You look like a mighty fine young professor."

Caleb opened *The Columbian Orator* to the first page and placed it on the teacher's little table. "I'm ready to go to work," he announced.

Nothing could have made Uncle Eph cackle louder. "Well, let me ring the bell then," he cried. "I never was one to hold a young colt back when he felt like kicking up his heels. Where's that cowbell?" Uncle Eph found it on a hook behind the door. Then he went outside and climbed a small knoll that rose behind the little log schoolhouse. At the top of the knoll he began shaking the cowbell with all his strength.

Caleb went to the window and waited. When Uncle Eph decided he had clanged the bell long enough, he returned it to the hook and calmly took his place in one corner, his hickory stick handy. About fifteen minutes later Caleb saw the first pupil, an eager barefoot boy, coming over the knoll. Presently another appeared. Then another. Then two girls in starched gingham dresses. It seemed like a miracle to have them appear that way when there were no houses or cultivated lands in sight. "Where do they live, Uncle Eph?" he asked in surprise.

"Back yonder 'tween the hills. There's right smart people back there in them bottoms."

"There must be!" Caleb exclaimed as a still larger group suddenly reached the knoll. They were chattering and laughing and seemed in a hurry to get to school. "I'm going to try to find a blue-back speller when I go back to Nashville." As the young people entered he went to the door and stood there awkwardly.

When the room was filled, Caleb started toward his table, but stopped when he saw Uncle Eph making his way to the front. The old fellow was shaking with laughter. "Well, children," he cackled, "here he is—the new teacher."

Caleb came forward. "Do you feel like singing?" he asked.

"Yes, sir. Yes, sir."

He laughed with them. "Well, make me know it then."

Their voices rose suddenly as they sang "Good News," and presently students and teacher and Uncle Eph were all completely at ease.

"You ain't done working yet," Uncle Eph chuckled several hours later when school was dismissed for the day and the last of the young folks disappeared over the knoll behind the schoolhouse. "The grown folks ain't going to like it if you don't hold school for them at night. They got to work in the field all day—them that ain't feeble like me and my old lady—but they been waiting for the new day too, these here old ones, and they wants to learn their letters right along with the children."

"I know what you mean, Uncle Eph," sighed Caleb, "but let's not take them on just yet. Wait till I go to Nashville this week and see if I can run across a blue-back speller. That'll give me time to get started with the young ones a little better too."

Uncle Eph looked disappointed. "It's going to be hard to put them off that long, son."

"They'll understand if you explain to them about the speller."

"They might understand, but they won't like it," Uncle Eph insisted. "But I'll put them off, if you say so."

"Right now," Caleb protested, "I'm tired and hungry as all outdoors."

"You got a right to be tired and hungry, son," Uncle Eph agreed. "You done fine today. Them children is sure going to learn a heap of letters and figures from you. And me and Aunt Delia going to see to it that you don't fold up in the middle. We aim to feed you plenty."

They closed the door of the log schoolhouse, and Uncle Eph led the way up the pine knoll. On the other side Caleb could see lowlands where crops were planted and a stream twisting between the hills. The countryside was dotted by clumps of trees under which tiny cabins nestled, and swamp thick with brush. Uncle Eph waited while Caleb's eyes explored the strange little community; then they started down the path together.

At Uncle Eph's cabin, supper was steaming in an iron kettle, and Aunt Delia stood in the doorway with her hands on her hips. She was a stern-faced woman, and her expression did not change when Uncle Eph greeted her with a chuckle. Even when he presented Caleb, the new schoolteacher, she remained erect and serious.

"I seen the children coming home from school half a

hour ago," she said. "Thought you'd be hungry enough to come right along behind them. I reckon Eph took up your time jawing and cackling about one thing and another. But I want to tell you one thing, young man, don't pay no mind to Eph. He'll make you miss your supper sometime."

There was an overtone of kindness as well as warning in her voice.

Caleb understood a woman like this; he had known several of them before. "Yes'm, Aunt Delia," he agreed. "From now on, I'll know who to pay attention to around here."

He went to bed early that night. The next afternoon he lost no time getting home for supper. But when he went outside to walk in the twilight by the edge of the swamp, he noticed that lights were already going out in some of the cabins. These folk were not like the city people of Nashville or Chattanooga or Charleston, who burned lamps or candles far into the night; it would be wise to follow the same plan while living among them.

The week passed quickly, and on Friday evening he returned to the tailor shop. At Fisk he found a student who consented to lend him a blue-back speller. Mr. White made a place for him in the young man's building, so Caleb slept at the school and had his Sunday meals with the other Fisk students, though he was not yet enrolled.

When he returned to the country school after the weekend in Nashville, he added the after-supper class for older folk. This filled his days so completely he had little time to think about his own problems and the plans he wanted to make for himself. All that must wait till after the school term ended and he received his pay. He would have plenty of time then to think about attending Fisk and to decide what he wanted to do with his life in the complicated world into which emancipation had admitted him.

It was all he could do now to answer the questions the young people and the old ones asked him about the alphabet and to try to teach them, as he had taught himself back in Mr. Harvey's tailor shop, how to get the meaning out of written and printed words, and how to make marks which themselves would have meaning for other people who saw them. This led many of them to bring him newspapers and books that had fallen into their hands; they wanted to know what was going on in the world.

Caleb read to them willingly as long as they cared to listen and tried to explain the news as best he could. He also told them what he had seen of the war and its aftermath in the cities in which he had lived. He talked to them about the school named after General Clinton B. Fisk and repeated the stories he had heard of the Christian soldier-teachers who had decided to devote their lives to helping the freed people. But he could tell them very little about the thing they wanted to know most, for he didn't know much about it himself.

Above all else, the emancipated country people wanted to know what other ex-slaves had been able to accomplish in freedom. Caleb could tell them about Frederick Douglass, the runaway slave boy who had become one of the great orators of his generation, a friend of leading American and British statesmen, and an advisor to President Lincoln on matters concerning his own people, but Douglass had emancipated himself thirty years earlier. He was not one of those who had been freed by President Lincoln's Proclamation. Douglass was a hero to Negroes everywhere, but these people were especially curious about the new freedmen who like themselves had just recently lost their chains.

In answer, Caleb could only tell them about the eager

young people he had met at Fisk. Then he would smile as if to say, "You'll have to keep your eyes on us and see how we make out," and he would open the blue-back speller and the lesson would go on.

While they watched him with pride, trying to see in the young teacher an example of the leadership they needed, he watched them—the people farthest down, the ones who would have to make the longest climb to achieve full citizenship in the land in which they had been born.

A month passed. Then a second month. On his weekends in Nashville Caleb sang with the group that Mr. White used as a choir for the Sunday services in the chapel of the school, but he was unable to practice with those who were learning *Nicodemus the Slave*. When the cantata was given before Fisk students, teachers and their friends in the city, he sat in the audience. He enjoyed the music, and he marveled at the voices of students such as Isaac Dickerson and Jennie Jackson, and the piano playing of Ella, but it only made him more anxious to be properly enrolled in the school and perhaps to blend his voice with those of the other singers in public programs. He was glad the school year in the country was short and that he would soon be able to claim his wages and enter Fisk.

Two weeks later he was reading a newspaper to the older group who came to school after supper when suddenly a sound of galloping horses was heard in the distance. The room became silent. Caleb put the paper down. He dashed to the window and looked out. Uncle Eph and several other men peeped out of the door. They saw nothing. Perhaps, Caleb thought, the horses had turned in another direction. He returned to the table, picked up his paper and began reading again.

Presently the galloping returned. This time no one

moved, and the sound came so near it seemed that the horses would thunder right into the schoolroom itself. When they were gone again, Uncle Eph, who continued to sit near the window, cleared his throat nervously and whispered, "Seems like I seen somebody dressed in white."

Caleb was as puzzled and frightened as anybody. As the teacher, however, he felt it his duty to keep calm. He paused only a moment before beginning to read again. The third time the horses and their riders swept through the cedars, a flash of musket fire startled the class and a bullet ripped the roof of the log schoolhouse.

A small, thin-faced man sprang from his bench and blew out the lantern. "We best be going home now," he said with fluttering voice.

"No need to run away," Caleb answered. "We're free now. We got a right to learn reading and writing. There ain't no overseers to stop us. No more patrollers on the roads. We got a right to stay right here and ask anybody what they want when they come riding by like that."

Uncle Eph tottered forward and put a trembling hand on Caleb's shoulder. "Ain't nobody paying you mind, son," he whispered. "Can't you hear them slipping away in the dark? Let's you and me go home too. We can talk about it some other time."

After all the others had gone, Caleb delayed long enough to lower the window flaps and close the door. Then he hurried out and joined Uncle Eph, who was waiting for him by a tree on the knoll.

That night all the cabins in the bottom lands between the hills and near the swamp remained dark, but not many of the folk who lived in them closed their eyes. The mystery of the nightriders had destroyed sleep. Aunt Delia and Uncle Eph sat with bowed heads beside their little wood fire. Finally Uncle Eph, who couldn't remain silent very long under any circumstances, began to mutter.

"I sure wish I knew what them rascals was up to, riding their horses like all that and shooting their gun at our schoolhouse."

"They must not want us to have school here," Aunt Delia reasoned.

Caleb scratched his head. He was stretched on the floor at the opposite end of the little sitting room. "We ain't bothering nobody," he puzzled. "We ain't causing no trouble. I can't see why anybody would want to stop us from teaching and learning. Everybody will be able to work and live better when they know how to read and write. Free people have to know how to take care of themselves. What would become of us if we didn't start learning?"

"You is young, son," Aunt Delia said softly, as if just remembering that the teacher was not an old man. "I got to tell you something. The war is over and all that, but some of the rebels ain't give up yet. They still fighting."

"They're not fighting the Union Army," Uncle Eph commented.

"No," the old woman said. "Looks like they done stopped fighting the Union and gone to fighting us."

Caleb sat up and rested his back against the wall. "It don't make sense."

Later that evening the small, thin-faced man who had been so quick to blow out the lantern when the horses approached, tapped at the door and slipped inside. His movements were stealthy and catlike, but his face showed no fear as it appeared in the dim glow of embers.

"What you find out, Percy?" Uncle Eph asked.

"Don't yet know what they was up to," Percy whispered, "but we got a good look at them, and we found out where they went. All of them was wearing bed sheets

141

and pointed caps to make them look monstrous. Seem to me like they was just out riding for devilment to scare folks. When they took off their sheets, a lot of them was just big, bad, overgrown white boys. But a few was grown men who didn't have no cause to be cutting up like that."

"Did you follow them?" Caleb asked.

Percy nodded. "We been passing the word along, too. I'll let you know if we find out anything else, professor."

The door closed softly behind the tiptoeing Percy. When he was gone, Caleb rose from the floor. "Well," he said, "we can't stop for nothing like that. I better get myself some sleep so I'll be ready to hold school in the morning."

He went to bed, but he didn't sleep much. Nevertheless, he rose on time in the morning, ate his breakfast and hurried across the bottoms, around the swamp and over the knoll to the schoolhouse among the pines. He was at the door when it occurred to him that the day was Friday.

Uncle Eph arrived as usual and rang the cowbell on the top of the knoll, but the young people did not show up immediately. Caleb waited a half-hour, an hour, two hours, but still he and Uncle Eph were alone in the small room.

"We wasting time," Uncle Eph said finally. "You just as well to go back to Nashville. Ain't nobody coming to school today. Maybe by Monday they'll be ready to come back."

Caleb agreed reluctantly. "Tell those you see that I'll be looking for them Monday," he added. "The grown ones too. I'll be back Monday for sure."

He struck off through the cedars toward the big road while Uncle Eph closed up the schoolhouse. By walking the first five miles and riding the next ten in a wagon with a family driving down from Gallatin, Caleb reached Nashville by early afternoon and went directly to the tailor shop.

That night at the Fisk school he told his experience to Mr. White and members of the choir with whom he rehearsed. All of them had heard about attempts by nightriders to terrorize freedmen.

Nobody was quite sure whether the masked men were up to pranks or mischief, but all took the report seriously.

"Has anyone told you about Professor Ogden?" asked Mr. White.

Several of the others indicated that they knew the story, but Caleb shook his head. "It's nothing to laugh at," Ella remarked.

"You're right, Miss Sheppard. It's serious—even if it does sound funny." The leader turned to Caleb again. "Professor Ogden has some very positive ideas, Mr. Willows. He woudn't mind my saying this, but I'm sure he wouldn't mention it himself. One of his theories is that none of us should keep firearms on the school property. If the South resents us and opposes our work in behalf of the freedmen, we will not improve matters by coming armed. However, our teachers have often been threatened by town people. You know about that?"

"I've heard about it, sir."

"Well, one of Professor Ogden's old companions-in-arms heard about it too. Knowing the former Wisconsin cavalry officer's present attitude toward firearms as protection, this friend sent Professor Ogden a small, shiny hatchet. All of us teachers considered it quite a joke, but Mrs. Ogden let the cat out of the bag when she revealed that her husband has been sleeping with that little new hatchet under his pillow ever since."

A surprised look came over Caleb's face, but he didn't laugh. "Has anybody ever bothered *you*, Mr. White?" he asked.

"Town people have said insulting things," the leader admitted. "They have jeered at me and Mrs. White and our two small children as we walked through the city.

Businessmen have made ugly remarks in the stores, but I haven't actually been molested. I don't expect *everybody* down here to like what we're doing. I don't expect many of them to help us with our work, but we're going right ahead. We're starting to learn another cantata this week. It's called *Queen Esther*. We'll give it in Nashville, and we'll invite the public. We'll tell our story during an intermission. If those who attend feel moved to help us by contributing, we'll be grateful to them. But if nothing comes of it, we won't stop; we have other ideas."

Mr. White broke off at that point. The choir members exchanged glances, indicating that they were used to Mr. White's habit of revealing his plans a little at a time. Caleb was too occupied with his own thoughts to notice the others. He was actually thinking how small by comparison was his little adventure in the country school.

"Is the rehearsal over?" Ella asked.

"No, no," Mr. White said. "We can't close on that note. Let's do 'Turn Back Pharaoh's Army.' Let me hear every word distinctly, and sing the song so as to reveal the hidden meaning. Are we ready? All right, Miss Sheppard."

On Monday morning Caleb arrived at the country school earlier than usual. The door was still closed. When he pushed it open, a slip of paper fell to the ground. It had been stuck in a crack, and when he opened the door it had been shaken loose. Caleb picked it up.

The paper was stained and old, but Caleb could tell by the blue and red lines that it had been torn from an old ledger or record book. On it was written a note in pencil by someone whose penmanship was big and bold, if not attractive. It said, KEEP THIS SCHOOL CLOSED. DON'T COME BACK NO MORE. Under these words a writer had attempted to draw something that Caleb took to represent a skull and crossbones.

Caleb put the note in his pocket, opened the window flaps, and, puzzled, sat down at the table to wait for his pupils to arrive. When an hour passed and not even Uncle Eph showed up, he began to feel restless and uncertain. He opened the note again and tried to imagine what could have been in the back of the writer's mind. Did this poorly educated individual really believe that a one-room log school for freed slaves was harmful or dangerous to himself?

Were these people who rode masked at night afraid of reading and writing? If so, why?

Caleb pondered awhile. Then he brushed the questions and answers from his mind. It all seemed so silly. Surely this was foolishness that people like Mr. Harvey or Mr. Coleman would never have taken seriously. Therefore *he* would not take it seriously.

But another hour passed, and still Caleb was alone at his little table. Whatever he thought about the note and the person who wrote it, he could have no doubt the folks between the hills and in the bottoms beyond the swamp had decided against sending their young people back to school at present. So he closed the room again and hurried over the knoll and down toward the house of Uncle Eph and Aunt Delia.

The old people were both smoking corncob pipes on their back steps, and Uncle Eph was whittling on a fishing pole.

"Well, I'm back like I said," Caleb greeted them.

Uncle Eph shook his head helplessly. "I'm sorry you come all the way out here for nothing, son."

"We know about the note," Aunt Delia explained. "Percy and some of them other menfolks you been teach-

145

ing seen it there yesterday. They managed to spell out the words."

"I want you all to know," Caleb told them slowly, "that I aim to keep school open till the regular closing time. The state officer gave me this job; I expect him to tell me when it's time to close up."

After a pause Aunt Delia took Caleb's hand and patted it tenderly. "You're my boy," she said kindly. "And you got some good notions too, but you can't hold school if the children and the old folks don't show up. These nightriders is acting mighty unpleasant; they done burned two houses already over the other side of the mountain."

"Percy found out they tarred and feathered some men in the next county and horsewhipped a woman," added Uncle Eph.

"The folks down here wants to learn reading and writing," Aunt Delia concluded, "but not if they got to have that much botheration."

There was another long silence.

"I'll walk you back to the big road when you get ready to go," Uncle Eph said finally.

Caleb began to feel helpless and defeated. He couldn't answer, but a few moments later he and the old man went off down the road together.

"Turn Darkness Into Day"

Caleb waited anxiously while the two men read the note. "I think General Fisk's headquarters will be interested in this threat," George White commented finally.

The principal shook his head. "No, Mr. White. We're not fighting the war any more. Even though we have named the school after the general, we don't need his military help in our work. We're here as missionaries and teachers. In trying to educate the freedmen, we are only doing for the South what the South will have to do for itself when it is not so weak. It would be unfortunate if we gave any other impression."

They were in the treasurer's office; George White was at his desk. Professor Ogden leaned over Mr. White's shoulder to read the crumpled and soiled note; now he resumed his soldier's posture and began pacing the floor. Caleb shifted his feet under his chair.

The treasurer frowned. "Yes, I know. But these ugly hints will have to be met somehow." He turned to Caleb. "Don't be disturbed, young man. We're getting used to this. Yours isn't the first case."

"That's right," the principal confirmed. "But we'll try to find out what it means."

George White's glance returned to the note. "Whatever it means, I calculate the state owes Caleb Willows some wages. By counting on that as a start, I think we can safely enroll him as a student at Fisk."

Caleb straightened himself suddenly. "But I'm not afraid to go back, sir. I'm not running away. If the state officer tells me to keep on . . ."

"Since Mr. White arranged the employment for you," Professor Ogden said, turning energetically and walking around the desk, "I think it would be better for him to bring it to the attention of the authorities."

"Whatever you say, sir," Caleb replied, his voice dropping to a whisper. But he couldn't hide his joy as he left the room a few moments later. He had entered the treasurer's office with a tale of woe; he went out walking on air. The knowledge that he could at last enter school as a regular student made him forget everything else. It was hard not to run as he went down the hall.

The rest of the day he sat with the students and listened to classroom instruction. He took no part in the recitations, of course, nor on the following day. But by the third day he began to realize that he was going to have trouble catching up. Miss Priddy noticed it, too, because she asked him to remain after the others left her class.

"You had a blank look on your face, Caleb."

"My mind was a blank too, Miss Priddy."

She took a moment to pin her nose glasses to her starched shirt waist. "I couldn't tell whether it was the Latin phrases or something else that worried you and gave you that bewildered expression."

"Maybe I ought not to start this late, ma'am."

"Not unless you're willing to put in a lot of extra time."

"Oh, I'll do that, ma'am."

"Well, come this afternoon, and we'll go back to the first part of the book."

Following Miss Priddy's lead, other teachers offered to work with him after hours, but it meant double studying for Caleb. He worked mornings and evenings. Every spare minute was used. He worked at his books sometimes till his head spun. While the singing class gave the cantata in town, he sat at a table by a kerosene lamp and agonized over the grammatical structure of several pages of English sentences. When Professor Ogden commended the singers in chapel the following day and thanked Mr. White publicly for his efforts to raise money for the struggling school, Caleb tried to listen; automatically he joined in the applause, but his mind was still grinding on a mathematical problem he was due to have solved by class time. And when a few days later the singers were away four days to present the cantata *Queen Esther* in Memphis, he scarcely noticed their absence.

During all this time the question of the country school and his return to it remained unanswered. "I've had a talk with the official in charge of state schools," Mr. White told him one afternoon on the school grounds. "He didn't give me much satisfaction. Looks as if you'll not go back this term. It's due you all right, but . . ." George White shrugged. "Are you making good use of your time, Caleb?"

An embarrassed expression came over Caleb's face. Good use of his time? But there was no way to communicate to Mr. White the agony it was costing him to catch up with the other students in the classes to which he had been admitted so late. "I'm trying, sir."

Perhaps George White realized that this was an understatement, for he paused before adding: "Whether the state office pays you for the full term or just for a month and a half, you'll have to wait till the end of the term for your pay. Professor Ogden and I understand that, and we don't expect you to pay your expenses till you get your money. But you needn't feel uneasy. Why do you smile, Caleb?"

"I reckon I'm glad to hear that, sir." Caleb hesitated as if reluctant to say what was actually in his mind, but presently he added cautiously, "Money is the thing everybody talks about. It's always money-money-money." Back on the plantation where he was born, there had seldom been talk of money. In Charleston and in Chattanooga where he had worked, he had seen and handled some money for his employers, but it had never seemed too important to him. He seldom connected it with the food he ate or the place where he slept or the clothes he wore.

"I suppose that's natural," the treasurer answered pleasantly.

"If I needed anything to remind me that I'm free," Caleb said, "all this talk about money and paying bills would do it."

"Let's call it part of the price of freedom. If you'd like to walk to my office with me, I'll tell you something else." They started toward the barracks unit that served for an administration building. "I can appreciate your eagerness to get an education," Mr. White continued, his voice growing more serious. "But I can't let you build up false hopes. Our experiences with the cantata have changed my outlook. I must tell you, Caleb—I must tell all the students who are struggling to continue their work at Fisk just as I've told the faculty several times in the last month—we can't go on as we've been going. With the limited work opportunities available to you in this community, very few of you will be able to keep up your expenses."

Caleb felt his heart sink. "You don't mean the school might close, sir?"

Back in the treasurer's office, Mr. White picked up the

wind-scattered papers on his desk. "These barracks are wearing thin." He took a moment to close the windows. They were out in the hall again when he considered Caleb's question. "School close? Well, if I didn't believe we were doing God's work, I'd say we didn't have a chance to keep it going."

"But you *don't* say that?" Caleb insisted with feeling.

They were walking slowly now. George White's voice confided, "No, I don't say that. All I say is it'll need a miracle. We might get through this year by cutting down further on the food in the dining room, by doing without fuel for heat and by asking teachers to go without pay, but the buildings themselves are falling apart. We can't go on camping like this. We need a miracle, and we need it quick."

The supper bell rang as they paused on the path outside the administration unit. "Well," Caleb tried to sound cheerful, "if you see it coming, I hope you'll tell me which direction to look."

The other sighed heavily. "There's only one direction: North."

But no miracle occurred during the remainder of that school year. Neither did Caleb fully catch up in his studies. The last weeks of winter remained cold, tedious and unpromising, and the early Southern spring brought no cheer. Caleb could see that the outlook for the Fisk school was growing steadily worse.

He also suspected that, as Isaac Dickerson had remarked, a bee was buzzing in the young treasurer's bonnet. To the students, as well as to the little band of almost discouraged teachers, it was plain that George White was pinning his hopes to something not visible to the rest of them. While all the teachers continued to work without faltering, several of them showed by their sad eyes and long faces that their own hopes for the school were dim.

Day after day Caleb listened as Professor Ogden tried to explain to the group of advanced students in the assembly room why their teachers were gloomy and worried. The number of students who tried to enter the Fisk school ran into thousands. All of them were begging for education. It seemed to him and his teachers a terrible thing not to be able to grant it. If schools like Fisk couldn't get enough money to carry on, the outlook for the children of the slaves was dark indeed.

These were disturbing words to Caleb, and he mentioned them to Isaac Dickerson, Tom Rutling, Green Evans and other boys of the singing class when they met one evening for practice. Except for Isaac, who was convinced that the treasurer had at least one more trick in his bag—a secret plan of some sort—they were as puzzled as Caleb was.

The subject had to be dropped when the girls entered the room, for they were followed immediately by Mr. White, and the practice began without further delay. Ella went to the piano, a dark shawl thrown over the shoulders of her school dress, rubbed her fingers to warm them and began arranging the sheets of music. The rest of the group drew their chairs into a semicircle around a small table on which a large lamp had been placed.

About an hour later Mr. White gave them a brief rest and left the room while they relaxed. "We don't sound good tonight," Maggie Porter complained. "I wonder if I'm catching a cold." She reached for an old brown coat she had thrown aside when she entered the room.

Jennie Jackson, a robust girl with a deep contralto voice, scoffed. "It's not that cold."

"We don't have the spirit," Minnie Tate suggested. The youngest of the girls, Minnie was also the prettiest.

Because she lived in the city and not in the dormitory, she wore a bonnet and had been accompanied by her mother, who now sat quietly in a corner. "We're not getting the feeling tonight."

"Maybe there's a reason," Caleb commented.

"A reason? What reason?"

Ella turned on the piano stool, "I believe the situation is worse than the teachers have let us know."

"Have you heard anything?" Isaac asked.

Ella bit her lip. "Well, I've been putting two and two together." She paused. "What I overheard was that Professor Ogden won't be here next year."

Suddenly all eyes turned toward the pianist. "Did I hear you right, Ella?" Tom spoke up.

"I wasn't making an announcement," Ella protested, embarrassed by the attention her remark had won. "It was just something I picked up while I was giving a music lesson yesterday afternoon."

"And what do you make of it?" Caleb asked.

"I didn't catch the reason, but I reckon it's because the money has run out."

Tom groaned. "Well, that's certainly the end of Fisk."

The door opened on the tenor's words. George White came in. "I'm shocked by that statement, Tom," he said.

Tom fumbled. "I only meant . . ."

Mr. White put Tom at ease with a gesture of the hand. "It's not a secret that we're going to lose our principal, but it is certainly bad news—to me perhaps more than to anyone. Another school wants Professor Ogden. None of us blames him for accepting this offer."

That calmed the group, and the rehearsal continued without further interruption. And with the coming of the warm spring days, heavy with fragrance, decked with blossoms, time moved slowly.

At the end of the term, Caleb was again faced with his

own problem. Had George White forgotten the country school? One afternoon a thunder shower and a sharp flash of lightning brought back to him the thunder of galloping horses, the flash of musket fire, and when the shower had passed he crossed the campus to the office.

The treasurer had lost weight in recent months. George White had also grown pale and high-strung in a way more becoming to a musician than to a business manager. Today he brushed aside Caleb's question with nervous impatience. "Don't let that trouble you any more, Caleb."

"I was thinking about school next year, sir," Caleb persisted. "I'd like to come back."

"You'll be back next year, all right. As a matter of fact, you're not going away." George White was obviously enjoying his secret. "The Fisk school will be without a principal for a while, but I'm still the treasurer, and I'll be responsible for keeping you in the dormitory over the summer."

"But I want to work if I'm going to be here, sir."

"Don't worry. You'll work. How you'll work! I don't mind telling you, Caleb, that I've fretted about Fisk's problems as long as I'm going to. I'm getting ready to try something else. And you—you're in my plans."

George White's excitement seemed to fill the office. Caleb got the impression that the young treasurer had worked himself into such a state that anyone would have trouble who tried to stand in his way. With another quick gesture, Mr. White dismissed him and began writing very rapidly on a sheet of note paper.

Caleb's heart pounded hard as he left the room.

Languid days followed in slow procession. Caleb knew, what many Southerners must learn, that the best way to endure summer heat and humidity is simply to yield to it. Fretting, complaints, pushing oneself to keep up a pace set by cooler days bring only misery. So Caleb yielded too; when he was not urgently busy, he sat down and fanned.

But George White couldn't relax. He was much too worked up over his secret. And before school closed, he called nine students together in the assembly room. Caleb noticed that they represented the best voices in the singing class: Minnie Tate, Jennie Jackson, Maggie Porter, Eliza Walker and Ella Sheppard, among the girls, and Isaac Dickerson, Green Evans, Thomas Rutling and himself of the boys.

"We're going into the North to sing," Mr. White announced calmly. "We are going to tell our story to the people up there. When they see you—they have never seen a group of eager, ambitious young colored students like you—they may get a better understanding of our devotion to this work. I believe they will be moved to make generous contributions. I believe it so much—well, you'll see how much I believe it. My plan is to have you ready to leave Nashville about the time school opens in the fall. Of course, all obstacles are not yet removed, but we'll have a new principal by then, and if I can count on all of you to make the adventure with me, we'll be on our way when the leaves commence to fall."

Presently the room was filled with assurances from the singers to their leader. Travel was nothing new to most of them. They had come to Nashville from states as distant as Virginia, Ohio, Louisiana and the Carolinas. And adventure, as George White called it, setting forth on new paths, not knowing what the end would be, was part of the daily life of the young and the recently emancipated. They were certainly not afraid of it.

There was nothing to do now but wait. Not until George White had discussed the project with a great many other people would he or the singers know how

155

their railroad fare would be paid and when they could expect to leave.

Meanwhile, it was necessary to practice. Every day Ella worked with the singers individually, making sure they learned all the part-harmony for the songs in their repertoire, and several times a week Mr. White called full rehearsals. Most of the time, of course, was given to learning such music as "Away to the Meadows," "Merrily O'er the Calm Blue Sea," "Friends, We Come with Hearts of Gladness," and "Hail, America," but no practice session ended without a few slave songs. The latter were not for program use. That argument had been settled by teachers and students alike. But since the leader loved the strong rhythms and rich harmonies of this folk music, his singers formed the habit of lapsing into it after the close of the practice periods. It stimulated them, too, so that everybody went out humming.

Between these occasions the singers saw little of their director. Mr. White was still holding consultations with people who might be able to help his project in one way or another. How well he was succeeding, the young people could only guess, but they did discuss it. They also discussed a number of other things for which Caleb had never before had much time. In these talks with the other students who, like himself, were counting on the singing campaign to keep them in school, he found himself growing better acquainted with these young people. They began to talk more casually of the experiences that had brought them to the Fisk school.

Ella Sheppard's story, for instance. One day when she seemed so tired that she could scarcely sit at the piano, Caleb suggested that he could possibly help himself if she would allow him. He had played the mandolin when he was a youngster in Charleston and thought he might pick out the notes on the piano. She moved aside, slumped into a roomy basket chair and watched him.

After a few minutes she commented, "You *are* musical, Caleb, really musical. How come?'

He gave a little shrug. "I don't know." He took a moment to tell her something about his life before he came to Nashville, then asked, "How about you, Ella? What's your story?"

"I'm not sure I can tell it as well as you told yours, but if we're going out to raise money for the school, I might as well practice. I suppose people will want to know about us."

"You were born right here in Nashville," he commented. "I've heard Mr. White and Professor Ogden say that much."

"My father ran a livery stable here before the war," she said. "He was a slave, but he got a chance to hire his own time, and saved eighteen hundred dollars to buy his freedom. But my mother was owned by Mississippi people, and about that time they decided to take her and me back to their state. Directly afterwards, somebody brought my father word that my mother had to work so hard she wasn't able to look after me and I wasn't expected to live. I was fifteen months old then." Ella closed her eyes, resting her head on the back of the chair. So her father had gone to Mississippi—she recalled as if telling a fairy tale—and purchased her from her mother's owners for three hundred and fifty dollars. He had brought her back to Nashville, and from that date her mother had been lost to her and him. Her father had later married another slave woman and purchased her freedom for thirteen hundred dollars, but again a complication had arisen. He was unable to get free papers for his new wife without journeying to a free state. By Tennessee law his wife remained his slave. That caused the trouble.

Yes, he could see how a woman wouldn't want to be her husband's slave, Caleb agreed.

157

"It was worse than that," Ella went on. "The trouble came when father's business failed, and he couldn't pay all his debts. The court held that my stepmother was my father's property and could be sold for his business debts. When my father heard what his creditors planned, he struck out through the woods with my stepmother and put her on the midnight train to Cincinnati at a little flag station called Guthrie. He and I left soon afterwards."

"So that's where you learned music?"

Ella nodded. "I went to school in Cincinnati and began taking music lessons. My father died when I was fifteen, and after that it was all my stepmother and I could do to make ends meet. The school classes and the music lessons had to be dropped. But every now and then I played for programs, and festivals, and somebody mentioned me to a prominent music teacher downtown and offered to pay for my lessons if the teacher would take me. When the teacher heard me play, he offered to give me lessons on condition that I use the back door and come late at night after all his other students were gone. And I wasn't to tell anybody that he was teaching me."

Caleb murmured understandingly, "Not so bad."

"Well, it was a little bit better than nothing. I was glad to get the music lessons, but nobody wants to be humiliated—even to learn music. The teacher always acted as if he was ashamed of himself too—always nervous, and jumpy, always explaining why it had to be like that and blaming it on his *other* pupils. Then the patron ran out of money. By that time I was able to get a job teaching school, and it was right down here at Gallatin, Tennessee, not so far from where you taught for a while last winter. I came out six dollars ahead for the term."

They laughed about this. One could only laugh. "So then you came to Fisk?"

"You see what I do here to pay my expenses—music lessons to folks in the city, helping Mr. White with the school music."

Caleb had always marveled at Ella's playing, the strong chords, the bright thread of melody, the unfailing rhythm, but he had never been able to see this slender, refined girl in his mind as a victim of slavery's humiliations. With so frail a body to have become the person she now was seemed to him quite wonderful.

Summer was here for sure now, and Nashville was an oven. It was impossible to feel comfortable even on the shady side of the barracks unit in which the male students lived. But that was nothing to Caleb now. It was impossible to think about hardships or failures or discouragements when one knew Ella Sheppard. Instead, Caleb began encouraging the other singers to tell him their stories as Ella had done.

Most of them were quite ready to talk about their experiences, and Caleb soon discovered that the slender girl named Maggie Porter, who was almost enough like Ella to be a sister, though a shade browner, had also been born of slave parents in Tennessee. But Maggie, who had come from Lebanon, had missed the harsher side of slavery because her mother had been a favorite house servant. Just before the war her master had moved to Nashville. It had been right here in the city that freedom had come to her. She was one of the three hundred pupils who had gathered in the old hospital barracks the very first day Fisk opened.

Then there was Jennie Jackson, the granddaughter of the body servant of General Andrew Jackson. This robust girl, darker in complexion than the others, had been free-born; General Jackson's will had set Jennie's grandfather free. But in her hometown free Negroes were

159

looked down upon, and when her father died, her mother was unable to protect herself or to get protection from a man who shamelessly defrauded her of her inheritance. So the little broken family moved to Nashville, and Jennie's childhood was mostly spent in service as a nurse girl. At fourteen she became a laundress, working with her mother, and after entering Fisk she continued to do this work during vacations. She paid her tuition by working in Mr. White's family.

Fourteen-year-old Minnie Tate, pert and small and pretty as a peach, had missed the harshness of slavery. Her free mother, living in Nashville, had taught her at home.

In contrast, the announcement of freedom had reached erect, dignified young Thomas Rutling on a plantation in Wilson County, Tennessee, where he had been born but six years before Abraham Lincoln was elected President. Tom's earliest memory was of painful separation from his mother, a woman to whom slavery was a hard yoke. His older brother and sisters were with him on the doorstep when their mother kissed them good-by and went away with her new owners. She was being sold as a penalty for several unsuccessful attempts to escape.

In the personality of little Tom, however, his owner's wife discovered a quality so pleasing that she began keeping him around the big house all day and sending him back to the slave quarters only at night. He carried wood and water, helped entertain the master's children, learned to wait on the table. He and his older brother did not leave the plantation immediately at the close of the war. Nearly a year passed before they heard that one of the older sisters was by then living in Nashville, and the two boys set out to find her. In the home of this sister, Tom learned his letters, and in Nashville he began to find jobs that a boy of twelve could do. After about two years he began attending the Fisk school, and in the three years that followed, his singing voice developed such a fine tenor quality that no group of students ever liked to sing without him.

Isaac Dickerson had been born in Virginia. In appearance he was a good bit different from Caleb and Tom, both of whom were slender and coffee-brown. Isaac was walnut, and he was heavier than the other two boys. His hair was softer, and he had already grown a small mustache. But Caleb found that Isaac's life before he came to Fisk was almost a duplicate of his own experience. Isaac, too, had made his way to Chattanooga after emancipation, and the two of them had worked in that city at the same time without ever meeting. Isaac had even taught a country school for a short while as had Caleb. Along the way he had learned to sing. His voice was not so deep as Caleb's, nor was it capable of the high notes that Tom could reach with such ease, but it was mellow and rich, and some of the Fisk teachers had called it the finest baritone they had ever heard. Isaac enjoyed jokes more than most of the young people in the school, but he never carried them too far, and at the proper time he could be as serious as any of the rest.

They were all courageous young people; they made good friends with whom to talk. Yes, good friends with whom to face an uncertain adventure.

When school opened in the fall of 1871, Caleb learned that arrangements for the singing campaign were practically complete. Professor Spence, the new principal, explained the situation to the students and teachers at a chapel period while Caleb leaned forward on the edge of his seat.

"A lot of people think we should not do it," the wiry little man chuckled. Adam K. Spence had been a professor of Greek and French at the University of Michigan for twelve years. When Professor Ogden, a "progressive" educator and a strong advocate of free public schools, left the Fisk school to accept the post in Ohio, Professor Spence was selected to succeed him. He was brought in to introduce the "college idea" and to "intensify the religious life" at Fisk. His eyes were blue and usually tranquil, but they brightened occasionally, and Caleb noticed that this was one of their bright moments. "These people think we are making a big mistake," the principal continued. "This campaign will tell the story of Fisk. We've emptied our treasury to help the singers put it over. There isn't anything left. If they don't succeed, the school will close. The American Missionary Association and the Freedmen's Bureau are both wondering whether they should continue their efforts to build a school in Nashville. They are worried about our buildings. These barracks are already wearing out, as you can see."

Caleb glanced up at the nearest wall. The boards were warped. Through the cracks came arrows of daylight. He turned and exchanged an understanding glance with Isaac, who was sitting next to him. They were remembering a recent night when Isaac had been forced to move his cot and set a washbasin to catch the drip from a leak in the roof of the men's building.

"That's not all they're worried about," Professor Spence went on, "but there's no need to talk about those things today. We've made our decision. It's up to the singers now. Since they plan to leave us tomorrow, I wonder if they wouldn't like to sing for us today."

Caleb went to the front with the other singers. Ella struck the chords, and they made the assembly room echo with "Battle Hymn of the Republic." After that it was impossible for anyone to feel anxious or uncertain about the outcome of the venture on which, as the principal had explained, they were all launched together.

Three carriages came to take the group to the station the following afternoon, and Caleb climbed into one with the other three boys. Considering the long trips he had taken during the war and immediately afterwards, it was a little surprising to him to feel his heart pounding with excitement as he set out on this new adventure. But he couldn't help feeling that this trip was different and, somehow, more important than the journeys he had made alone and just for himself. This one was for the school. It was—how could he say it?—it was for all the emancipated folk who were trying to learn how to live as free people. That was what made it important. That was why he felt so excited.

Professor Spence, Miss Priddy and the other teachers and students came to the roadside to say good-by, and the principal quieted them a moment so that he could say a prayer. The words sounded like a poem, and Caleb noticed that Professor Spence rose on his toes and lifted his outstretched hand as the carriages began to move. "Go turn darkness into day," he called after them.

Teachers waved handkerchiefs. Students cheered. A moment later Caleb and his companions answered them in blended voices:

> "Going to ride up in the chariot
>   Soon-a in the morning.
> Going to ride up in the chariot
>   Soon-a in the morning
> And I hope I'll join the band.
>
> "Going to chatter with the angels
>   Soon-a in the morning.
> Going to chatter with the angels
>   Soon-a in the morning
> And I hope I'll join the band."

Jubilee
Singers

Caleb heard an echo of those words two weeks later, but by that time the melody seemed very far away. A rolling countryside flowed past the window of the coach in which he was riding. It was a lovely country, but it was not like Tennessee. It was not like the Carolinas or any other part of the South. And this was not the train on which he and his companions had left Nashville. In two weeks everything had changed; even the faces of his fellow students looked different to Caleb as he sprawled uncomfortably in his seat.

Ella and Maggie, accompanist and leading soprano, appeared nervous and worried. Jennie Jackson, the deep-voiced contralto, and Eliza Walker seemed disappointed, if not discouraged, and Caleb could see that Eliza, who was only fourteen and looked as if she might have been a younger sister of Jennie's, had been crying. The faces of Minnie Tate and Phoebe Anderson were hidden, but their heads inclined forward and they were certainly not talking.

Nor did the boys have anything to say at the moment. The two tenors sat with eyes closed, but Caleb did not think they were actually asleep. And he suspected that Isaac's mind wasn't on the newspaper he was pretending to read. But suddenly Isaac crossed the aisle and offered Caleb the paper.

164

"Great day," he remarked, "your face is as long as a mule's. You look like you've lost your last friend. We had had bad luck at Chillicothe, but Chillicothe ain't the whole country."

Caleb accepted the newspaper and began twisting it. "We didn't do much better in Cincinnati."

"You mean we didn't raise much money."

Caleb nodded. "I happen to know that Mr. White used the last red cent of it to buy our tickets to Springfield. He don't have nothing to pay our board and lodging with tonight."

For a moment even the optimistic Isaac showed concern. "But you forget we got an engagement at Black's Opera House in Springfield. We'll do better there. I know we will. There'll be money for expenses after that."

"And if not?"

Isaac smiled hesitantly. "Don't worry so much. We'll have a good crowd in Springfield."

"I don't know what makes you so sure."

"Stop twisting that newspaper and read it. Look on the back page."

Caleb opened the paper and turned to a column headed *Mozart Hall Concert*. Presently his eyes caught the words, *It was probably the first concert ever given by a colored troupe in this temple of music.* "This is about us!" he exclaimed.

"Keep reading," Isaac grinned.

"I didn't think they'd put it in the newspaper." Caleb found his place again. *The sweetness of the voices, the accuracy of the execution, and the precision of the time, carried the mind back to the early concerts of the Hutchinsons and other famous families who years ago delighted Cincinnati audiences and taught them with sentiment while they pleased them with melody.* By this time Caleb's hands were shaking with excitement, his eyes skipping words, phrases and whole lines, but he didn't miss the comment that Jennie Jackson's rendering of "Old Folks at Home" had been *rapturously received*, nor the one that praised Isaac Dickerson's singing of the "Temperance Medley." Further on he picked up something about an *organlike bass voice* heard only in the choral numbers.

"That's you," Isaac laughed, noticing where Caleb's eyes had finally stopped. "You're the one with the organlike bass voice."

Caleb folded the paper. Outside, the rolling countryside was still sweeping rapidly past the train window. After a long pause he said, "Maybe you ought to show this to the others. It might make them feel better."

"Does it make *you* feel better?"

Caleb's eyes twinkled. Isaac took the paper and carried it to Jennie. Maybe, Caleb mused, maybe there was some truth to that old saying about a bad beginning making a good ending. Maybe the discomforts of their week in Chillicothe, their difficulty in finding a hotel that would accept a company of colored singers and the poor quality of the rooms they finally secured, would yet be balanced by greater hospitality in other places. Perhaps the small audiences that had attended the two concerts in that city and the small amount of money raised in Cincinnati were leading to something more favorable ahead. Caleb sighed. Perhaps.

Suddenly someone laughed across the aisle. Big, robust Jennie was waving the paper in the air. "I'm going to pass this around," she boomed. "I want everybody to read it."

"What does it say, Jennie?" Ella asked merrily.

"Oh, you got to read it, chile. Everything good."

A few seats away Mr. White stood up to rearrange the heavy gray shawl on the back of his seat, and Caleb could see that he too was smiling wanly. There was no doubt that George White had read the newspaper comments on the program. Nor, if Caleb was any judge of facial expressions, could it be doubted that the leader of the singers was still anxious and uncertain about the next step of the journey. The other singers crowded around Ella's seat, laughing and reading over shoulder, but Caleb turned to the window again and to the low, rolling hills.

He was afraid to let himself feel happy.

A few hours later the singers and their leader assembled in a wing of Black's Opera House in Springfield, Ohio. With them was a Miss Wells, a teacher in an A.M.A. school in Athens, Alabama, who had joined the company as preceptress for the girls. She appeared to be a devoted, though stern-faced and plainly dressed woman, much like Miss Priddy at Fisk. Waiting for the concert to begin, Caleb could not help noticing the dresses worn by the girl singers. His experience as a tailor's assistant made him unusually observant of clothes.

The dresses were of many colors and styles. This caused some of the girls to appear much older than others. Not all of them were flattered by their costumes, and Caleb suddenly remembered the explanation for these odd get-ups. None of the students who accepted the invitation to take part in the singing campaign owned suitable clothes for the tour. The problem had been solved in a way by Miss Priddy and other women of the Fisk faculty. These teachers, who during the past four years had suffered every possible hardship without complaining, had volunteered to divide their own clothes among the girl singers in order that the trip could be made. Not all the fits were perfect, and some of the styles favored by pale, middle-aged missionary ladies from New England created rather surprising effects when worn by peach, plum or chocolate girls under twenty.

The suits worn by the young men were less noticeable, though some had been acquired in the same way from the men teachers at Fisk. All were plain and dark, and Caleb felt that his own was quite satisfactory.

"Why are we waiting?" Isaac asked suddenly. "Isn't it time to start the program?"

Caleb turned to George White. "Isn't it time, sir?" he repeated.

The leader looked at his watch. "It's past time. I'll go out and see what we have." He removed the gray shawl from his shoulders and placed it on a chair as he left. The wings of the opera house were definitely drafty, but Mr. White's shawl was the nearest thing to an overcoat in the whole company.

Anticipation kept Caleb warm, but he noticed that thin, sensitive Maggie Porter was biting her finger nails. "Cold?" he asked smiling.

"Not cold, scared," Maggie confessed with a shiver. "Waiting like this gives me stage fright."

When Mr. White returned a few moments later, his face was drawn, his eyes troubled. "Awfully disappointing," he muttered in a tired voice. He stroked his dark, silky beard. "Awfully disappointing. We'll wait a little longer." He drew the shawl around his shoulders again and began pacing the floor. A puzzled silence fell on Caleb and his companions.

Fifteen minutes later the leader went out again. He was gone longer this time. When he finally returned, he was accompanied by the manager of the opera house.

"Something wrong?" Caleb asked anxiously.

"Mr. White is going to make an announcement from the stage," the manager said.

"There are less than twenty people in the audience,"

the leader told the singers. "If we give the concert, we'll have to pay for the opera house. We don't have any money left, as you know."

"I have suggested that you call it off and return the money that was collected at the door," the manager commented.

Another uncomfortable pause followed. "Where does that leave us?" Caleb asked.

George White looked miserable and dejected. The manager spoke. "Maybe I can help Mr. White find a place for you to spend the night."

"I'll make the announcement now, sir." Without bothering to remove the old shawl this time, Mr. White turned slowly and walked out to the stage like a man going to the gallows.

Caleb didn't try to hear the words he spoke to the little handful of people. Instead, he and Isaac and the other two boys moved toward the stage entrance while Miss Wells gathered the girls around her. The company waited outside till the building was darkened and locked. Eventually the manager and another shadowy figure joined them and then led the way down a dark street.

They stopped first in front of a dwelling house, and one of the men went to the door and knocked. He returned presently with a lighted lantern. Caleb and Isaac followed behind the rest, muttering and kicking the ground in disgust.

"Discouraging, he calls it. Humph—it's a plague sight worse than that."

Isaac laughed mirthlessly as he slapped his friend on the shoulder. "You're always singing about how nobody knows the trouble you've seen. Well, you'll be able to put feeling into it now. It's root, hog, or die for sure, big bass. But you won't die; you'll just root."

They fell so far behind that when they reached the

building in which they were to stay, the others had gone upstairs, and only the man with the lantern waited outside to show them in.

"This looks like a store," Caleb observed.

"On the first floor it's a feed and grain store," the man explained. "Upstairs there are rooms. The owner used to live there before the building was condemned. Nobody can live there now, but with singers and traveling folk like you I don't reckon it'll make any difference. You got to get used to rough spots when you're just knocking around. How about it?"

Neither of the boys answered. They followed him up rickety steps and down a hall to a room in which a candle was already burning. George White, Tom Rutling and Green Evans were exchanging puzzled glances across the flame. The man with the lantern left Caleb and Isaac at the door.

There was one bed and a rocking-chair in the room. Neither piece was in good repair, and Caleb began to wonder how five young men could arrange to sleep under these conditions.

"Do I see something crawling on that wall?" Green asked, his large eyes rounding suddenly.

"You do," Caleb assured him. "And it's just what you think. But that's not what I'm worrying about."

"We'll have to sleep in shifts," Isaac suggested.

"I'll sit in the chair," Mr. White offered. "I'm used to nodding that way. You boys can have the bed."

"I won't be able to sleep with things like that crawling around me," Green complained.

"Isaac and I will kill them while you and Tom sleep," Caleb volunteered. "After about an hour we'll wake you up, and you and Tom can kill bugs whilst we sleep."

It wasn't a pleasant prospect, but no one objected, and in a few minutes Caleb and Isaac were silently slaying pests while their companions dreamed.

When daylight broke through the cracks of the room, these two were standing guard for the third time. Mr. White opened his eyes and stretched his legs. A moment later he got up and put on his hat. "I think I'll go out and look around," he whispered.

As soon as he left, Caleb slid into his chair, and Isaac, practically asleep on his feet, shoved the two sleepers on the bed over a little and crowded beside them. They were in these positions when Mr. White returned.

"I apologize for disturbing you." The leader's voice sounded less dismal than it had the previous night, but it was far from cheerful. "I know how you feel after that struggle last night, but I've got news. Not much, but some. A Synod of Presbyterian ministers is meeting here. They will allow us to sing and present our cause if we can get the company there for the early session."

"Have you called Miss Wells?" Caleb asked.

George White nodded. "The girls are getting ready now. I hope you can sing on empty stomachs."

They could, and they did. They sang mightily, and a sorrowfulness of disappointment came into their voices. Caleb noticed some of the ministers leaning forward in their seats. The atmosphere in the church auditorium grew tense. When the group of songs was completed, Mr. White got up to talk, but the ministers wouldn't let him.

"No speech. More songs, more songs!" they cried.

After the second group by the singers, the men forgot that they were clergymen attending a Synod. They stood and applauded, and some cheered.

George White tried to talk above the noise, tried to say this was the end of the trail for the singers from the school in Nashville because their money had run out, and they hadn't been able to raise enough to pay expenses and keep them going. He wanted the ministers to know that the young people had had no breakfast and didn't know how they would get home. Everything was lost, he tried to say.

But the ministers wouldn't listen. "Nonsense!" someone cried.

Caleb heard another shout, "Nothing of the kind!"

Mr. White dropped his arms helplessly, but before he could return to his seat or the singers could leave the platform, a heavily built minister came down the aisle and addressed the chairman of the meeting.

"Mr. Chairman," he said in a ringing voice. "I propose a resolution by this body commending this noble band of sweet singers from the Southland to the favor of the Christian community in Ohio." That sounded pious but rather empty to Caleb. The strong-voiced minister paused, then added, "And this matter of expenses—let's not let them go away feeling bad."

The chairman chuckled. "I hadn't aimed to pass the plates this early in the morning, but if our young friends haven't had breakfast yet, maybe we shouldn't keep them waiting any longer. Will the ushers come forward?"

The plates went around during the next song, and at the close the amount was announced—one hundred and five dollars.

Ella's left arm was locked in Caleb's right and Maggie's right was in his left, and beyond these were the gay, tan Isaac with his foppish little mustache, the dark, sad-faced Tom and the rest of the singers, all locked in a line that reached from one side of the tree-shaded lane to the other. Two weeks had passed since that morning in Springfield when they sang on empty stomachs to the Presbyterian Synod, but Caleb still felt elated. Suddenly his big bass boomed, and the other voices filled in the harmony as they swung along.

"The wind blows east, and the wind blows west,
  It blows like the judgment day,
  And every poor soul that never did pray
  Will be glad to pray that day.

"Didn't my Lord deliver Daniel?
  Well, why not every man?

"He delivered Daniel from the lion's den,
  Jonah from the belly of the whale,
  And the Hebrew children from the fiery furnace,
  And why not every man?

"Didn't my Lord deliver Daniel?
  Well, why not every man?

The final chords faded. "Too bad we can't put that song on our program," Ella laughed. "There's so much—so much get-up-and-go in it. I really believe . . ."

"Don't say it, Ella," Isaac interrupted. "We've got enough other troubles without starting that argument again."

"No argument, Isaac. Not this fine day anyhow. I was just going to say I believe the slave songs have something about them—but—you know what I mean."

"Of course we know," Caleb assured her. "We all understand. But *you* know how Maggie and Green feel."

"I don't mind being laughed at sometimes," Green spoke up, "but songs like 'Swing Low, Sweet Chariot,' 'Steal Away' and 'Go Down, Moses' meant the world and all to my ma and pa when they were slaves. I won't have white people laughing at them just because the grammar ain't always right and the melodies seem strange sometimes. You'll never get me to sing them in public." His large eyes showed his hurt feelings.

173

"That's right, Green," Maggie approved.

"I think you're both wrong," Caleb cut in thoughtfully, "but let's don't argue about it now. This is too pretty a day."

They fastened their arms more firmly and began to walk faster. Autumn leaves were falling. Corn had been gathered in the fields. Among the shocks lay great golden pumpkins. Ohio's bounteous countryside, so rich in color, so favored by freedom that runaway slaves had nicknamed it "God's country," aroused only harmonious feelings in Caleb. He didn't want to continue the one subject of discussion that was always sure to throw the singers into a wrangle.

Half a mile away was the Ohio State Normal School, where Professor John Ogden was now principal and where the company of Fisk singers had been invited to rest for a week and get ready to hit the road again. And a welcome rest it was too, with time to read and write letters in the morning, pleasant walks in the afternoons, and evenings of friendly conversation after an hour or two of rehearsal.

Caleb had begun to feel weary himself at the time of their arrival in Worthington, and he was sure the others were equally worn-out. The singing campaign had been a touch-and-go affair since that morning in Springfield, not so discouraging as before, perhaps, but by no means good enough. One new town began to look much like another, and the trip had lost its first excitement. Audiences ran together in Caleb's mind. He could scarcely remember where it was that the bootblacks, occupying a row of seats in the back of the hall, started tapping their feet and bootjacks to keep time with the song and then joined the singers in the chorus of "John Brown." He believed it was at Xenia that colored students from the Wilberforce School came to the church programs given by the singers and then took the group back to their own school for meals and made them feel at home. He believed it was Xenia, but he wasn't sure. In any case, he was glad for the interlude at Worthington provided by the heavy-bearded, soldierly schoolmaster who had admitted him to Fisk when he arrived in Nashville more than three years before.

He also enjoyed the evenings in the Odgens' parlor. It interested him to hear George White and John Ogden and Mrs. Ogden recall their experiences together along with even earlier memories, and today as the afternoon walk came to an end, he began to hope that those stories would be continued once more after supper.

In this he was not disappointed. The evening rehearsal was held in the Ogden parlor, and the singing had scarcely ended when George White found a soft chair and began talking. "I was the village blacksmith's son back in Cadiz, New York," he mused. "The Cadiz grammar school is my only alma mater. But it wasn't the skimpiness of my schooling that I minded. What hurt me most as a boy was that I couldn't go on with violin lessons. Music was my real love—then as now."

"Don't think we haven't suspected it," said Caleb.

"But it's worse than you know." Mr. White shook his head dismally. "I'd never have been drawn into the treasurer's job at Fisk if Mrs. Ogden hadn't kept talking about the rich voices of some of the students and their undeveloped musical talents."

When Caleb showed surprise, Mrs. Ogden explained, "I taught a few piano lessons at the school when it first opened. Maggie here was one of my piano pupils. There was also a singing class."

"We haven't forgotten that class," Minnie Tate assured her.

"Thank you, Minnie. That was four years ago. You were much smaller then."

"But I was an advanced student."

CHARIOT IN THE SKY

Caleb noticed that Professor Ogden smiled in agreement. "You were the youngest advanced student," the schoolmaster explained. "Of the thousands of young people and older folk who tried to enter the Fisk school while I was there, not more than forty could read and write well enough to be classified as advanced."

"I reckon that was mighty discouraging," Caleb commented.

"Not at all, not at all. Learning to read and write without help is hard enough at best. When it is a crime subject to punishment you don't expect very many people to keep working at it. That requires a rather special incentive."

"And special courage," Mrs. Ogden added.

Caleb felt that the last two remarks were partly aimed at him. "Not enough to brag about," he laughed. He thought a moment. "At Fisk we talk about courage and fear and such things. In slavery time nothing like that ever crossed my mind. I just did what I was obliged to do, what I could do."

Professor Ogden shifted his feet under his chair. "You've given a pretty good definition of courage, Caleb," he stated. He seemed to be turning it over in his mind as he added, " 'What you're obliged to do—what you can do.' Yes, I'll accept that definition." Four of the girls were crowded on the sofa. Ella turned around on the piano stool. Tom and Green sat in the window seat a little withdrawn. There were chairs enough for the rest. "When you're doing what you have to do, when anything else is unthinkable, you get a different feeling, don't you? It isn't fear. It isn't bravery. I think I've had that feeling at least twice in my life, Caleb."

"Tell us, sir."

"The first was when bloodhounds forced me to climb a tree in Georgia after my escape from Macon prison. I went into the war as a lieutenant of cavalry. Later I was commissioned captain and assigned to recruit a regiment of Negro soldiers behind the Confederate lines. That's what I was doing when I was captured. Another prisoner and I tunneled out of the prison and made a dash. We traveled at night and slept during the day, depending on the folks in the slave quarters to feed us, hide us when necessary, and keep us moving in the right direction. Our luck ran out eventually, however, and we found ourselves up in a tree looking down into the eyes of howling, leaping dogs. I was sure my time had come, but I wasn't afraid. I waited for my captors to arrive and tried to reason with them. They treated us pretty rough this time, but we lived through it.

"Then not more than two years ago Klansmen invaded the school property at Fisk and rattled the windows of the barracks unit in which Mrs. Ogden and I lived. There were dozens of hooded figures, and they rode their horses right up to the school buildings. The wind was blowing that night with shingles rattling, and somehow the riders failed to awaken the rest of the teachers or the students. It was not their purpose to stir up a lot of commotion. I heard them say distinctly that they had come to get the 'Professor.' Mrs. Ogden and I had gone to bed early to save kerosene oil in our lamps. That's what saved us. Our rooms were all dark. The intruders began muttering something about the professor being out. They peered through all the windows without discovering us and then mounted their horses and rode away. My young wife slept through it all."

"But why didn't you tell me, dear?"

"That was before the baby was born—remember? I didn't want to frighten you."

She smiled. "But *you* weren't afraid."

"Actually no," Professor Ogden replied. "I knew the

177

danger, and I expected the worst, but I didn't feel fear."

"I think I know what you mean," Caleb whispered.

There were whispers of agreement around the room. All the young people could recall similar moments.

Before the group left Worthington, the Ogdens arranged a program for them in town, and enough money was raised to carry them a little farther on their journey. The following morning they gathered in the Ogden parlor again. The girls wore their hats. Outside, horses were tied to the hitching posts, and carriages waited to transport the group to the railroad station. Austere and silent as usual, Miss Wells, dressed in black, sat in a straight-back chair near the door.

"You've both been wonderful to us," Mr. White said to his hosts.

Mrs. Ogden blushed as she removed an apron she had put on while clearing the breakfast table. "Nonsense," she smiled. "We're as poor as church mice ourselves. We haven't done anything, but we've enjoyed having you."

"So where are you headed now?" her husband asked.

"We're moving in the general direction of Oberlin," Mr. White disclosed. He stroked his beard thoughtfully. "Sooner or later we'll have to ask ourselves a serious question."

"Yes?" Professor Ogden asked.

Caleb edged as near as possible. Mr. White had revealed none of his plans since that bad night in the rooms above the grain store in Springfield, and neither Caleb nor his companions had felt like asking. They believed that he would talk when he decided the right time had come. Now he appeared to be ready, and Caleb didn't want to miss it.

"After Springfield," he explained, "the question was whether or not we could go any farther. The money we received there and the contacts we made with the Presbyterian ministers have enabled us to keep going this far. Now we must decide whether we are justified in continuing the campaign for the bare expenses of food and travel. Our aim is to raise money to save our school.

"The National Council of the Congregational churches will be held in Oberlin—let me see, when is that date?"

"November 15," Mrs. Ogden said.

"It occurs to me," her husband added, "that a meeting like that ought to give you a good opportunity to set your sights. Leading Congregational ministers and laymen from all over the country will be there. They have a special interest in schools like Fisk."

"That's what we have in mind, sir." George White's tone indicated that his hopes were modest. "If cold weather doesn't catch us," he said, "we'll try to make Oberlin. Ella's shoes are thin. We'd be in a fix if our accompanist got sick."

"Another thing," Professor Ogden offered. "Mrs. Ogden and I have been thinking that you might do your cause a lot of good if you would include some of the slave melodies in your program. Hold on now, I know what you're going to say, but I want to tell you that people love those songs—those who have heard them. They are not just more of the same thing they have been hearing all their lives. They're something new under the sun."

Miss Wells stood up stiffly. "Don't you think we'd better be leaving, Mr. White?"

"We have enough time, Miss Wells. I'm interested in Professor Ogden's suggestion."

Maggie Porter crossed the room with a proud air. "I'm sure I would never consent to sing those plantation songs in public. We're trying to forget slavery, Professor Ogden—slavery and everything that went with it."

The small, usually quiet Green Evans almost sprang

out of his chair. "I'll never sing them in public, sir. People would laugh, and that would hurt me too much. I couldn't stand to hear giggling and laughing whilst we sang music that was sacred to our parents in slavery."

"I know what you mean, young man," Professor Ogden assured him quickly, "and I'm sorry I can't promise you that people won't laugh at some of the words. They are not used to the idea of colloquial speech in pathetic melodies. They'll smile because they are surprised, but I think they would cry more than they would laugh. But don't let me upset your minds. It is just a thought."

"Some of us do think the way you do about the slave songs, sir," Caleb explained calmly. "We're all mixed up."

Mr. White made another fold in his shawl. "Anyhow, thanks again for everything."

The singers began shaking hands with Professor Ogden and his wife. A moment later the carriages were moving toward the train station.

Several times before they reached Oberlin they ran into cool rains, and Caleb shivered for Ella as he noticed her cloth slippers. Green and Tom turned up their coat lapels and stuffed their hands into their pockets. When Green began to sniffle, Mr. White decided something had to be done at once. He collected all the extra money in the company, including even the pocket change which a few of the singers had, and bought overcoats for the two boys who seemed to be suffering most from the cold. He also bought a pair of shoes for Ella. After these expenditures in Cleveland, there was just enough left for train fare to Oberlin.

Persons attending the meeting looked with friendly smiles on the group of poorly clad strangers from Nashville. Caleb heard kind words as he strolled under the bright autumn leaves of Oberlin's trees. But no one seemed to be in a hurry to hear the group sing. Mr. White insisted that they attend all the general sessions of the council, occupying a row of seats in the back of the auditorium, because the chairman had promised to call on them for a number when an opportunity presented itself. But the sessions dragged on and nothing happened. A day passed, two days.

Caleb was convinced that the chairman, absorbed in the problems before the council, had forgotten his promise to the singers from Fisk. By ten o'clock of the third day, Mr. White was of the same opinion. "But we'll sing before noon today. He's forgotten us, but we *will* sing. Watch for my signal. We'll sing right here where we're sitting. We'll do 'Steal Away.' Pass the word along."

Maggie Porter gasped when Caleb whispered to her. "But that's a *slave song*. He's not asking us—here before all these people?"

Caleb nodded positively.

Perspiration appeared on Green Evans' forehead when he received the word. "Not 'Steal Away,'" Green pleaded in a whisper. "Of all the slave songs . . ." His words faded. He seemed ready to cry.

The protest on the faces of Green and Maggie could be seen in a less marked way on others, but Caleb was convinced that the singers would not actually rebel in public. Nevertheless, he waited anxiously for the signal. Presently there was a lull in the deliberations down front. The speaker took his seat and the chairman leaned over and whispered something in the ear of the minister at his side. The members of the council took a deep breath and stretched their legs in front of their seats. At this instant Mr. White glanced at his singers and motioned with his fingers.

A whisper of strange harmony rose in the back of the

auditorium. Members of the council in the front seats looked around in puzzlement. What was it? Where was it coming from? The tone increased in volume as the ministers listened, and their eyes showed that it was wonderful to hear. By the time it reached full voice, there was no longer any secret about its source. It was not from another world. It came from the neglected, oddly clothed band of colored students in the back row. The weary and perplexed members of the council turned their heads in pleasant surprise.

As they did so, Jennie Jackson raised her eyes to the ceiling and cried in an agony of deep melody:

> "My Lord he calls me,
>   He calls me by the thunder;
>   The trumpet sounds within-a my soul:
>   I ain't got long to stay here."

That soft, strange choral harmony rose again:

> "Steal away,
>   Steal away to Jesus.
>
> "Steal away,
>   Steal away home.
>
> "I ain't got long to stay here."

The second verse, as Jennie sang it, sent a chill down Caleb's spine, and he judged by the expressions he saw that he was not the only one so affected.

> "Green trees a-bending,
>   Poor sinners stand a-trembling;
>   The trumpet sounds within-a my soul:
>   I ain't got long to stay here."

It was a slow song with many lines repeated, and it faded as hauntingly as it had begun. But it left the audience in a bewildered attitude. Some mouths that had been opened to say "Ah!" couldn't seem to close. Heads that had turned to see the group of young people on the back seat remained turned after the song ended. And the chairman rose and began stammering, "I w-wonder if that was as remarkable as I thought it was."

A dim-eyed old clergyman interrupted from the floor. "I'm here to tell you, brethren, that you just listened to something the likes of which you never heard before."

"Maybe—maybe," the chairman continued, "maybe we should recess for a while and ask these young people to come to the rostrum here and favor us . . ."

The suggestion received hearty approval, and a moment or two later Caleb and his companions were standing before the council and blending their voices in "Swing Low, Sweet Chariot," "Rise, Shine, for Thy Light Is A-Coming," "Deep River," and "Roll, Jordan, Roll."

When the audience finally let them stop singing, it was lunch time, so Mr. White had to make his remarks brief. But he managed to explain the purpose of the singing campaign and to recount its ups and downs to date. Should they give up the effort now and go back to the school that would have to close if they failed to raise money? Or should they continue on their way, hoping against hope? These were questions that had to be answered, Mr. White told the audience in a disturbed voice. These were the questions he wanted to leave with them as they went to their lunch.

Much happened behind the scenes during that lunch hour, and it continued to happen throughout the afternoon and into the evening, but Caleb had no clear notion of what it was. All he knew for sure was that the prominent men who were leading this council were discussing him and his fellow singers. The longer this went on, however, the more serious he took the discussion to be. What could they be talking about all this time?

He and his companions huddled together under a large tree on the campus. Later they scattered and explored the countryside around Oberlin, and it was not till the next morning that the outcome of all this deliberation was revealed to them. Caleb was drumming on a piano in a music room, picking out tunes by ear. Isaac was reading a newspaper, and among the others two separate conversations were in progress, one centered near the window seat, the other around the sofa, when the door opened.

Miss Wells entered, followed by Mr. White, two patriarchal men with white beards and octagonal spectacles and a bouncy younger man whose red hair needed trimming. All of them looked exhausted, but the men were smiling. Only Miss Wells seemed displeased. The boys rose promptly and offered their seats.

"Never mind about the seats," one of the ministers said, extending his hand to Ella. "We only want to wish you well." He began shaking hands. "I'm Rev. George Whipple, from New York," he explained. "I expect to see you there soon."

"Some of you remember Rev. Cravath," Mr. White reminded them. "He was in Nashville the day our school opened. He represented the American Missionary Association and Professor Ogden represented the Freedman's Bureau."

Caleb had not been present, of course, but he had heard about the founding of the school, and he could see by their expressions that most of the others recalled the event. "I'm Mr. Pope," the bouncy young man chirped. "I'm Mr. Pope. I'm going along with you."

"With us?" Caleb asked bewildered.

"Somebody will have to tell them what's been decided," Miss Wells said sternly. "It isn't as if it didn't concern them." She found space on the sofa and seated herself between two of the girls.

"We'll leave that to Mr. White," Rev. Whipple smiled. "I'm afraid I'll have to have a nap now, but first I wanted to let the singers know that we are with them. We've decided to stand behind them. We haven't talked all night for nothing. You'll excuse me now?"

Standing by the piano, Caleb was the last to shake hands with him. "Thank you, sir," he said. "That's all we wanted to hear."

"But there's more to it than that," Miss Wells spoke up.

Mr. White's shoulders sagged. He looked exhausted. "I'll explain," he promised. When the other men left the room, he sank into a chair. "You heard what Rev. Whipple said. Well, that's it. We are continuing our campaign. We are going to sing our way to New York. We are going to tell our story in churches along the way. A collection will be raised for us here; that will enable us to buy more coats and start out. That's the story."

"What songs are we going to sing?" Green asked.

"Slave songs," Mr. White answered. "That's the understanding."

Green rose from his chair and walked to the window, turning his back on the group.

"I don't think I like that so well," Maggie snapped.

"I didn't think you would," said Miss Wells.

"I've said my say about the slavery-time songs," Green announced, his voice breaking. "It won't do any good for me to say it again. But I'm not going to sing that old music in public, sir. As soon as you can get somebody else to take my place, I'd like to go back to Nashville." With this he broke into tears and covered his face.

185

CHARIOT IN THE SKY

A stunned silence followed Green's outburst. Caleb could almost have cried himself, out of sympathy for Green and the sincerity of that boy's feeling, but he could not bring himself to feel ashamed of singing the slave music. He had never felt that way about it, and he had never understood people who did. Ella Sheppard coughed softly.

"And when you can find another preceptress for the girls," Miss Wells said calmly, I'd like to return to my teaching post in Athens, Alabama."

Another long pause.

"So that's where we stand," George White sighed. "We respect the opinions of all of you, and we won't argue any more. Some of us will continue the campaign. I'll send telegrams tonight and try to replace those who don't wish to go on."

Somewhere between Oberlin and New York City, Edmund Watkins, a surprised-looking dark fellow with a big voice, replaced Green Evans in the company and Susan Gilbert, an attractive young A.M.A. teacher, became traveling preceptress for the girls. Somewhere between these points, too, the students from the Fisk school began calling themselves the *Jubilee Singers*. G. S. Pope, the young man whose red hair needed trimming, went ahead of the company now as an advance agent and made arrangements for concerts. Caleb began to notice that as a result they were singing to somewhat larger crowds.

None of this seemed terribly important, however, for Caleb's hopes and the hopes of his fellow singers were now centered around New York; it was there that they expected to meet the real test of success or failure. Everything that had gone before, their ups and downs, their humiliations and hardships, the snubs they had received from strangers and the conflict of opinion within the company that had resulted in two changes in personnel—all this was preparation for the one event that would decide the whole matter.

In the days that followed the Oberlin meeting, it all boiled down to this: They would stand or fall on the slave songs that had thrilled the ministers attending the council. If this music should be approved by a large and critical New York audience, other audiences in smaller communities would want to hear it. This would mean that more tickets would be sold, money would be raised for the school, and the efforts they had all made would not be wasted.

Naturally Caleb felt nervous as the train arrived at the Grand Central Station. It was now December. The first snows had fallen, and New York looked like a big and unfriendly place in which to be stranded. He didn't have to be reminded that the company had used up all Mr. White's money, all the school's money that they had borrowed at the beginning of the trip, and all the money they had raised in concerts along the way. After paying expenses and buying a few clothes, they were again penniless.

But all was not lost yet. They had their experiences together to keep them from feeling discouraged. More important still, Rev. Whipple assured them as he met the train that they would not have to wait long for their big test.

"Sunday night in Plymouth Church in Brooklyn," the minister chuckled. "Plymouth Church in Brooklyn—do you know what that means?"

The singers exchanged excited glances on the platform. "I'm afraid we do," Caleb exclaimed. "Plymouth Church —whew!"

The students from Nashville knew, as did everybody

else in the United States in 1871, that Plymouth was the church of Henry Ward Beecher, the most famous preacher in America. Everybody knew about the Beechers. Two of them were powerful preachers, known for their strong attacks on slavery, and their sister was Harriet Beecher Stowe, who had written the novel *Uncle Tom's Cabin*, which had done so much to arouse opposition to slavery and to bring the struggle for freedom to a climax. In December of 1871 no name meant more in America than Beecher, unless it was the name of Lincoln.

"I help you to say *whew!*" echoed Isaac.

But there wasn't time to talk about it on the train platform. Carriages were waiting, and the group had to disperse to the homes in which they were to stay while waiting for Sunday night.

As usual Caleb and Isaac were roommates. They slept late on Saturday morning, and toward noon they went out to walk and see more of New York—marvelous, tall and frightening New York. Caleb felt smaller than an insect among its massive buildings, its streams of carriages and its rushing crowds. How could a little band of nine students from a small school for Negro youth in Tennessee make any difference to all these hurrying people? What interest could those important folk in carriages possibly have in songs of slavery? Caleb said nothing to Isaac about his fears, but his heart began to sink. Only a miracle could save the Jubilee Singers. How could he and Mr. White and the others have ever dreamed of anything so unreal, so impossible? What was Rev. Whipple thinking about when he and his fellow ministers encouraged them at Oberlin?

On the other hand, how could he explain to students and teachers at Fisk just what it was about New York that doomed the effort of the singers to failure? How could he explain to them what he felt as he and Isaac walked through the crowds? It would be mighty hard to go back and tell his classmates why he and the other eight had let them down.

"You're mighty quiet," Isaac said suddenly.

Caleb shook his head. "I'm just looking. Ain't it something?"

Before they returned home, they bought newspapers, and that evening Caleb discovered that each paper carried an announcement made by Mr. Beecher at his Friday evening praise service. The minister had told his people that he would present the Jubilee Singers from Fisk to the Sunday night audience. He promised that these children of slaves, these infants of freedom, would be worth hearing, and he urged all to come out and give them a fine welcome.

"Well, now!" Isaac exclaimed. "They must put every word Mr. Beecher says in the newspapers."

"He's a powerful man. I sure hope . . ."

"Now, now," Isaac laughed. "Buck up. Faint heart don't become you, Caleb."

Caleb swallowed hard, but not until the next evening, when the Jubilee Singers were grouped on the rostrum in the huge Plymouth Church, standing solid to secure the most perfect harmony, their heads erect and tilted back a little, their eyes upward or nearly closed and quite oblivious to the packed audience—not until then did he whisper his reply to his roommate. "Faint heart, huh?" he muttered without moving his lips. "Who's trembling now?"

In another second his thoughts were centered on the bass notes of "Turn Back Pharaoh's Army." Ella struck the chords and the program began.

At no time was the Sunday evening audience in Plymouth Church wildly demonstrative, but Caleb didn't have to be told that the hushed attention given to the

189

songs showed unusual interest on the part of the listeners. During intermission, Rev. Whipple came to the room in which they rested and tried to cheer them up.

"This is a cold, critical Brooklyn audience. They're hard to please, but I think—I hope you're getting to them. We'll know later. A number of music critics and reporters from the papers are in the audience. I just spoke to the man from the *New York Tribune*."

A few moments later they went out and did the rest of the program. No sooner had they completed the last number than a great waving of handkerchiefs began and Mr. Beecher himself rushed to the rostrum to say something to the crowd. Caleb failed to hear the words. He was too excited by the sudden demonstration by the audience, and too, the singers had begun to leave the platform.

The room behind the rostrum was now in an uproar. People had begun to crowd through the door. A stately gray-haired man reached Caleb first. "Sure, I cried," he smiled. "I'm not ashamed. Those melodies—they'd bring tears out of a rock."

When Caleb looked around, he saw that each of the other singers was in the hands of an equally enthusiastic stranger. Others were almost wringing George White's hand off.

Rev. Whipple returned presently, bursting with pride. "This is it," he exploded in Caleb's ear. "This is the real thing. They're still bringing in money out there—bushels of it. You may sleep well tonight, Caleb, you and your friends. The Jubilee Singers are a success—a very big success. And the Fisk school is safe. I guarantee you it will never have to close."

Old
Friends

Caleb reflected a long time on those proud words spoken by Rev. Whipple in the excitement of the choir room behind the rostrum of Henry Ward Beecher's Plymouth Church in Brooklyn. "The Fisk school is safe. I guarantee you it will never have to close." But nearly three months passed and many big crowds heard the Jubilee Singers before its full meaning penetrated his mind.

Indeed, it was in Nashville that the key to the riddle was provided. Caleb and his companions were surrounded by schoolmates who had come to the railroad station to meet them, and it dawned on him that all the people he saw on the platform could not have been Fisk students and teachers. Why half the city must have been there!

Many of those who shook his hand seemed as unfamiliar—as unfamiliar as the people who came backstage after their concerts in New York, New Jersey and Connecticut to compliment the singers and wish them well. The handsome brown youth who was moving toward him now, for example, was certainly not one of the students at Fisk school seven months ago when the singers set out on their campaign. On the other hand, he was not quite a stranger either. Where had Caleb seen that face before?

The fellow smiled. "Everybody in town wants to see you. The Jubilee Singers are famous."

"We didn't have it so easy at first," Caleb confessed.

"I know."

He knew? Caleb's forehead wrinkled. "You kept up with us?"

The other boy laughed. "A lot's happened since the last time I saw you, Caleb, but I hoped you'd remember me just the same." Caleb remained puzzled. "What became of that copy of *The Columbian Orator*?"

The crowd was now moving along the tracks, but Caleb stopped abruptly, dropped his traveling bag and overcoat and began pumping Phillip Sazon's hand. "I'll be John Brown! Where'd you come from, Phillip?"

"Don't ask me now. It's a long story. Besides, this is *your* day."

Caleb didn't try to pretend he wasn't excited. "What do they say about us, Phillip? Do they think we did all right?"

Phillip made a big gesture. "Look up ahead there. Look at the crowd, the carriages—doesn't that give you an idea? I'll take your bag."

Part of the welcoming group was already a block ahead, and Caleb could see them crossing the tracks and heading for the school. The singers were scattered among them, each surrounded by his own friends and admirers. Caleb took time to greet all who were near him before joining in the homeward procession. A few moments later, the first hubbub somewhat calmed, he and Phillip turned a corner and came in sight of the dingy cluster of wooden barracks that was the Fisk school.

"We didn't look for all this," Caleb remarked. "They must have turned out the whole school."

"And this is just the beginning." Phillip had always been a serious boy, but he laughed easily now. "Twenty thousand dollars is a lot of money. It calls for a celebration."

"Is that what it amounted to?"

"Didn't you keep a record?"

"Mr. White kept account, I reckon," Caleb shrugged. "What I can't get over is finding you here."

"Oh, I'll tell you about it sometime. What have you got in this bag, rocks?"

"Here, let me carry it a piece," Caleb offered.

Phillip's eye showed mirth. "I didn't say I was tired. I just wondered what made it so heavy."

"There's a new winter suit in it," Caleb smiled. "Shirts, shoes, galoshes, underclothes—all such as that."

"That reminds me. I got something that belongs to you," Phillip remembered suddenly. "An African drum."

"You shouldn't have bothered."

"My mother thought you might want to have it to remember your mother and father by."

"I'm much obliged," Caleb said. They reached the grounds of the school and took a path toward the remote barrack that served as a dormitory for boys. "The old place looks good," he sighed.

"I'm glad to hear you say that," Phillip remarked as they reached the door. "Of course, I don't mind it. I've been at sea most of the time since I saw you last. I'm used to a rough life. But you've been living in fine hotels for the past seven months."

"Fine hotels?" Caleb mused. "Only since December— since we struck New York and the Plymouth Church. That would be more like four months."

Phillip laughed. "Four months is enough to soften you up. Come in and get used to sleeping on a hard army cot again in a room with twenty other fellows."

"Gladly. Gladly."

They went through the entrance hall to the long room in which the cots were arranged in two rows and Phillip pointed to one that had not been slept on recently. It was at the end of the row. "Does that look familiar to you?"

Issac, Tom and Edmund were already sitting on the sides of their cots, yelling from one end of the room to the other and making a lot of noise. Caleb took off his coat and hat, went to the window and looked out. The view consisted of a windowless board wall about thirty feet away, a wall that Caleb recognized as the rear of the unit in which assemblies and large classes were held. "Yes," he said to Phillip as he turned around, "it's all familiar." He paused, then remembered something. "Say Isaac—you and the others here—Phillip wasn't here when we left. He's from my hometown. Phillip Sazon."

Everybody tried to do something for the nine students to whom the school owed such a great debt. Miss Priddy directed the cooks to prepare a special supper; she herself decorated the tables with spring flowers. After the meal, Professor Spence announced that there would be no classes the next day; instead, there would be an all-day picnic at Fort Gillem, the Union stronghold on a hill west of the city. The burst of applause that followed his statement was so loud it astonished Caleb.

"You'd think," he chuckled a moment later, "that he was Abraham Lincoln and that he had just read the Emancipation Proclamation—the way they cheered him."

Even Miss Priddy had to smile.

The picnic itself was soon under way, for the singers went to bed directly after supper, and by daylight they were well rested. A forty-minute walk from the school grounds, along twisting paths, through woodland, over two small hills and up a higher one, brought the procession to the old ramparts. There the ranks broke and games started.

By noon Caleb was as glad as anyone to find a place

under a tree within easy reach of food and refreshments. He was still there, his back propped against the trunk, his stomach full, a blissful drowsiness beginning to touch his eyelids, when Professor Spence spoke up suddenly.

"I wonder if we couldn't persuade our returned ambassadors," he said with a twinkle, "to tell us some of their experiences before we start playing again."

Caleb groaned softly. "Not me," he pleaded under his breath. "Oh, please, not me. I was just about to get a nap."

The group under Caleb's tree included George White, Miss Priddy, Ella Sheppard, Isaac Dickerson, Phillip Sazon and about a dozen other students. All had finished eating. They sat on blankets or mats.

"Splendid!" Caleb heard Miss Priddy's voice. "A very good idea." A chorus of approval arose.

Then the principal's quiet, firm voice again: "It would be easier to thank our singers if we did not owe them so much. There are no words for our feelings today." He hesitated. "When we received Mr. White's telegram after the program in Mr. Beecher's church, we knew that the Battle of Jericho had been won and that presently the walls would come tumbling down. I read this message to the students. Later we posted newspaper clippings on the bulletin board, especially that item from the *New York Tribune*, which called the songs 'the genuine soul-music of the slave cabins' and the 'only true native school of American music.' But your letters were too short. We want to hear more about the trip."

"There are some things we don't want to tell," George White remarked. "Some things we'd like to forget."

Miss Priddy's reply was prompt and sharp. "Don't hold out on us, Mr. White. We're entitled to know everything."

Caleb knew that nobody ever denied Miss Priddy anything when she spoke in that tone. He glanced at Ella and then at Isaac. They seemed to be waiting for him to speak. "You explain it, Ella," he urged.

"One of the things Mr. White is probably thinking about," she said, turning to Professor Spence, "is the trouble we had finding places to stay. In Chillicothe, our second stop, two hotels refused to accept us. The third was none too anxious."

"I'm sorry to hear that." A hurt expression came into Professor Spence's gentle eyes. "But you did get rooms?"

Ella hedged. "There were special conditions. The proprietor moved out of his quarters to make space for us, and it was understood that we would use the dining room only after other guests had finished eating. Chillicothe was just an example."

"You might call that the dark side of the singing campaign," Caleb commented lightly, hoping to introduce a brighter note. "But it was always with us," he added honestly. "We kept meeting people who, for some reason or other, were bent on keeping us from eating or sleeping. I'll never understand that."

"The breaking of bread together," Professor Spence remarked calmly, "is one of the oldest symbols of human friendship and brotherhood. The other attitude—well, it's the opposite."

Isaac, who was sprawled on the ground, pulled himself up on one elbow. "The worst thing of that kind happened in Newark, New Jersey, while we were having one of our best weeks. Maybe that's why I felt it worse. After New York we went to Connecticut, you know. Up there we sang for everybody—the governor, the Senator, the folks at Yale—everybody. In New Haven we had so many people there was almost nobody at a lecture which Mr. Beecher had scheduled on the same night. So he dismissed his few, postponed his engagement and came to our concert and told the people there how happy he was to see the day come when a group of freed slaves could draw such a crowd that a big thousand-dollar-a-night lecturer like himself would have to call off his address. He was wonderful that night in New Haven, full of fun, really overjoyed. Well, it wasn't much more than a week later that we reached Newark. We arrived at night. Our reservations had been made, so we went right to our rooms. Then, after midnight the proprietor discovered that we were not a blackfaced minstrel troupe, as he had imagined. He couldn't wait till morning to put us out of the hotel."

"But that's just part of what happened in Newark," Caleb added quickly. "We were pretty uncomfortable, plodding around in the snow that night and then sitting up in the railroad station, but the hotel keeper didn't come off so well either. Next morning all the newspapers reported what he had done to us, just the night before our big concert there, and many of his other guests moved out the next day in protest. More important still, the city council met on it and took that occasion to admit colored children to the public schools of Newark. On top of all that, our Newark concert was very successful."

"Yes," Ella added, "and it led to our singing before President Grant in the White House."

"You deserved that honor," Professor Spence said. "You were very brave. I hope the President liked your singing."

Ella smiled. "He said many kind things, sir."

"He kept us longer than we were supposed to stay," Isaac added.

The principal pondered the last remarks before he spoke again. Finally he said, "I'm not sorry you told us about the hardships of your trip. They make us just that much prouder of your success. And your achievement

197

hasn't ended yet. We are still receiving messages of praise and gifts as a result. And I can let you in on an important secret now."

Caleb's eyes brightened. "A secret!"

"Well, it has been, but it need not be any longer. One of my reasons for having the picnic here at Fort Gillem was to give everybody a chance to consider it as a possible site for the Fisk school. We can buy this entire hilltop with the money you have raised. General Fisk is willing to make the arrangements. Do you like the view?"

Everyone under the tree stood up suddenly to explore the surroundings. In the distance Caleb could see the other hills around Nashville and the one in the center of town. None seemed higher or more attractive than the place where he stood. "It will make a fine location for school buildings and grounds," he ventured.

"I didn't say anything about buildings," the principal smiled. "I said we could buy the hilltop with the money you raised. But a building—that's something else."

"Is it true," Phillip asked, "that there was a slave mart here before the Union Army built the fort?"

Ella nodded. "I can remember it."

"I was just thinking," he said, "first a slave market, then a fortress in the war to end slavery, then a school for children of emancipated slaves. It makes an interesting history."

Caleb turned to Professor Spence again. "But a building will be necessary," he insisted.

"Yes, Caleb," the principal replied. "A building will be necessary."

Later Caleb and Phillip entered the ramparts and inspected the interior. No soldiers were around now, but two workmen were loading metal into a cart. The boys drew nearer and discovered a pile of rusty shackles, some with length of chain attached. Caleb did not have to be told that these were the chains of bondsmen.

"It's been a long time since I saw anybody wearing one of those things," Phillip observed.

Caleb reflected. "Let me see—six years. Doesn't seem like the war's been over that long."

"It's been eight since I saw any slavery. Remember?"

"I've been meaning to ask you about that. What happened after you left us that night in Charleston?"

The sun was dropping behind the ramparts. "We'd better keep moving," Philip advised, "or we'll be left behind." Weeds had begun to grow inside the fort, and Caleb could not fail to observe that the place was being abandoned. The boys made a quick tour of the gun emplacements, the neat pyramids of cannon balls, the flagpole and the observation tower, and returned to the gate at which they had entered. "Your father put me on a ship," Phillip recalled.

"He told us that."

"It turned out to be a French trader. I had free papers, and I had money for my passage. The trouble was that I didn't know where I wanted to go. Between Charleston and New York I made friends with some of the crew, and I went with these fellows to a seaman's boardinghouse when we went ashore. Some of them were white boys, some brown, some black—they were from all nations. We spoke French mostly; I'd got used to hearing French at home, as my father talked it sometimes. Well, talking French with these fellows, eating with them and hearing them tell about the places they had been and the wonders they had seen—all this started me thinking. When it was time for them to put out again, I went back to the ship and asked the captain if he would sign me on. That's how it began."

"Did you see the world?" Caleb asked. Back at the main entrance to the fort, he and Phillip went through the gates of old Gillem, walking slowly. The rest of the picnickers had started down the hill, following the wagon path, and most of them were out of sight.

Phillip nodded. "Paris, London, Lisbon, Brussels, Barcelona, Rome—I saw them all. Africa, the slave coast, the pirate islands. We crossed the equator time and again. And I can remember orange trees overlooking beaches, harbors edged with coconut palms, waves bubbling by old sea walls, little red-roofed towns looking down at the water, sailors singing in all kinds of taverns."

"I'd like to travel," Caleb admitted.

"What are you talking about?" Phillip laughed. "You just came back."

"Across the water, I mean."

"There's a lot to see on the other side. Kings and castles, cathedrals—you wouldn't get tired of looking."

"But *you* didn't stay?"

"Home is in Charleston. My mother's still there, that's where my father's buried. It's the place where I was born."

Caleb understood. "Just another homesick boy!"

"I guess that's what you call it. Anyhow, when I got home, my mother told me about this Fisk school, and next thing I knew I was on the train. What do you expect to be, Caleb?"

"A teacher, I reckon."

"You teach them. I'll try to cure what ails them. I'm going to be a doctor," Phillip said with a twinkle.

The sun was sinking rapidly. Caleb noticed that the voices up ahead were fading. "We'd better walk faster," he suggested. "They're getting away from us up there."

The boys quickened their steps. Neither spoke for a few minutes and by the time they reached the school, they were just behind the rest of the tired students who at that moment broke ranks and dispersed to their own buildings.

"I believe it's cooler now," Phillip noticed. They crossed the grounds toward the boys' unit of the barracks. "Who's that character?"

A little dark man was sitting on the steps, twirling a hat on his finger as the boys approached. Caleb thought he looked familiar. "I believe it's somebody I know," he said. A moment later, when he was near enough to make sure, he threw out his hands and exclaimed, "Uncle Eph! What are you doing here?"

His old friend broke into giggles. "You wasn't expecting to run across me so soon again, was you?" he laughed. Uncle Eph had to stand up to talk.

"You're a long way from home."

"Shucks, Nashville ain't no trouble to me. I'm apt to show up almost anywheres." The old man seemed to bounce with his words. He never actually stopped laughing.

"But you haven't changed," Caleb added. "This is Phillip Sazon from my hometown."

That tickled Uncle Eph too; he had trouble suppressing chuckles enough to acknowledge the introduction. When he finally got the words out, they were very charming, of course. "My compliments," he said. "I'm pleased to make your acquaintance, Mr Sazon."

Phillip shook his hand. "How do you do, sir."

"How's Aunt Delia?" Caleb asked.

"Mean as ever," Uncle Eph laughed. "Just as big and bad as she was when you was staying with us in the country. She's the cause of me being here this evening."

The boys smiled broadly. "Well, if she sent you," Caleb declared, "it's all right. I'm on Aunt Delia's side all the time."

"I don't know," the old fellow hedged. "Wait till you find out how come. One thing the old lady told me: 'Don't take no for an answer.'"

"Come on now, Uncle Eph," Caleb smiled. "What are you all up to?"

"Sit down here on this step," Uncle Eph said. "We got to talk business."

"Is this private?" Phillip asked.

"No, you stay too," Uncle Eph told him. "You his friend; I want you to hear it. It's right serious." He paused and began twirling his hat again. The boys sat beside him on the step. "We heard how you been singing with the Jubilees, professor."

"I'm glad to be back," Caleb sighed.

"Now that's where we come in," Uncle Eph chirped. "You back home now, and you ain't got nothing much to do—leastwise not till your school opens again next fall— and that set my old lady to thinking."

"If there's something I can do for Aunt Delia, I'm bound to do it, Uncle Eph."

Old Eph's laughter exploded again. "Looks like we getting together here." He paused and nodded toward Phillip. "Is your friend a professor too?"

"I'm going to be a doctor," Phillip told him.

"You'd make a mighty fine professor. We need a heap of 'fessors out in the country. Near about all our folks want to read the newspapers. They want their young ones to get educated."

Phillip smiled. "They need doctors sometimes too."

"You right about that. If ever you change your mind though—" Uncle Eph broke that sentence in the middle and turned toward Caleb again. "We ain't had no professor since you left us, son," he said. "Things is quieted down now and a passel of them nightriders is moved away or gone to jail or thought up other ways to waste their time."

"Hold on, Uncle Eph," Caleb protested, putting his arm around the little old man's shoulder. "For you and

Aunt Delia I'd do anything, but I know you're not fixing to ask me to come out there and let the Klansmen take another shot at me."

"General Forrest done disbanded the Klan, son. For a fact—ask anybody. Ain't no more Klan. We been thinking about this right smart. Percy and the rest of them got the same idea. We want you to come back and open up school again. If the man in the state house won't pay you, we'll get the money ourselves. We got lots of children up there ready for school. We'd be mighty proud to get you back, professor."

Caleb's expression became one of indulgence and sympathy. "I know, Uncle Eph," he said. "You all are nice to me. But I aim to go to school myself. While we were out raising money for the Fisk school, we were raising money to pay our own way. I don't know enough to be a good teacher yet. I got to learn a heap more myself."

Uncle Eph became very serious. He put his hat on the ground at his feet and prepared to argue. "Looka here," he said, spreading the fingers on his left hand and making a pointer of the index finger on his right. "What's today?"

"May 23," Phillip volunteered.

"All right," Uncle Eph went on, looking Caleb directly in the eyes. "May 23. Two more weeks, and your school here will be closing down for the summer. Ain't that right?"

Caleb nodded. "I see what you mean."

Uncle Eph giggled triumphantly. "We'll just be ready to open up then. The cotton is all chopped. Nothing much to do in the fields till picking time. We could hold school from June to September if you'd come along and help us out." He turned to Phillip. "Wouldn't that work out nice?" he asked.

"Looks like he's got you, Caleb."

"I thought I was going to have this summer to rest up," Caleb lamented, half in earnest. "But if Aunt Delia thinks I ought to come up there and try to keep school, you tell her I'll be there."

Uncle Eph rose from the step and began bouncing again. "She told me not to take no for an answer," he repeated. He was laughing all over himself now. "She'll be mighty proud when I tell her you're coming."

"I'll be there directly after school closes here."

"Percy will be tickled too. Him and the others. But I better let you all go inside now. It's getting late."

In another moment Uncle Eph was off in a hippity-hop. Deep twilight enfolded him as he turned into the street.

Caleb and Phillip stood on the steps a few more minutes, then opened the door.

The Gates
Of Gillem

Caleb slept soundly that night. After the games in the
open air and the long walks to and from Fort Gillem he
was tired. He woke in the morning feeling happy. Was it
the shining silver in the windows that made him feel so
contented? Or was it simply that he was among old
friends again? Suddenly he remembered Uncle Eph's un-
controllable laughter, the old man's bouncing delight as
he left the school grounds the night before, and he knew
at once that it was the thought of going back to the log
school in the country that made the morning seem so
fine.

His former experience in that situation had ended on
such a tragic note that Caleb could not help feeling
thankful for a chance to try again. He thought of the
cedar trees on the hill, the cotton growing in the bottoms,
and the unpainted, tumbledown cottages in which the
country folk lived. He thought of Aunt Delia's pungent
mustard greens, game meat—rabbits, quail and possums,
caught in traps or shot with blow gun or knocked out of
the trees with sticks and pounced on by dogs, and the
fish Aunt Delia and Uncle Eph caught while Caleb was
at school. Certainly the food out there was more abun-
dant and appealing than the plain fare in the Fisk dining
room, but Caleb knew he wouldn't have said yes just on
account of Aunt Delia's cooking.

CHARIOT IN THE SKY

No, it was the other reason. Out there under the cedars he had left a job unfinished. He would not be satisfied till that school was running again. When he went there to work before, he went to earn money to pay his way at Fisk. Now he didn't have to worry about school expenses. The singing campaign had taken care of all that for the students concerned. He was going now just for the good he could do. It was a happy thought: Going back to complete a job he had left more than a year before.

The other boys in the long rows of beds were still asleep. Caleb turned over and began to remember other unfinished matters in his life. His own schooling needed to be completed. Yes, he would have to come back to Fisk in the autumn and study hard. But that would not be difficult now that the expenses were taken care of. A much harder problem came to mind; perhaps Phillip reminded him of it. It was the task of finding his mother and father. At the close of the war he had gone all the way to Charleston from Chattanooga to look for them. Now that things were more settled and Phillip had brought him the drum, he thought of them again. He would have to try to find his parents. Somewhere—somewhere they would be looking for him. They would be older, and they would expect a young man like himself to try to find them. Maybe they needed him.

He wouldn't think about it anymore now because it made him sad, and he didn't want to show a long face to the other boys; he would keep it in the back of his mind till he returned to the country school. Out there among the cedars he would think about his parents again and try to figure out a way to find them. He threw the cover back and put his feet on the floor. In the same instant the rising bell rang and all the boys began to squirm on their cots and rub the sleep out of their eyes.

A few beds away Isaac began to groan. "No, no. I

can't, I can't. It's cruel." He rolled over and put the pillow on top of his head.

Caleb was on his feet now, and he responded by going to the bed of his singing companion and snatching the pillow from Isaac's hands: "What's wrong, big friend?"

"I'm ruined." Isaac lamented. "The singing campaign has spoiled me. I'll never be able to get up at such hours as this again."

Phillip laughed. He was on the side of his cot, pulling on socks. "You should have gone to sea instead, like I did."

"Maybe a little cold water would help," Caleb taunted.

Instantly Isaac was wide-awake and sitting upright. "Never mind, Caleb. None of your helpful notions, thanks."

From one end of the room to the other bed covers were flying, bare feet thumping the floor and nimble, long-legged boys were stepping into their school pants, reaching for towels, racing to the washbasins or waiting for turns. Caleb, who had been awake longer, remained a step ahead of the rest. He finished washing and began drying his face.

"About that drum," he said to Phillip. "Where'd you say you put it?"

Phillip knelt on the floor and reached under his cot. "Glad you reminded me," he said, bringing the old tom-tom out. "Do you aim to take it to the country school with you?"

Caleb thought a moment. Then he shook his head. "I believe I'll ask Professor Spence to keep it."

Now Phillip was at the washbasin, pouring water from a pitcher. "Too bad you have to leave so soon," he said as Caleb returned to his cot and began to put on his shirt and necktie.

"Leave?" Isaac called. "Where you going, Caleb?"

Caleb laughed. "The country school, where I was before."

"But your expenses are taken care of now," Tom spoke up.

"I might as well be doing something while I'm waiting for school to open in September."

"He can't get out of it," Phillip explained smilingly. "The old fellow was waiting for him at the door last night."

"Hope you don't come back faster'n you go," Isaac commented, remembering his own experiences as well as Caleb's earlier attempt to teach school in the outlying communities, where there was still passionate opposition to any efforts to instruct freedmen.

"If I get in a tight spot," Caleb grinned, "I'll send for you."

Moments were passing rapidly. Breakfast would soon be on the tables in the dining room. The boys were all keenly aware of this. The room grew steadily noisier. Presently the uproar put an end to all connected conversation. Less than five minutes later Caleb and Phillip were leading the line of boys headed for the dining room.

That afternoon Caleb knocked on the door of the principal's office. Professor Spence's soft, cultivated voice invited him to come in.

"There are two things, sir—if you have the time," Caleb said hurriedly.

"Of course I have time, Caleb. What's that under your arm?"

Caleb placed the African drum on the desk. "This is one of the things I'd like to mention." He noticed a pile of papers and letters in front of the principal. "I hate to take your time, sir."

"Sit down, Caleb," Professor Spence said rather positively. He shoved aside the heap of letters. "We'll worry about these later."

Before accepting the chair, Caleb thumped the drum a few times. "It's African," he explained. "My father . . ." He broke off. "I didn't find my people after the war, sir."

"I understand, Caleb."

"Last time I was with them, my father thought I might like to keep this thing with me. If you can tell me what to do with it, sir, I'll sure be much obliged." He smiled. "I don't want to throw it away. Same time, I don't know how I'm going to keep up with it."

"A real African drum?"

Caleb nodded. "My father worked on the docks in Charleston. Sometimes the sailors gave him things they brought across with them."

Professor Spence's eyes turned toward the window where a square of intensely blue sky was framed. He seemed completely unhurried. "If you'd like to leave it with me, Caleb, I think I can find a use for your keepsake," he said deliberately.

"I'll be much obliged to you, sir."

"That building you mentioned at the picnic, Caleb," the principal continued. "I'm still thinking about it. These old barracks are wearing out. Look up there." He pointed to a crack where daylight peeped through the ceiling. "That's not all. The weatherboarding is falling apart. But even if the units were in good repair, as they were when the Union Army put them up, they would still be a poor excuse for a school. They aren't built right. I don't have to tell you that—after all the schools you've seen while traveling in the North with the singers."

"These are just a little bit better than no building at all, sir."

Professor Spence rose from his chair and went to the window, his hands locked behind his back. A wistful expression appeared on his features. Caleb was sure the man was dreaming. After a long pause he confessed, "I'm thinking about the building, Caleb. I can see it on the spot where Fort Gillem stands. It will be a beautiful building with a bell tower on one corner. Inside there will be handsome stairs. And the woodwork—I'd like to see wood from the trees of every land in that building. Perhaps the wood in this drum can be used to represent Africa."

"But it won't be a wooden building?" Caleb glanced again at the place where the barrack's wall was coming apart.

"Oh, no, Caleb. I'm thinking about a brick building." After another pause Professor Spence returned to his desk. "You mentioned *two* things."

Caleb pulled himself up in his chair.

"I had a visitor last night, sir. He was waiting on the steps of the boys' building when we came back from the picnic." Caleb waited a second for Professor Spence to react to these words, but the principal's expression did not change. He was waiting too, waiting for the rest of the statement. "He was from the country, sir—this man— from the school where I tried to teach after my first year at Fisk."

The principal was still waiting. "Yes?"

"He asked me would I come back and try to open the school again now."

"What did you tell him?"

"I promised I would." Suddenly a wrinkle appeared in Professor Spence's forehead. If his face did not show disapproval, it certainly showed puzzlement. "I keep worrying about how I had to leave the school last time," Caleb explained. "Seemed like this would be a chance to make up for—for the way it ended before. I might not get much pay but . . ."

"I understand, Caleb, and any other time I'd be ready

to praise you for your attitude, but—but I'm afraid your life is becoming more complicated." Again he rose and went to the window. This time Caleb stood too.

"I don't understand, sir."

The principal took so long to answer that Caleb became aware of footsteps passing in the hall and voices in other rooms, beyond the thin walls of the office. "I'm glad you told me about this," he said finally, "but it does raise a problem. For one thing, it makes it necessary for me to tell you something that I wanted to be a surprise. I hope you will help me keep it a secret for a while."

"Oh, of course . . ."

"Well, it's like this, Caleb. That pile of letters you see on my desk is not routine mail, not by any means. And if you'll move the letters aside, you'll find something else of interest." When Caleb lifted the letters, he saw the telegrams, perhaps a dozen of them. "All of that in one day."

"What does it mean, sir?"

"In a way it means a building for the Fisk school, a building not made with hands. It means a Fisk University with all that goes with it. It means a new step forward for the freedmen of the South. It means, but I mustn't start dreaming again. Caleb, these are telegrams and letters urging us to send the Jubilee Singers out again. There is one from Philadelphia asking you to give a concert in the Academy of Music, one of the finest halls in the United States. It is signed by John Wanamaker and other prominent men of that city. Another is from the mayor of Boston on behalf of the group promoting the World's Peace Jubilee there next month. You are asked to sing in their Coliseum as part of that great celebration. Others are from Baltimore, Chicago, Cleveland—there is scarcely a city from which we haven't heard.

"Furthermore, the American Missionary Association's

headquarters has been flooded with requests for more concerts by the Jubilee Singers. Why, Caleb, there have even been letters from concert managers in London, Berlin and Amsterdam offering to promote a tour of the Jubilee Singers through Europe. I see in all this—but don't let me wander too far, Caleb. What concerns you immediately is that we have decided to ask Mr. White to get the singers ready for another tour at once. It will be necessary for you to leave next week in order to make a few stops and still reach Boston in time for the World's Peace Jubilee. Do you see what I mean, Caleb? That's why I say your life is becoming complicated. You can't do as you like now, even when the thing you plan is good."

Caleb smiled helplessly, "I thought I was free, Professor Spence."

That seemed to amuse the principal too. "Not entirely," he meditated. "Not entirely and not for long. We all give up a part of our freedom when we give ourselves to a thing we believe in. From now on you belong to the Jubilee Singers, Caleb—and to Fisk University."

"I'll have to talk to you some more, sir."

Caleb stumbled out of the principal's office, his mind in a daze.

Certainly the world was marvelously confused, he thought as he and Phillip left the school grounds the following Saturday morning and started across town toward the Gallatin Pike.

"Are you sure we can get a ride?" Phillip asked.

"Most of the wagons will still be coming this way," Caleb acknowledged, "but some of the country people are bound to be finished with their business and heading back toward home."

"That sun's a little too bright for a real long walk."

Caleb agreed. "But there's shade on this side as far as the river."

"And beyond the river?"

The mile to the Cumberland was nothing. Long, swinging strides carried the tall boys through the center of Nashville, and the smokestacks of boats tied at the landing came into view before Caleb got around to the explanation he owed Phillip.

"This is no wild-goose chase," he apologized suddenly. "And I'm not going to walk you too hard in the sun."

"I'll take your word for it. But you have to admit it's pretty mysterious as far as I'm concerned."

They reached the public square, crossed a street and began to weave through a congestion of wagons and carts. A comparable hubbub surrounded the markets on the waterfront. "The ferry's on this side," Caleb observed. "We won't have to wait."

A couple of minutes later they discovered that it was not only on their side of the river but loaded and ready to pull off. Caleb and Phillip hurried aboard. "They need another bridge here," Phillip commented, noticing the crowding of carriages, drays and riding horses.

"They'll get one soon, I reckon," Caleb mused, his mind wandering. "But about where we're going—it's not a secret. We're going out to see Uncle Eph and Aunt Delia."

"I guessed that," Phillip said dryly. "What I'd like to know is why?"

"Professor Spence made me promise not to tell one thing, but he'll announce it in chapel before we get back, so I can mention it to you now." Caleb paused. "The Jubilee Singers are going out again, Phillip. Right away. This week. I got to go with them."

Phillip seemed only slightly surprised. "What's the rush?"

"You should see the stack of telegrams and letters. We have to hit while the iron's hot. Fisk needs a new building. We're going to Boston to sing at the World's Peace Jubilee. After that, I can't tell you where-all else."

"Do you think Uncle Eph will understand?"

"I thought he might if you came with me."

"You're a slick one," Phillip smiled. "You're taking me along to back you up." He shook his head positively. "No, you'll have to do your own explaining, Caleb."

Caleb's face became serious. "That's not what I mean," he said. "I was thinking that maybe you'd be willing to take my place, once you saw the schoolhouse out there among the cedars and met the folks that live in the bottoms and tasted some of Aunt Delia's cooking."

"Wait a minute now," Phillip protested, holding up one hand. "You're taking me too fast. Remember, I'm no schoolteacher. I'm not even planning to be one. What's more, I never lived in the country. I don't know how I'd take to it, or it to me. I don't think you'd better bring that up. Just tell the old folks what's happened. You're sorry, and that's that."

Caleb did not answer. They left the ferry on the far bank of the river and started walking again. Presently Caleb heard a clatter behind. When he turned, a mule-drawn wagon appeared in a cloud of dust, and he couldn't help thinking of the prophet's chariot that came down from the sky and that was mentioned in so many of the slave songs as a symbol of deliverance from bondage. The shape of the sun-lit dust cloud around this wagon and the alertness of the two white mules made it look as if it had just touched the ground. "This is for us," he told Phillip.

The driver of the wagon pulled his team to a stop as the boys hailed him. He was a city man in appearance, and Caleb now saw that his wagon had springs under its two seats. A moment later he noticed fishing poles sticking out the back. "I'm heading for Indian Lake," he announced cheerfully. "You can ride as far as I go."

"Much obliged." Caleb and Phillip climbed over the wheel and slid into the back seat. "That suits us fine. We walk from there."

A bird dog, sleeping on the seat beside the driver, rose up with a growl, looked the boys over and then closed his eyes again. Caleb noticed a squirrel gun on the floor of the wagon beside the fishing poles. There was also a lunch basket, a jug, pails of bait and other equipment. The driver, who smoked a pipe and whose hat tilted forward to shade his face, was a picture of contentment as he shook his lines and clucked to the white mules. "I'm going to have myself a time," he explained. "Nobody but me up there on Indian Lake, but I won't be lonesome. I got everything I need. I even got my guitar covered up under them blankets. These next two or three days is mine—mine!"

The boys laughed with him. "I know how you feel," said Phillip.

"Yes, sir, I'm going to fish till I don't want to fish no more. Then I'm going to set my lines and take my dog and go hunting. I'm going to have fish for breakfast, squirrel for lunch, and birds for supper. Then I'm going to play my guitar and look at the stars and go to sleep." A warm glow seemed to come over the well-dressed city man. He was dark and middle-aged. "What'd you all say back there?"

"We didn't say nothing," Caleb answered.

"I better hush my fuss before I get too happy," the driver laughed. "Come on, mules. Let's go from here." He gave the lines a strong shake.

Caleb and Phillip exchanged glances as they settled back for the long ride. "He's got a right to feel good," Phillip whispered.

Caleb nodded as the mules went into a trot.

It was late afternoon when they left the man who had everything he needed for a happy weekend. He waved to them from his wagon as he turned into a side road, and they continued down the pike. In another hour they were on a country lane. Soon they came to a crossroads store, with riding horses tied to the hitching bar in front and half a dozen carts under near-by trees. There was a bench in front of the store. Some of the faces he saw looked vaguely familiar to Caleb.

"I don't like their looks," Phillip said critically.

Caleb shrugged. "Country people always stare at you. You get so you don't notice it after a while."

They continued another mile on a twisting wagon path and then took a footpath into the woods. Half an hour later they hit a big road again, and Caleb saw two horses tied in a thicket. He did not comment, but it struck him as odd that riders were not in sight. A moment or two later the explanation was clear. The thicket rustled, and two quaint, dimly recollected characters parted the twigs and stepped onto the road.

"Remember us?" a thin voice piped.

Caleb and Phillip paused. One of the men was tall, pimply and carrot-colored. The other was so short he seemed to be squatting. He was midnight-dark. Their clothes were flashy, especially the vest and caps. Where had Caleb seen this pair before? Suddenly he remembered: Pinky and Blue, the fellows who had tried to strike up an acquaintance with him in front of the Fisk school when it seemed as if he would not be able to attend because of lack of money.

"I didn't hardly know you in those riding clothes," Caleb fumbled.

Blue's manner became oily. "Still your friends," he whined.

"Well, step aside then; we're in a hurry," Caleb said.

They showed no intention of moving. "How come you can't let well-enough do?" Blue asked impatiently. "Ain't you the one the nightriders run away from here?"

"Is it any of their business?" Phillip asked sharply.

Caleb shook his head. "None that I know of."

Pinky's eyes shifted. "I wouldn't say that. We your friends. That makes it some of our business."

"Sure," Blue piped. "We don't want you to get hurt."

"Get out of the way," snapped Phillip.

Pinky looked at Caleb. "Better talk to your friend there. He sounds like he wants to get bad. If the night-riders don't want no school here for colored folks, that's the way it's got to be. We can't do nothing about it."

Caleb saw Phillip's jaw set, his teeth held firmly together as he hissed angrily, "You low-down varmints. Who're you trying to help? Get from in front of me, you snakes." The words were scarcely uttered before his fist shot out. It landed on the side of the tall fellow's face, and Pinky had to take two steps backward to keep from falling.

"Oh, that's how it is!" Blue squeaked gleefully. "They want to play rough, huh? Well, I'm a bad boy myself. Count me in on this, professor." He doubled his fists as he moved toward Caleb. His rounded shoulders looked uncommonly powerful as he advanced, but by now Phillip had hit Pinky again, and there was nothing for Caleb to do but face the menace. Blue's left hand flicked toward him, and Caleb ducked. As he did so, he felt Blue's other fist planted solidly against his stomach. Caleb gasped, but he managed to shove the fellow back. In another second he had his bearings again, and fists began working from both sides.

Presently Caleb lost sight of everything but the crouched, belligerent figure with which he had to deal. He was taller than Blue by half a foot at least, but his

217

weight and width could not match those of his opponent. Blue's arm muscles bulged his coat sleeves, and he came forward like one who was used to this business. His head lowered, the bill of his cap turned sideways, he maneuvered confidently in a weaving motion. Caleb, however, had only his anger to guide him and his determination not to be bullied by these strange individuals who seemed to have their own reasons for annoying him and getting in his way.

When Blue hit him again, a sharp thump against the head, even this went out of his mind, and he charged madly into his foe. Where the blows fell and how much damage they did, he could not see. He was half-blinded by Blue's last punch. Other blows were coming at him, and the time to think had passed. His enemy was crowding him. Caleb's fists tightened. His own arms started working like pistons.

Sometimes he fanned the air. Sometimes his arms became entangled with Blue's so that he clinched and wrestled momentarily. But when he broke away, he promptly began pumping his fists again. Sometimes— sometimes they struck home. His knuckles began to smart as if they had been in contact with something hard. Had it been Blue's head?

The action was furious for a while—Caleb couldn't tell how long. Then it slowed down, his head cleared, and he realized that his arms were weary, his breathing hard. He could also see that Blue was panting, that he had lost his cap. Blue's arms, too, were hanging wearily, and one of his eyes was closed. Caleb began to think: He's played out. He's whipped. I could—I could—

Suddenly he heard Phillip laugh. "Well, Tall-and-ugly, Squatty-and-mean—you two had enough or do you want some more?"

Seeing Phillip standing triumphantly at the side of the

road, while Pinky muttered and cursed under his breath, completely revived Caleb's confidence. He raised his right fist for the finisher, but paused. "Get out of the way," he commanded. Blue didn't move, but the boys could see there was no fight in him.

They were kneeling beside water a few minutes later, washing their hands and faces and trying to look presentable. The sun was low behind the hill, and the cottage of Uncle Eph and Aunt Delia was only a few hundred yards away. The trip they had made since morning had been long and tiring, but it was the encounter with Pinky and Blue that had exhausted them finally and accounted for their messed-up appearance.

"Well," Phillip said, "they got what was coming to them."

Caleb rose slowly, dried his face with his handkerchief and rolled his sleeves down. "They were still mumbling when we left."

"Fools like that never know when they've had enough."

"I didn't count on running into anything like this," Caleb apologized.

"Never mind about that. It's helped me to make up my mind."

"How you mean?"

They were now walking along the water. "If those rascals want any more trouble, I'm their man," Phillip said angrily. "I'll stay here and open up the school if you want me to. It would do me good to meet up with that pair again."

At that moment Caleb saw a lighted lamp appear in the window of the cottage they were approaching. "I believe you're braver than I am."

Phillip smiled. "Not braver, crazier. I just get madder, I think."

They reached the door and Caleb knocked. Aunt Delia

welcomed them with open arms while Uncle Eph's laughter rose in the background. The house was fairly bursting with cooking odors.

There was a musical note in the old woman's stern voice. "You're in time for supper," she said.

"I ought to warn you," Phillip said, "we haven't eaten since breakfast."

"And we've come a long way," Caleb added.

This pleased her. "I'll just be a minute," she sang. "Everything's ready." She left them in the front room with Uncle Eph, and the boys sank into the chairs he offered.

"We wasn't looking for *two* professors," the old man chuckled, "but we glad to have you both. Powerful glad. Fact of the matter, it might take more than two of you to keep school open." It was obviously a serious matter, but if you didn't know Uncle Eph's way of talking, you might have thought he was joking. His remark ended with a little laugh that trailed off gradually.

"What you mean, Uncle Eph?" Caleb asked.

The old man rubbed his hand over his face to remove the smile. "Things ain't quite as settled now as they was when I talked to you all last week."

Caleb wondered what bearing the presence of Pinky and Blue in the community had to do with it. "I'm sorry to hear that," he said.

"We going right ahead though," Uncle Eph assured. "We ain't stopping for nothing this time. Percy and me done talked to all the families round here that's got young ones that ought to be learning, and the biggest part of them is lined up with us. We going to have a school for you."

"There's something I have to tell you," Caleb said. "I brought Phillip along—"

"I'm ready to feed you now," Aunt Delia interrupted from the kitchen. "Come on in, you all."

"We better not keep her waiting," Caleb smiled. "I can tell you about this other after supper."

Neither Caleb nor Phillip mentioned their trouble with Pinky and Blue during the meal, and for some reason not entirely clear to Caleb the two old people remained rather quiet. Maybe, he thought, they were as tired and hungry as he and Phillip were.

The meal itself was not one that Aunt Delia would have considered special, for she had not expected company. It was mainly a stew, but there were many things in it and all of them wonderful to taste. "Caleb told me about your fine cooking," Phillip said when his plate was about half empty.

"This ain't nothing much," Aunt Delia protested. "I got a dessert for you though, so leave room."

Again conversation lapsed. The desert turned out to be a strawberry shortcake, and Caleb's eyes popped open as he was served. "I'll help you to say you got a dessert!" he laughed. "I'm glad you warned me. The way I was going on that stew I might not have had a place for it by now."

"I was going to say," Phillip added politely, "that Caleb didn't exaggerate a bit. It's wonderful."

"You said something," Caleb recalled, turning to Uncle Eph, "about things not being so settled out here now."

Aunt Delia answered for him. "You remember the night-riders that caused the ruckus when you was here before?" she said.

"But the Klan's disbanded, isn't it?"

She nodded. "There's still some troublemakers around," she explained. "Percy and the others keeps up with them. The white ones at the bottom of it has got some colored ones from the city working with them. They don't want to be bothered with no school. They've started something they call 'shares.' They put the families on the land and tell them to work it. End of the year, if they raise enough cotton, there'll be something left for the family. If they don't raise enough, all the money will go to the owner. The owner does all the weighing and the counting though, and nobody but him knows if he counts it fair or cheats. Me and Uncle Eph and Percy thinks that that's how come they don't want the school to open—so nobody will learn to figure and keep up with the owner. Looks to us like a scheme to get the colored folks back in slavery without anybody knowing what's happened."

Caleb and Phillip exchanged knowing glances. "I think we understand," Caleb said. "It makes me more anxious than ever to want to help out. But there is something I have to explain. Phillip here—"

A knock at the back door interrupted him. It was a sharp, excited knock, and Aunt Delia was out of her seat instantly. Percy entered, almost as agitated as this bearer of bad news had been the last time Caleb saw him. He nodded briefly to the two boys and then turned to Uncle Eph.

"We got to have a meeting tonight," he announced out of breath. "They're back again. The same two. They been talking to the folks at the store. Got them all worked up and scared. Seems like—" Percy couldn't suppress a note of satisfaction. Then a thought struck him. He pointed to Caleb and Phillip. "I wonder if it could have been these two."

"What you talking about, Percy?" Uncle Eph asked. "Don't you remember the professor? This other'n is his friend from the Fisk school."

Percy was thin and ageless. He might have been twenty, thirty or forty years old; it was impossible to guess. "That's what I mean," he went on. "Seems like somebody caught the scoundrels on the big road and give them what-for. They looked like they been in a cage with panthers or something. Anyhow, they're mad aplenty now. They got some kind of devilment up their sleeve. We got to hold a meeting."

"Where at?" Aunt Delia asked.

"At the schoolhouse, I reckon."

Uncle Eph began to bounce eagerly. "Anytime you say, Percy. We got us two professors here. Seems like we oughta could hold a meeting on Saturday night if we feel like it. You want us to go now?"

"The quicker the sooner," Percy said.

Uncle Eph and the boys rose from the table. "Come along, y'all," he chuckled.

Aunt Delia had no intention of being left alone. She quickly blew the lamp, closed the doors and joined the boys on the path. With her along, the others could not walk fast, and it took twice as long to reach the hill as it required when Caleb walked it alone. When they were near the top, the old woman suddenly sniffed the air. "I smell something burning."

"Just wood smoke," Uncle Eph said.

"No house ain't near here," she insisted. "Just the school on the other side of the hill. How come a wood fire would be burning there?"

Nobody answered, but all rushed to the top of the hill, leaving Aunt Delia several paces behind. Sure enough, Caleb discovered, there was smoke coming out of the schoolhouse, a lot of it. There was so much smoke, in fact, that it could be plainly seen in the early darkness. A moment later he saw a glow at one corner of the building. He and Phillip and Percy raced down the slope.

Under the cedars a distance away he heard voices, and

he began to put the fragments together. "They've set the school on fire," he shouted.

"The devils," Phillip cried. "Let me get my hands on them." He dashed madly toward the shadows from which the voices came.

"No, Phillip," Caleb cautioned. "Wait. We'll all—"

"Hold on," Percy whispered fiercely. "You can't tell about them. They might—"

Phillip kept going. A second later a shot rang through the trees. Caleb felt a shudder, but he couldn't let Phillip do this alone. He followed in the same direction. A second shot followed.

Then it was that Caleb heard the horses and the galloping into the trees.

"Where are you, Phillip?" he called.

"I'm—I'm—here—" The voice was strained, filled with pain.

Caleb knew that Phillip was hurt, badly hurt. When he reached him, Phillip was sinking against a small tree. Out of the darkness behind came Percy and then Uncle Eph and then—a moment or two later—Aunt Delia. Flames from the burning schoolhouse filled the cedar woods with a golden light.

Phillip, the friend from Charleston, Caleb's only friend remaining from the days before freedom, clutched at the tree like a shipwrecked sailor clinging to a floating spar.

The Horizon Beyond

The death of his friend was such a blow to Caleb that he wanted neither to see nor talk to anybody for several days. He had returned to the Fisk school, of course, and the body of Phillip Sazon had been sent to Charleston at the request of Phillip's mother, but by then the second tour of the Jubilee Singers had been announced and the other members of the company were busy packing their bags.

Caleb did not pack. He did not attend rehearsals, and his fellow students respected his wish to be left alone with his thoughts. Even George White and the Jubilees avoided mention of his absence and went about getting ready for the trip as well as they could without him.

Then, on the afternoon before they were scheduled to leave, after Caleb had returned from a solitary walk into the country and was sitting alone on the steps of the assembly building, he became aware of someone in the doorway behind him.

"I didn't aim to disturb you," a girl's voice said.

Caleb turned around slowly. "Oh," he said, surprised. "I thought it was one of the singers."

Precious Jewel had a serious expression on her face. "The singers are rehearsing inside. But we all sympathize," she added softly, "the rest of us, as well as the singers." She waited till he raised his eyes again. "But it won't help anyone for you to go on grieving about Phillip."

"I've been trying to decide what I oughta do," he told her. "Everything's so mixed up."

"But the singers are leaving tomorrow, Caleb. Maybe you'll be able to think better on the road, when you are away from Fisk and out of Tennessee."

He shook his head sadly. "I'm not going on the tour. I can't leave here just yet."

"But they're counting on you. Besides, there's nothing you can do about Phillip now."

"They can find somebody else to sing bass. And what I'm thinking about's not just Phillip. It's the folks up yonder in the country and the burned-down schoolhouse and everything. It's all those young ones I was trying to teach. Phillip's dead and by now he's buried, I reckon, but I'd be ashamed of myself if I went off and let them— them mean rascals have their own way about closing the school after Phillip lost his life fighting for it. They did away with Phillip all right, but I'm still here, and I don't feel like quitting. I'm going back and open up school again. We can find a place to teach. Somebody will let us have a cabin, and I'm going to finish out this summer there like they asked me to."

"But those men, those two—"

"I met Pinky and Blue once, and I don't mind meeting them again. I believe I'll have more help next time."

"How about the nightriders?"

"I'm not letting any nightriders stop me either." He smiled as bravely as he could. "Tell Mr. White for me, please."

When he stood up, her hand touched his arm and he felt that Precious Jewel approved. "I'll tell him," she promised. "I'll tell the others too—they're waiting inside now."

So that settled the question where Caleb was concerned, and he decided not to let himself feel too disappointed about not leaving with the singers on their important second campaign. A fellow couldn't be in two places at once, no matter how much he wanted to, and Phillip Sazon's death among the cedars near Indian Lake had left him with an obligation that was more urgent than anything else.

He left Fisk school next morning as crowds of students were beginning to head for the railroad station to give their famous classmates a hearty farewell. In the excitement, not many of them thought about Caleb. Even the teachers were too busy to call him aside and say whether or not they thought he was doing the right thing, and Caleb was glad to be overlooked. He turned down a side street and began walking rapidly.

The journey to the country was uneventful, and he arrived at the cabin of Uncle Eph and Aunt Delia by mid-afternoon. Two mornings later he began teaching seven bright-eyed youngsters under the pride-of-China tree near the front doorstep while Uncle Eph nodded on a barrel-stave hammock near by.

By the end of a week he had thirteen pupils, and Percy suggested that the meeting place of the class be moved from time to time. First under the China tree, next in an abandoned smokehouse, then on benches by a well—never long enough in one place to become a target for the enemies of learning.

In the third week the number of his pupils reached twenty, and Caleb began teaching a few of the older folk in Aunt Delia's front room at night. He also received a letter that week which was delivered to Uncle Eph at the crossroads general store where the old man occasionally bought sugar and coffee or flour.

School was over for the day when Uncle Eph handed

the envelope to him, so Caleb went down by the creek and sat on the bank to open it. He had scarcely begun reading when his heart started to pound wildly. The news was fine.

The singers had been giving programs in cities of the Midwest, Isaac wrote. No longer were they troubled by not knowing where they would sing next or whether or not there would be an audience to hear them. Everybody seemed anxious to hear the Jubilee Singers now. Large audiences came wherever they appeared and large amounts of money for the new building at Fisk were being raised.

The singers were looking forward to the great celebration in Boston, of course, as the high point of the tour, and it made them all sad to think that Caleb, their fine bass singer, who had shared their hardships on the first tour and helped them make their present reputation, would not be with them when they came onto the stage of the Coliseum for the World's Peace Jubilee. They understood how Caleb felt about the unfinished teaching assignment, but that didn't keep them from feeling sad.

Well, it was a fine thing to have true friends like Isaac and Ella and the rest of those singers, Caleb mused. But he must not feel sorry for himself. He must not let himself wish that he had gone along with them. He would not be doing his job and keeping faith with Phillip, if he did. All he could say to the Jubilees, even under his breath, was good-by and good luck and may they bring home money for a fine new building at Fisk.

One other thing he might do, of course, would be to calculate as nearly as possible the exact time when they would be on the platform in Boston and sing along with them, though more than a thousand miles away, the words of the "Battle Hymn of the Republic." Isaac mentioned that they had been asked to prepare that number and that they were practicing it diligently. Yes, Caleb could do that much at least.

So the following week, when his class was meeting under the China tree again, he suddenly surprised the youngsters by saying he had a song he wanted them to hear. He rose before them, closed his eyes and began singing in a strong and very musical voice:

"Mine eyes have seen the glory of the coming of the Lord;
He is trampling out the vintage where the grapes of wrath are stored."

The children were delighted. They clapped their hands when he finished, but Caleb did not tell them why he had done it.

The three months of school in the country were nearly over when Caleb received another letter from the Jubilees. His class had grown as big as it had been before the schoolhouse was burned, and Percy and Uncle Eph and Caleb had begun cutting logs to build another schoolhouse.

"We'll make believe this here's a church we's building. That'll keep the devils away maybe. Then next summer maybe a professor'll just happen up and we'll just happen to hold school in it." Uncle Eph chuckled.

Caleb smiled. "You're all right, Uncle Eph. Nobody's ever going to outsmart you. If you'll excuse me a minute now, I got another letter to read."

"Go right 'head. I hope it's good news."

Caleb went around the house, sat on a chopping block by the woodpile and opened the envelope. Three separate letters fell out. One was from Ella Sheppard and told how forty thousand people had crowded Boston's Coliseum on the afternoon when the Jubilee Singers were presented. She was sorry to say that not all this audience was friendly to the little group of colored students when they first appeared on the platform. There had been some hissing, for in this huge gathering there were many people who had not heard the songs of the Jubilees and who could not imagine young ex-slaves singing in such a way as to interest or entertain them. But the hissing died away as the students from Fisk raised their well-trained voices, and when they finished the "Battle Hymn," the applause was deafening. The musicians in the orchestra waved their fiddles and whacked their cellos. People in the audience waved their handkerchiefs and tossed their hats into the air. And one of those who applauded most vigorously was Johann Strauss, famous composer of wonderful waltzes.

So the singers had been a great success at the World's Peace Jubilee. "We thought about you and wished you could have been here," Ella concluded. "Did you think about us that day?"

Caleb opened the second letter. It was from Isaac, and he told a few more details about the Boston experience. But mostly he wanted to let Caleb know that his singing friends were terribly anxious to know how the teaching work was coming along in the country and whether or not there had been any more trouble.

After next week, Caleb thought, he would write his answer. When he was safely back in Nashville, he might be able to say how he had made out, but not yet. There was still enough time left for the nightriders to cause trouble if they wanted to. He began unfolding the third letter.

Caleb couldn't fail to recognize the handwriting of the treasurer of the Fisk school. Mr. White's note was brief and businesslike. The Jubilee Singers, he said, had been invited to tour Europe: London, Paris, Brussels, Berlin, Antwerp. They planned to accept the offer. After filling engagements in Philadelphia's Academy of Music and in a few other large American cities, they planned to sail from Boston on the *S. S. Batavia.* But they were not entirely satisfied with the bass singer who had taken Caleb's place. Mr. White wanted to know if Caleb would consider joining the group in Boston after finishing his term in the country school.

Caleb put the letters back into the envelope and returned to the shade of the front of the cabin. Uncle Eph was in his hammock now, fanning with a palmetto leaf.

"Did you get good news?" the old fellow chirped.

"Real good, Uncle Eph," Caleb replied, smiling broadly, "real good." He didn't think it was necessary to tell the details. "My friends are getting along fine up there in Boston."

Uncle Eph stopped fanning. After a moment he murmured, "Is you sorry you didn't go 'long?"

Caleb shook his head slowly. "No, Uncle Eph. I'm not sorry, not any more."

The next week he finished his teaching and returned to Fisk, and a few days later Caleb caught the train for Boston.

"Always did want to cross the water," Caleb chuckled as he and Isaac stood outside the hotel having their shoes shined on the day of departure.

"Aren't you afraid of seasickness?"

"I'll take a chance on that."

The luggage of the group was piled in the lobby of the hotel. Half an hour later bellboys began loading it into carriages.

A crowd of admirers met the singers on the deck. Most of these were strangers to Caleb, and he found himself shaking hands without getting more than a vague impression of the people he greeted.

In the midst of these farewells, however, when he was beginning to feel a certain going-away melancholy, two familiar faces suddenly loomed before him. They were the faces of a Negro man and woman, perhaps in their fifties. They were the same height, but the man looked short because he was heavy and broad-shouldered. His wife seemed tall because she was slender and taller than the average woman. Both faces were deeply lined, but they had not changed so much as to make it hard for Caleb to recognize his parents instantly, even in their strange attire and in these unfamiliar surroundings. He threw his arms around his mother, and presently the little reunited family was lost to all the others on the deck.

"We heard some talk about these Jubilees," the father remarked finally. "But we didn't expect you to be one of them."

"Not till we seen a picture," the mother added.

"I went to Charleston to look for you," Caleb explained. "After the war I went home first thing. Nobody could tell me what became of you."

His mother continued to press his hand. "Don't talk about it, son. Don't say a thing. We came back looking for you, too. Nobody we seen could tell us nothing."

"We came up here from Charleston on a boat," his father continued. "I'm working on the dock here now. Your ma—she can't work no more."

"It's this hand." Caleb saw that her left hand had no strength in it. "Kind of a light stroke, I reckon."

"I hope it will be well by the time we get back from Europe."

"Don't you fret, son. Me and your pa is doing first rate. We got two rooms here, and I can still keep house a little."

"I'm proud to see you, Ma. You too, Pa."

"I can't get over this big boat you fixing to sail on," his father beamed. "My, my, my! Going across the water."

"Europe," Caleb said.

Sarah's brow wrinkled. "How come you going way over there?"

"I'll tell you all about the Jubilees sometime, Ma," Caleb smiled. "It's a long story though, and the ship's fixing to sail now." He glanced around and saw his companions going aboard.

"You got a few more minutes," his father whispered.

"What songs you going to sing when you get over yonder?" his mother asked.

Caleb relaxed a moment, his arms around his parents. "Slave songs. Same ones you and Pa sing at home all the time."

"You reckon they'll like that kind of singing—them folks in Europe?" Moses asked.

Caleb nodded confidently. "I bound you they'll like them all right." Suddenly the remark seemed boastful, and Caleb was sorry he had put it in those words, so he quickly added, "Not on account of us, you understand, but the songs—they ain't just slavery-time songs. I've learned something about these songs since the last time I saw you, Pa."

Both his parents showed surprise, but it was Sarah whose eyes questioned him pointedly. "How's that, son? What you mean?"

"A heap of people don't want to sing slave songs nowadays," he explained. "They're the ones that's getting educated, mostly. They talk about forgetting what's past and gone, and they think slave songs remind them of slavery. They don't want to sing them themselves and they don't want nobody else to sing them." Caleb could see that the old folks were baffled, so he added lightly, "It's kind of funny when you think about it."

But Moses did not smile. He asked seriously, "Did you ever think anything like that, son?"

"No, Pa," Caleb answered honestly. "Of course, I didn't have any reason except that I always liked to sing the songs that I knew best, but here lately—well, I think I'm beginning to know how come."

"I'd hate to see you get so educated you couldn't enjoy good singing," Moses smiled.

"Good singing is good singing," Sarah remarked. "That's about all there is to it."

Caleb laughed warmly. "I been thinking the same thing, Ma. I was fixing to say that these songs we sing, these songs that meant so much to us back in slavery— well, they mean a lot to other folks too. Near about everybody is trying to get free of something. Down inside, people are all alike. Leastwise, all those we been singing to acted the same. Take a song like 'Good News, Chariot's Coming.' We sing that everywhere we go."

"And what happens?" Moses urged, his eyes brightening. "What happens when you sing 'Good News'?"

"Pretty soon we hear feet patting. Most generally we don't look right at the folks when we sing, but every now and then I peep out to see how the audience is behaving, and I can tell you they all do about the same way when they hear us sing 'Good News, Chariot's Coming.' Their eyes sparkle and their teeth shine. Poor folks and rich, city people and country, old slaves and old masters, and the ones that never had anything to do with slavery— all of them rock back and forth when the singing commences. All of them smile and pat their feet like it was their own song they're hearing, their very own. You understand what I mean?"

Of course they understood, and it delighted them to

hear their grown-up son talk with so much feeling about the familiar songs of bondage, songs it had never occurred to them to question in any way. Their boy had become a man since they last saw him. More important, he had found something in which he could believe, something fine and beautiful. He was learning to defend his belief. They understood.

"Sure, son," Sarah murmured. "We know, but the time's too short to talk about all that now. Looks like all your friends is up on deck."

Caleb glanced around anxiously. "I forgot to introduce them," he remembered. "I reckon I was too excited, running into you like this, so unexpected. Maybe I better go on board too."

His father caught his arm to hold him as long as he could. "They won't leave without you," he promised, knowing more than the others about ships and sailings. "They'll ring a bell and let you know when it's the last call."

"Tell me who you aim to sing to over across the water," Sarah asked, lovingly putting her arm around him.

Caleb drew his parents to him as if to whisper a secret. "We're going to sing for the queen," he confided. "Queen Victoria. And if we do right well, we'll keep on going. The Netherlands, Germany, France—all over Europe."

"The queen!"

"I'm scared to death, Ma. I'm afraid I won't know what to do in front of royalty. We been—most of us been slaves, you know."

Suddenly his parents stiffened.

"Don't you say that again," Moses snapped, drawing away. "Don't ever say that no more." There was growing sternness in his voice. "Did you hear me? Don't ever say that again."

"I'm sorry, Pa. But it's more'n a notion, going over

235

there to London and all those cities—it makes you tremble."

Sarah's hand shook more than usual as she took hold of his arm. "You just as free as anybody else, son. Mind what your pa says. And don't you go in front of the queen trembling neither. Walk in proud when the time come—you and your Jubilees. Sing your songs like sweet children. Don't you be afraid."

"I'll try not, Ma."

"And another thing. Don't forget about Jesus. He'll be listening. Be humble in front of Him."

At that moment the all-aboard bell sounded, and Caleb heard his companions calling him from the deck. When he looked up, he saw that Ella and Isaac were trying to say something which he could not make out. So he hugged his parents again, then turned to go.

"Good-by, son," Moses called, as he stood proudly watching him.

Caleb paused. "I'm coming to see you when I get back. I got plenty of things to talk about, and someone I want you to meet."

Sarah smiled and took Moses' hand. "Something tells me maybe it's a girl he wants us to meet. That's good."

"Now how you know that?" Moses asked, but stopped his questioning when Sarah pointed toward the ship.

Caleb was joining the others on deck. "Did you want to get left?" Ella chided above the din. Most of his companions were breathless with excitement.

"Who are those people, that man and woman?" Isaac asked.

Caleb felt his voice choking up suddenly. He could think of no words to express what he felt. For a moment he was in a daze. It was not till Ella nudged him standing at the rail that he recovered enough to answer, "My ma and pa—down there on the wharf. Look. Look at them there, waving. I didn't get a chance to make you acquainted."

A strange throbbing silence fell on the young singers. They all knew Caleb's story, just as he knew theirs. Their past experiences had often been shared, and it was not necessary to tell them now how the excitement of this moment had been compounded for their tall bass.

"They look like mighty nice people," Ella said, after the pause. She touched his arm, and he could see that her own eyes were cloudy. "You're lucky, Caleb," she said. "It must be wonderful."

"When we get home, you'll meet them, Ella. You'll like them, and they'll love you."

For a moment Caleb wondered if he deserved so much, remembering that Ella and others among them had lost not only parents but brothers and sisters whom they had given up hope of ever finding. Yes, he was lucky, and he had no right to stand there by the rail like a fellow in a trance, keeping his joy to himself. He pulled his hat off and began waving it, his eyes fixed on his parents on the pier.

As the *Batavia* moved away, he tried to convey to the little group around him how pleased his parents had been to hear that the melodies that consoled them in slavery were being received so warmly by Americans in all walks of life. And now they too would be anxiously waiting to hear how Queen Victoria and her people would take them. "We mustn't be afraid," he added quickly. "They told me that too. When we sing in front of kings and queens—" He paused, and Ella interrupted laughingly, "We'll just be ourselves, and sing and act the best we know how."

"You sound a lot like Ma, Ella, sweet and good."

It was the first time Caleb had said anything quite so

personal, or nice, thought Ella, as she stood beside him not wanting to spoil the moment with words.

Caleb began humming an old song. When he turned to Ella she could see contentment in his eyes. Sensing his thought she said, "This has been a good day for you, Caleb, finding your father and your mother."

Caleb nodded and smiled. "Yes, Ella, a fine day, finding my ma, my pa—and you." And his arm went around her as they stood together looking out over the water until the dock and the people on it dropped completely out of sight.